MW00615891

CALL HER FREEDOM

A Novel

TARA DORABJI

SIMON & SCHUSTER
New York Amsterdam/Antwerp London
Toronto Sydney New Delhi

Simon & Schuster
1230 Avenue of the Americas
New York, NY 10020

NOTE: This work is the S&S imprint's winner of the
Books Like Us competition, originally titled *Fire*.

First Simon & Schuster hardcover edition January 2025

SIMON & SCHUSTER and colophon are registered
trademarks of Simon & Schuster, LLC

For information about special discounts for bulk purchases,
please contact Simon & Schuster Special Sales at
1-866-506-1949 or business@simonandschuster.com.

The Simon & Schuster Speakers Bureau can bring authors to
your live event. For more information or to book an event, contact
the Simon & Schuster Speakers Bureau at 1-866-248-3049
or visit our website at www.simonspeakers.com.

Interior design by Lewelin Polanco

Manufactured in the United States of America

1 3 5 7 9 10 8 6 4 2

Library of Congress Cataloging-in-Publication Data is available.

ISBN 978-1-6680-5165-8
ISBN 978-1-6680-5167-2 (ebook)

Contents

"You know, they straightened out the Mississippi River in places, to make room for houses and livable acreage. Occasionally, the river floods these places. 'Floods' is the word they use, but in fact it is not flooding: it is remembering. Remembering where it used to be. All water has a perfect memory and is forever trying to get back to where it was."

—TONI MORRISON, *The Site of Memory*

"My nights are tormented and I cannot sleep, the bodies and graves appear and reappear in my dreams . . . the sound of the earth as I covered the graves . . . bodies and faces that were mutilated . . . mothers who would never find their sons. My memory is an obligation." Atta Mohammad, a Kashmiri gravedigger at Chehal Bimyar who buried 203 unidentified bodies from 2002 to 2006.

—A. P. CHATTERJI, P. IMROZ, ET AL, *Buried Evidence: Unknown, Unmarked and Mass Graves in Indian-Administered Kashmir*

CALL HER FREEDOM

PROLOGUE

SMOKE. I CAN'T smell smoke without thinking of you, Father. You left me after the fire. I was seven years old. As a child, I tried to understand what happened, but all I could remember was the grief. The fire rips in jagged ways through my memory. I could barely breathe through the thick gray clouds. Mother held me. Orange flames licked her scarf. The weight of her body suffocated mine.

The fire left a scar on my calf. It's a pale white line, splitting my birthmark in two, running like the border that crosses our home, militarized on both sides. My body, like my birthmark, partitioned by colonial forces, so all we remember is war. Father, you were the one who said my birthmark was shaped like our country, Charagan, like a moth struggling to flutter its wings and be free. When the colonial rulers left, they divided the land that our rivers flow through in the name of Nadistan's "independence." I studied my scar and found where our village, Poshkarbal, lands on the border.

Fire. Our story begins with fire, an element that humans have learned to create, contort, and manipulate. This story ends with water. Most of the human body is comprised of water. I am a grandmother now. But I will never ask my grandchildren to come to my grave after I die and tell me that our freedom has come. I live my life as an act of freedom, as I did from birth.

Freedom is our natural state of being. Call us freedom.

part 1

SCHOOL

AGE 8

1974

In the village of Poshkarbal in Charagan

On the border between Nadistan,
Daryastan, and the Middle Kingdom

1

AISHA

AS A CHILD, Aisha opened the carved wooden shutters each morning, letting light stream in. Strings of dried fish hung from the ceiling, glass jars filled with healing herbs sat on the shelf, and a mortar, yellowed with turmeric, lay next to the stove. She bent over the stove to light it. Flames burst forth, reaching toward her as if she were kerosene to feed on.

"Aisha." Her mother's voice made her jump. She hadn't heard her enter the room. "You will go to school today. I'll finish the breakfast."

Aisha turned toward her mother in shock. Her cousins were returning to school after the winter closure, but she'd assumed that she'd stay with her mother. "Why didn't you tell me before?"

"You'd just worry yourself thinking about it."

Her parents had always fought about school. It was the fight that caused the fire. Aisha was sure of it. Her mother's shrill voice rose above her father's. Her father insisted that Aisha was too young for school.

Her father was right. A year after the fire, at eight years old, Aisha still wasn't ready for school. She should stay with her mother. She'd already learned how to mix herb tonics. When her mother delivered babies, she was there with the blankets, thermometer, whatever her mother needed. Still, there were times her mother left her alone at the house, saying she was too small to come along. Aisha would beg her mother to take her with her, but her mother only said, "You are too young to sit with death."

How did her mother know who would live and who would die?

Aisha grew curious about the face of death, how it might look when it entered the room. She'd asked her mother once, expecting to be reprimanded. "Death is a smell you learn to breathe in," her mother said. "I prefer not to see it, but we all find our own way with it."

School, too, seemed far away, a blurred image.

"Fetch some drinking water," her mother said.

Aisha could not move. Her feet sunk into the ground. The argument rang in her ears. Her father had said she wasn't ready. The fire somehow petrified his words, encased them like glass.

"Go," her mother said firmly.

Aisha grabbed the water jug and headed out the door away from the orchard. The rising sun cast the field in yellow. The mountains surrounded them on all sides and the cottonwood trees, growing along the river, swept up to kiss the sky. Canals dotted their land, small eddies that siphoned water from the river to flood the rice paddies that terraced the hill. Walnut and apple trees grew near the house, with mulberries at the borders. Above the rice fields, the arid soil gave way to a blanket of pine trees. Up this steep trail there was a fertile swath of land where her mother grew poppies, not the few that were mixed in with their vegetables, but a field that bloomed in summer, stretched between the folds in the mountain. A place she never spoke of. Aisha only went up there when she was sure her mother was far away.

She climbed over a fallen log and then hopped over a remaining patch of snow, arriving at the spring where the water bubbled up. Her reflection stared back, her long brown hair hung around her face, still messy from sleep. She had her mother's full lips and father's dimpled chin. She stood up tall, spreading her lanky arms so her reflection reached the other side, then filled the jug to the top and turned back toward home.

The wind blew gently as she crossed through the apple trees. The branches swooped toward her, daring her to climb up into them as she always had with her father. During the harvest, he'd lifted her up into the branches so she could climb to the top and get the apples. The sour taste exploded in her mouth as she ate the ones with wormholes, tossing the best ones into baskets. He'd taught her to recognize the signs of moths nesting in the leaves and how to prune in the fall so the trees wouldn't get sick.

They'd always fished in the river together. Her father taught her to cast into the eddies, where the fish gathered in the evening. In the mornings, they clustered in the still water. Once, Aisha had landed a fish all by herself. Her father unhooked it and squeezed the belly of the fish, causing a stream of translucent eggs filled with red-eyed fish to pop out. They had caught the mother. Her father threw her back in the water and said, "Better let this one go, and eat the children when they grow up."

Every time Aisha caught a fish in the river, she knew it was one of the babies, all grown-up, something her father left behind for her. But now the fish were getting harder to catch. There were fewer and fewer of them. Soldiers on both sides of the border caught the mothers, as if they'd never learned the right way to fish, or how to care for a river.

She closed her eyes, attempting to push away the image of her father's face—the crinkle that formed at the corner of his eyes when he laughed, the bristle of his beard against her cheek when he hugged her.

Aisha was forbidden from mentioning her father and the fire. She'd spoken of him once and could still feel the sting from her mother's slap. "He will never come back." His absence settled around them, bright like the sun at noon, something that illuminated everything, but couldn't be directly looked at.

Aisha went inside the house and found a gift from her mother waiting on her sleeping mat: a perfectly white dupatta. There was also a winter cloak, the gray wool tightly knit with lotus flowers along the sleeves and neck.

"Thank you, Mom." Her mother did not look up but continued sweeping. Aisha did not want to touch the gifts, afraid that her fingers would leave marks. She felt taller and smarter as she dressed. Her mom brushed Aisha's thick brown hair, which came to a peak on her forehead, just as her mother's did. Usually her mother used the white plastic comb with the missing tooth to rip the knots out of Aisha's hair, but today she used the tortoiseshell brush, adding the smallest bit of oil so that the knots came out with ease. Even the oil smelled sweeter. Aisha wrapped her new dupatta over her head and around her neck and carefully pinned the fabric by her ears.

Her mother rubbed her back. "You must pay attention at school. Education can never be taken away."

Maybe school wouldn't be that bad. Maybe the other children would be kind. Maybe her mother was right.

Her mother handed her the final gift: shoes. They were not heavy winter shoes, but shiny black leather with the most delicate straps. Aisha wanted to grab them, but instead she reached for the round middle of her mother and buried her face in the folds, breathing in her scent of cardamom.

Her mother hugged her back. "Put on your shoes."

It took three tries before Aisha could buckle them. Her mother towered above her, impatient, but Aisha was determined to do it on her own. The shoes were stiff and a size too big. As they went down the hill, a blister formed on her baby toe.

The houses around them grew closer together and larger in size as they descended. A herd of goats grazed under poplar trees, near a smattering of spring snow. For every one of her mother's steps, Aisha took three, counting them in her head. No mud splashed on her shoes.

Instead of following the path to the center of town where the fabric store, private school, mosque, and market were, they went toward the mountain that led to the government school. On the mountain across the way, the army outposts marked the border.

Some days gunfire erupted, but today the clouds hid the other side, leaving only the closest guards visible. The soldiers came from far away. They were short and squat, with flat noses and guns. Mother kept her away. They rarely walked on the paths where the soldiers were.

The dirt path led to the school, a huge gray building with paint peeling off. Just before entering, her mother grabbed Aisha's wrist. "At school, stay away from the boys, understand?"

Aisha nodded.

"Never look at them or go near them. God is watching and will know if you disobey."

Surely, boys must be terrible if God himself were watching to make sure that she stayed away. Besides, she already avoided the other children so that they wouldn't make fun of her. She inhaled deeply and entered the classroom. She was late. All the other children were seated.

"Welcome, I am Mr. Malik." The teacher wore a shirt that buttoned down the center, and dark pants instead of a traditional cloak. His face was narrow and clean-shaven, with thick-rimmed glasses.

A boy pointed at her and said, "It's the mute girl." The whole class laughed. Aisha felt her cheeks turn red. She wasn't mute. She just didn't talk to people other than her mom.

"Silence," said the teacher. His dark hair was thin and parted at the side. Aisha had seen him at the mosque before but had never spoken with him.

This was a bad idea. Why was her mother doing this? She held her hands behind her back as she glanced around the room. The children toward the back were bigger, some as tall as the teacher. They were all boys, except for three little girls up front by the window, one of whom was her cousin Mina. Please, let Mina be nice today. Ever since her father left, Mina had turned on her, saying ugly things and pinching her. But maybe today would be different. Maybe at school Mina would defend her from the other kids.

The teacher pointed to an empty desk in front of Mina, next to a girl with a missing front tooth and white leather shoes. Mina stuck her tongue out. Her auburn hair slipped out from under her cream dupatta. Aisha wanted to go home, but instead, she sat on a wooden chair, folding her sweaty hands into her lap.

"Come, sit." Murad Malik hadn't anticipated a new student today. Aisha was a miniature replica of her mother, Noorjahan, the same full, dark hair and heart-shaped face. Noorjahan was supposed to meet with him in advance of having Aisha join the class. But Noorjahan always wanted to do things her way.

"You are wearing black boy shoes," Mina whispered, and the missing-tooth girl giggled. Aisha glanced around. The other girls were wearing white shoes. The missing-tooth girl pressed the white tip of her shoe into Aisha's calf. Her scar burned. Aisha pulled her legs away and tried to conceal her shoes, placing her right foot on top of the other, leaving a ribbon of mud on her shoe's shiny black surface.

A few more students trickled in, including Omar, the tall boy who lived three houses down. He was surprised to see Aisha. His mother had told him to be kind to her, but other kids said that Noorjahan got possessed by the evil eye and that's why her parents were dead. When Noorjahan came to treat his mother when she was sick, Aisha played outside with his cat but refused to speak to him. Strange people.

The teacher tapped a baton on his desk. The students quieted. "We have a new pupil joining us," he said, looking to Aisha. "Please, introduce yourself to the class."

Aisha's heart beat into her ears. She opened her mouth, but no sound came out. Why did her mother make her go to school? She knew that she couldn't speak to anyone else. Her father had known that it wasn't right.

The missing-tooth girl leaned over so her lips were right against Aisha's ear. "Just say your name."

Thirty pairs of eyes stared at her as if she were stupid. She opened her mouth. No sound came out. Aisha slouched at her desk for the rest of the class, wishing herself invisible.

Murad shook his head. Poor child. How could Noorjahan have sent her daughter to school if she didn't even speak? It was hard enough teaching girls, but this was absurd.

The morning passed slowly. When lunch finally came, Murad told the class, "In three months, we will have our exams for this term. At the end of the tests, you will bring your father to collect your results."

The blood drained from her face. She had no father to come with her. Aisha felt the sting of her mother's slap when she'd asked where he was. She knew if she were good enough and worked hard enough, her father would surely return.

At lunchtime, Aisha sat by herself under a cottonwood tree. She couldn't see the path that led back to her house because of the thick trees.

She opened her lunch tins. The lentils were still warm and the rice let off a bit of steam. She ate, relieved at being unnoticed, until her gangly neighbor Omar approached her. His cheeks were flushed from the cold and his nose arched off his face like a mountain. His brown hair grew thick around his head. "Why don't you talk?" he asked, putting his face up to hers. "Is it because your mother is a witch?" Omar pinched her arm. "Say something." He grabbed under her dupatta and pulled her hair.

Aisha howled, jumped up, and rammed her head right into his stomach. Omar screamed and released her. She ran toward the school-house. He tried to grab hold of her dupatta, but it slipped through his muddy fingers. He had surely just stained it. Just like her shoes, everything was ruined.

2

MURAD

MURAD, THE SCHOOLTEACHER, sipped his cardamom tea on the porch. An almond swirled at the bottom of the golden tea. The mountains to the west dissolved into the purple twilight. Crows flew overhead, crossing a stand of silhouetted poplars. A few crickets started a song. This was his favorite time of day, when the dark took over the light. But tonight, he could not enjoy it with the pounding in his head.

For years, he had been plagued with headaches. They began just after he started teaching. The village doctor gave him a monthly dose of pills to manage the pain, but he'd used them all last week, and two weeks remained before he could get his prescription refilled.

"Would you like a biscuit?" Murad's wife, Haseena, asked from inside the house.

"Please," he said, perhaps some food would help. He turned toward her, but he could not make her out from behind the shear turquoise curtains, a gift from their wedding, now dusty with age.

The door to the house hung open. She always forgot to close it, even in the cold. Alim, their son, brought out the biscuits on a silver tray. He was thin like his father and had his long nose, too. Murad patted the chair next to him, but Alim shook his head.

"I have to study, Father."

For all the time that boy spent studying there were no results. He ranked in the middle of the class. Haseena came out onto the porch and sat beside him. Her thick black hair was freshly brushed. When they first married, Murad brushed it for her. She wore a loose-fitting teal kurta that hung down to her knees. Murad couldn't even make out the shape of her breasts under it. Her plump cheeks were red from the chill of the night, and even though she had not gone out all day, she'd applied kohl to her eyes, accentuating the shape. "Are you feeling alright?" she asked, pouring herself some tea.

"It was a challenging day at work. The little girls just aren't pre-pared for school." He tightened the woolen scarf around his neck to keep the cold out.

"What do you mean?"

It was rare that Haseena took any interest in his work. He turned toward her, taking in the cleft of her chin.

"The boys were distracted by the girls, and one is even mute. Can you imagine? What am I to do with a child who doesn't speak?"

"I went to school," Haseena said. "You think this education was wasted on me?"

The pounding in his temples grew deeper. "I'm not talking about girls from good families, but what sense is there in having a child from a poor, broken family be educated? It's hard enough at these govern-ment schools to educate the boys. Why make it more complicated?"

Haseena was silent as she finished her biscuit. "You are talking about Aisha?" Of course the poor child didn't speak—after what happened to her grandparents. They said that the fire was an acci-dent. But who would believe that?

"Yes, Aisha can't even speak. What am I supposed to do with her? And all the children make fun of her." But he couldn't blame

Noorjahan. Her husband had left her, after all. What could she do? Her husband, Babak, was a man from an upstanding family who had married a field worker. Their story was destined for tragedy. Such a silly part of their youth, believing love could conquer caste, and that Charagan would be free.

"Are you listening, Murad?" Haseena placed her cup on the table. "There was a bombing in the capital, near the university."

Haseena only ever spoke of the news when she was afraid. She worried Murad would be next. The government propaganda in the newspaper had framed this bombing as militants from Daryastan killing civilians, but it was Nadistan's army killing civilians. Of course, these same papers never reported on the roundups, the young men taken in the middle of the night.

"I just get worried," she said.

"I know."

"You must really be careful with what you are teaching your students." She squeezed his hand. His fingers tensed under hers.

"I will not teach them government propaganda." The new textbooks arrived last week, stamped with the prime minister of Nadistan's seal. The book referred to him as "our leader," dedicating a full chapter to his biography. Yet the actual governor of Charagan, who by Nadistan's own constitution was Charagan's autonomous leader, was not even mentioned. The constitution guaranteed the right to self-governance for Charagan, but the military presence flouted the law.

"It's just not safe for you, for us. Think of our son if not yourself." Her voice rose higher.

"Do you want me to not even mention the governor's name? Pretend that we are Nadistan's colony?" He pulled his hand away. This year's textbook eliminated the chapter on land reform that Charagan instituted after the colonial forces left. "What future do our children have if they are raised on lies and don't understand our history? If they don't even understand how they got the land that they stand on?"

"Be reasonable, Murad. You know they are arresting teachers. Just follow the government textbooks. For me. Please?"

He turned away from her and looked out at the trees beyond their property, sloping up to a ridge. He'd saved half the old textbooks when the Ministry of Education had come to collect them. He didn't let the children take them home, but he used them in class.

"Think of your family." Haseena picked up the tray and loaded it with their cups. He was stubborn—wed to his dreams.

In the distance, the lights from the army posts dotted the mountain that marked the cease-fire line. A bat fluttered overhead, and the neighbor's dog barked as someone left. Murad made out a woman. Why was she alone at this time? The snake of her hair was distinct on her back. Was it Aisha's mother? His heart beat faster; it was Noorjahan. He needed to talk with her about Aisha. It was ridiculous to have a student in school who wouldn't speak.

He waited until Noorjahan left the neighbor's, and then followed her, going through the gate of their backyard to avoid Haseena's questions.

Noorjahan was ahead of him. He walked quickly to catch up to her on the road. "Good evening," he said when she was within earshot. Seeing her awoke something inside him. When he was young, all the boys noticed Noorjahan when they saw her working in the fields. They'd made excuses to go and buy wool and leather from the goat herders who lived on the mountain above her.

That was when he was young and idealistic. Even the local government had believed in dreams then, and legislated land reform, forcing the landowners to give their land to the poor who worked it. Anything seemed possible—even marrying a girl from a poor family. But she chose Babak, and a good thing, too, as these things never lasted.

Noorjahan turned to face him. She had high cheekbones, her hazel eyes the green of the land. Her hair was covered in a sheer blue scarf that he could see the line of her ear under. She moved ever so slightly toward him, an indication that he could continue even though they both knew that he should not be approaching her alone.

"I wanted to speak with you about Aisha," he said, trying to block the pain pounding in his head.

Noorjahan's lips stiffened. "Yes?"

"I'm not sure that she's quite ready for school."

She crossed her arms. "What do you mean?"

Murad swallowed, feeling suddenly nervous. "She doesn't speak. How can I teach her?"

"She knows how to speak. She is just afraid outside the home." Her eyes pierced his. "Be patient with her. She will learn."

Why was she telling him how to teach his class? He was the teacher. "The other children are cruel to her. Wait another year."

"You are being cruel." She started walking up the road, but then she turned and added, "Why on earth would you deny her an education?"

He wasn't denying Aisha anything. He had only meant to help. "Of course, she is welcome in the classroom. I am just concerned that she is being teased so much." He walked after Noorjahan.

Noorjahan sighed and slowed down, letting him catch up to her. "She has been through so much. Just give her some time."

Noorjahan looked so vulnerable and alone. Murad wanted to take her hands in his. "I could maybe offer her additional lessons. That is, if you would like that."

"No thank you." Her voice was stern. "We will be just fine. Is your head bothering you?"

His cheeks flushed and he stammered as if he were a boy again. "Bothering me?" What was she implying? Why had he even come after her and tried to help? She was such a difficult woman.

"Why not say what you need?" She shook her head and reached

into the leather pouch at her side. "It's my help you want. Why bring Aisha into this?"

Murad's throat tightened. What on earth was she talking about? "I'll be on my way, then."

She pulled something from her bag, some kind of dried herb, and rubbed it between her hands, then shoved it under his nose. "This will help."

"I don't believe in such rubbish." He blocked her hand from his nose. The feeling of her skin against his sparked against his spine.

"Just inhale it when your head hurts. You can also add it to boiling water and breathe in the vapors."

Murad took the herbs and sniffed them skeptically. Relief flooded his sinuses.

"That should take care of it. This time, I won't charge you."

The pain from his headache dissolved.

3

AISHA

RETURNING HOME FROM her first day of school, Aisha found the house empty. She scrubbed her shoes with an old cloth. The dirt came off, but the leather was scuffed and damaged. Trying to hide the ruin, she placed the shoes in the shadow of her thick winter boots.

Where was her mother? It was late. Maybe someone was sick and her mother had gone to help? She kept glancing out the window to see if her mother was coming up the road.

Aisha removed her dupatta and assessed the damage. Her stomach tightened. Omar had stained it with his muddy fingers. A huge red stain like a moth opening its wings tainted the white fabric. The best thing her mother had ever gotten her was destroyed.

She changed into a long shirt and wool pants and went outside and tried to wash out the stain, but the moth refused to give away. Instead, bits of the fabric snagged and tore. The silhouette of the moth remained. There was nothing to do but hide the soiled dupatta where her mother wouldn't see it.

She checked the pots on the stove—there were some crusted lentils left, but no rice. She measured a cupful, washed the rice until the water ran clean, and put it on to boil.

The front door creaked open, and her mother came in. Aisha ran over to her and hugged her. How beautiful she was; her mother didn't need to wear makeup. Everyone told Aisha how much she looked like her mother, but she never saw it.

"I made rice," Aisha said, hoping to distract her mother from the ruin of her dupatta.

"What would I do without you?" her mother said, releasing Aisha from her arms. "You must be hungry."

Aisha nodded. She skipped over to the stove and pulled the wooden step stool over to reach the bowls, and then served them. They ate in silence. Her mother formed the rice into little balls and grunted her thanks. Aisha hadn't realized how hungry she was until her stomach warmed with food.

"How was school?"

Her hand froze. "Good."

"You are a very smart girl. It is important that you do well in school and get high marks on your exams."

Yes, she'd do well. So well that her father would arrive to collect her scores. She knew that her father was alive, that he was going to come back for her.

"Where is your dupatta? Why aren't you wearing it?"

Aisha's breath constricted in her chest. "It's hanging under my old ones so it doesn't get damaged." She felt bolstered by the story. It made good sense. "I'll wear it only for special occasions."

Her mother's eyes softened. "You are such a good girl. I'll do the dishes tonight. You must be tired from such a long day. Go, get ready for bed."

Aisha finished her food and then slid off to bed.

As the week passed, Aisha settled into a new rhythm with school. She missed going with her mother and seeing all the babies. The best days were ones like today, when her mother was home.

Noorjahan stood at the stove cooking dinner, while Aisha rushed through her homework so that she could play outside while it was still light. As soon as she finished, she put her schoolwork away, headed to the door, and grabbed her yellow dupatta.

"Why don't you wear your white one?" her mother asked her.

Her heart dropped. "I don't want to dirty it." Aisha forced herself to meet her mother's eyes.

"Why don't you wear it to school?"

"I do." Aisha pulled on her boots, grabbed her jacket, and fled.

The door slammed over her mother's words: "Don't catch cold."

Skipping away from the house, past the orchards, she climbed up the hill. Her cheeks flushed as she reached the top. The trees in the orchard below were small little dwarfs with green sprouting limbs. Aisha ran down the hill, hands in the air, screaming, imagining she were being chased. She ran so fast that she was flying, arms outstretched. At the bottom, she dropped to the ground, eyes open to the clouds. A bear in the cloud turned into an owl and floated away. She rolled on her belly, grabbed a stick, and poked at a bush. There were two bugs on a leaf. She blew on them, and one flew away; the other landed on a nearby plant with four purple flowers. These were special flowers that warded off the evil eye. Aisha leaned closer and squealed with excitement. Gathering as many as she could, she slipped them into the pocket of her woolen cloak.

Her mother would be so happy with the flowers. Aisha ran home, singing all the way, eager to give her mother the gift. When she entered the house, her mother sat in the corner, cross-legged, smoking her grandfather's water pipe.

"Mom, I have something for you."

"What is it, love?"

Aisha pulled the flowers from her pocket.

Her mother looked down and smiled. Smoke curled above her

head. "What a wonderful surprise. A mother without a daughter is like a boat without oars."

Aisha beamed.

School ended, and her mother would be working late, visiting newborn babies. When her mother was away, Aisha often went down to the river to catch fish, but some days she felt bolder, venturing down the hill toward town all by herself.

Aisha watched Mina head down the hill toward their grandparents' compound with a cluster of boys eager to play cricket. But Aisha was not invited, and her mother forbade her from visiting her paternal grandparents after her father had left. Omar headed up the hill with the missing-tooth girl, Mina's brother, Padmal, and the Gujars' children, who lived high in the hills, herding goats.

When the coast was clear of the other children, she started up the path home, kicking a pine cone. After weeks of use, her shoes were now worn, and the scuffs from the first day no longer mattered. She'd not worn the dupatta since Omar had stained it, and her mother stopped asking about it. She washed it each week, in an attempt to remove the muddy stain, but it hovered over the fabric, leaving half-spread wings.

The pine cone skidded up the trail, hit a rock, and then rolled by her down the hill. Aisha turned around and ran after it, kicking it with all her might, expecting it to explode into a million pieces. Instead, it gained momentum and tumbled farther down the hill. It was not going to get away. Her legs pumped fast against the ground as she ran after it, the wind cold against her.

She ran past the pines and large boulders, but could not catch the pine cone; it was gone. As she approached town, the pines gave way to poplars, rice paddies terraced the hills, and corrugated metal fences lined the roads. She crossed the metal bridge over the river into the town. Long embroidered shirts hung in the entryway of a shop, vegetables were heaped in stainless steel bowls, flat breads were being toasted in a metal skillet, walnuts mounded alongside golden raisins, and shawls were stacked by size and quality.

Aisha went to the vendor selling bread and bought two pieces. She crouched down at the side of the stall and ate the bread toasted with poppy seeds. She used to come here with her father. Her mother would get mad at them for wasting their money on the bread when she'd made it at home, but neither Aisha nor her father could resist.

Every week, her father used to take her to visit his ancestral home, but her mother never came. Her father's brothers and one sister, Mina's mom, still lived at their parents' compound. Even before her father left, something had separated her from her cousins whose parents lived on the family land, building their houses on the undeveloped parts. Still, she liked playing with her cousins, building forts from sticks, climbing trees, and eating fruit before it was ripe. The older cousins used to pull Aisha and Mina in a wagon down the hills, bumping them over rocks and potholes.

After her father left, the visits ended. She ate the bread alone, remembering how when she became tired, he'd lift her on his shoulders and they'd pretend she was riding a horse, Aisha telling him which way to go. Aisha finished her bread and headed down the path toward her father's ancestral home. She could ask his parents where he'd gone. She needed him to come to school for exam day.

Passing the private school, a stately A-frame building with intricately carved shutters, she watched the children march in the front courtyard in their starched uniforms, khaki and white, the same color as the mountains peering out from the snow. All her cousins, except for Mina and her brother, Padmal, went there. But now that her father was gone, her other cousins pretended not to know her and did not run up to the fence and wave like they used to. Once, her cousin Zeina had slipped a sweet through the fence into Aisha's outstretched hands. She didn't chew the candy, but let it melt in her mouth.

Arriving at her grandparents' compound, Aisha continued up the driveway. The stairs to their house creaked as she ascended them. The radio blared, children squealed from behind the house, and onions popped as they fried. Her grandfather, Baba Chacha, sat on the porch, smoking. His eyes lit up when he saw her. "Aishaji, come."

Aisha ran and hugged him. He smelled of sweat and wool. His sweater scratched against her cheek. His brown eyes were creased with wrinkles and his beard and hair were streaked with gray. He wore a gray wool cap and long sweater over brown pants.

"Let me get a look at you," he said, releasing her. "So tall now."

Aisha stood up straighter, smiling.

"We have missed you around here," he whispered, a secret for just the two of them to share. "You are looking more and more like your mother. Sit." He patted the seat beside him. Aisha sat down. She imagined the framed photo of her father hanging on the wall inside her grandparents' house.

"Where is my father?" The words came out with a stutter. Aisha covered her mouth with her hand, stunned at her own voice.

"He is in the city. He sends letters and asks of you. It is so good that you have come to visit, so I can give him some news. What shall I tell him?" Her grandfather took her hand, his cracked with age.

There was so much Aisha wanted to ask: When would her father return? Why did he leave? Will he come to school to receive her grades? The front door opened, and Aisha turned as her grandmother came out onto the porch, wringing a thin cheesecloth in her hands. The curds clung to her wrist. She narrowed her eyes at Aisha. The tiniest hint of gray threaded the line below her eyes. Aisha was sure that her grandmother was made of steel.

Aisha's knees knocked together and she stumbled over the uneven wood on the porch toward her grandmother. "Isn't it late for you to be so far from home?"

Her throat closed. Only a stutter came out.

"Speak up, child. I don't have all day. She doesn't speak?" Her grandmother spoke to her grandfather. "I told you. Something is wrong with her."

Aisha froze, stunned. She longed to curl up under a blanket and disappear. She took a step back, her legs shaking, and looked toward Baba Chacha. "It is getting late, Aisha. Does your mother know you are here? Shall I walk you home?"

"I need the table moved in the kitchen," her grandmother said.

His eyes held hers for a moment. Aisha shook her head, turned, and ran down the stairs, not looking back, even though Baba Chacha called to her. Her muscles took over as she ran up the hill. Her tears turned to sweat; her stomach cramped. In the center of town, a few shops were still open, but the streets were mostly empty. In twenty minutes, she would be home.

As she headed into the forest, the sound of male voices stunned her. She slowed down to hear better, the language foreign. She glanced around, searching for a place to hide. The voices grew louder.

Aisha moved as quickly and quietly as she could, heading off the trail and down the mountainside toward a ravine, where she curled up behind a boulder. Her belly pressed into the dirt. She prayed that the men would pass quickly and not see her.

Five men came around the bend. Aisha wriggled for a better view. Yellow teeth, eyes black as river stones, and fur-rimmed hooded jackets cast them in shadows. These must be the men of the north—guns held ready. They had a captive. Aisha held her breath and squinted to see who it was. Her cousin. One of the men held a knife against Padmal's back.

Aisha forced herself to be quiet and still.

Padmal looked so small against the men's heavy frames. The man with a thick black beard leaned forward, bringing his knife down along the side of Padmal's head. Padmal screamed. Blood flowed down his neck.

Aisha bit her lip to keep from screaming. Everything began to spin. Padmal's screams were inhuman, sharp splinters of noise.

And then a dozen men from the village ran down the path and into the clearing with guns of their own, swords, sticks, stones, and kerosene lamps burning in the twilight. They came from the top of the mountain, tall and brittle like pine trees. Omar's father and grandfather approached, swords in hand.

The men who held Padmal captive looked up in shock. The bearded man gave Padmal a kick, sending him crashing to the ground, and then ran toward the border; the men of Poshkarbal chased behind them.

A few men stayed back to tend to Padmal. Omar's father knelt down beside Padmal, pushing a cloth against the side of his head to stop the bleeding. The grandfather searched the ground and grabbed something.

Aisha stayed hidden, watching as Omar's father slung Padmal over his shoulder and headed up the path. Aisha ran after them, terrified to be left alone.

The men spun around when they heard her approach, knives raised. It was Omar's grandfather who recognized her first.

"What are you doing here, child?" the grandfather asked. "Were you coming home from school?"

She nodded, dropping her eyes to the ground.

Omar's grandfather shook his head. "Look at the danger this child was in." He turned toward Aisha. "You mustn't be out so late. Things have changed. You are to walk home with the boys in your class from now on. If your mother had any sense, she wouldn't be sending you to school in all this danger."

Padmal hung listlessly over Omar's father's shoulder. Blood trickled down his body. Aisha tried to look away, but she couldn't avert her eyes. His ear was gone. They'd sliced it off. She followed behind the men as they headed toward her house, where her mother would help Padmal.

As they approached her house, her mother stood by the door, arms crossed, waiting for them. Aisha followed the men into the house and was met by the stern impasse of her mother. She was late. She was with men. Aisha slunk past her mother, hoping to become invisible in the chaos unfolding around them.

As soon as she slipped off her shoes, her mother said, "Put water on to boil." Aisha's hands shook as she lit the stove and heated the water. Her mother thrust some herbs and honey toward her. "Mix them."

Aisha nodded, taking too long to find a bowl.

Her mother pressed a cloth against Padmal's bleeding wound. Padmal curled into her mother's lap. Omar's father was sent to gather ice from the mountain. When he returned with a handful of snow, they put the blue ear on ice.

When the bleeding slowed, her mother pressed the ear against his head and stitched his ear back on. Padmal gritted his teeth. Aisha pressed her hands over her ears, imagining the stabbing pain. Tears flowed from Padmal's eyes, but he did not scream. The blue ear under the pleading pressure of her mother's needle turned to pink—once again a part of his body.

When the men left, Aisha's body tensed, prepared for her beating.

Instead, her mother hugged her. "I was so worried about you. You must be a good girl and come home right after school, even if I am away."

"I'm sorry." Aisha bit her lip. "Maybe I shouldn't be in school."

Her mother sat down on the mat and pulled Aisha into her lap. She rested her chin on her head. "No, baby, you have to go to school and study hard. You are so smart."

Aisha's body relaxed against her mother's. She wanted to tell her mother how lonely school was, how she needed her father to receive her test results, how scared she was that she would get attacked by the men, that when she closed her eyes, all she saw was blood.

Instead, she reached up and grabbed the warmth of her mother's neck, inhaling her sweet scent.

4

MURAD

EVERY TUESDAY, MURAD watched Noorjahan across the street, visiting with the neighbor's new baby. He imagined the infant nestling against her chest.

Haseena shuffled into their room. He dropped the curtain and turned from the window, going over to their nightstand where he grabbed the nearest book.

"Alim is having trouble with his homework. Could you help him, Murad?"

"He doesn't want my help. I asked already."

"Maybe if you were more patient with him, none of this would be a problem. He barely passed his last quiz."

Murad took a deep breath. Haseena always blamed him. What about how she pampered the child? Alim refused to focus on his studies and there was never a consequence.

"I heard Padmal is deaf in his ear." She hadn't been able to sleep the last few nights. The poor child. Who would they take next? Nothing like this had ever happened before.

Murad looked up at Haseena. "The ear is healing, and his hearing is just fine. It really is quite a miracle." He'd heard that Noorjahan had bravely stitched Padmal's ear back. The men were taking turns stationed at gaps in the border, watching for intruders. It was no longer safe for their children.

He longed to go back to the window to watch Noorjahan. There was something so sweet and tender about her.

"Maybe you could teach at the private school next year." Haseena already discussed this with her uncle. They had a position opening and the pay would be more. Why was he being so stubborn?

Murad tensed. He didn't want her family's handouts. He could earn his own way. Leaving the school wouldn't solve anything. "Padmal was taken because of his parents." He was targeted because his father was Hindu. It was easier to believe that they would be safe and only the mixed families were in danger. "Don't worry; we'll get through this. We're keeping watch on the village."

"With all the soldiers around, you'd think that you wouldn't have to." She hated it when Murad went out at night to look out with the other men. The hours passed without sleep as she imagined him being taken by bandits or shot by the army.

"These soldiers are not here to protect us." Nadistan's military never seemed to interfere with armed bandits crossing the border. Instead, they interrogated the village men as if they had attacked Padmal. Everyone knew that it was operatives from Daryastan paid by drug lords that wanted to control the opium industry.

"It was so different when we were children," Haseena said. "We never had to worry like this."

Murad stood up and took Haseena's hand in his.

"Why are you wearing your jacket?" Haseena asked. He wasn't signed up for patrol.

Murad's stomach tightened. Her hand stiffened. "I'm going to see my brother."

"What about Alim?"

"He didn't want any help." Murad slipped into the night, hoping that he hadn't missed Noorjahan.

His timing was good. As he rounded the bend, Noorjahan was just ahead of him. He walked loudly so that she would hear his approach.

She turned around. The dusk cast her face in purple light. "Yes?"

Murad closed the gap between them and stood before her. "You shouldn't be out so late alone."

"Is that why you've come? Or is it about Aisha again?"

"She is clever, just like her mother." Murad was amazed at her progress over the past weeks, but poor Aisha was so traumatized by what happened to Padmal, she kept drawing pictures of children being stabbed by men with swords. "Have you seen her drawings?"

"They are so lovely. She brought me the bird."

"She is talented, but I think what happened with Padmal frightened her."

"It's scary to live in this world where people will hurt a child just because of how their parents love. What can we do?"

"I just worry about her walking alone."

"She was out late. It won't happen again. I told her to go right home after school."

"Why doesn't she walk home with Omar? And on days he can't, I can go with her."

"Save her from the bears, feed her to the wolves. I know how to protect my daughter."

Then why was Aisha out alone, watching Padmal taken hostage by goondas? "It is getting late." The moon slipped out from behind a tree and shone on them. "I only want to help you."

She shook her head. "I should be going."

"Next week, we'll meet again?" He hadn't meant to be so forward, but suddenly he was sure of it. Sure that he could help her. Sure that she needed him.

The next day in class, Murad's headache was back.

"Children, pencils down," he said. "Mina, please collect the work."

Mina jumped when the teacher called her name, startled. She wanted to cry. To go home and be with her mother. She'd heard her grandparents last night. Her grandmother said her mother should have never been allowed to marry her father—that this was all Baba Chacha's silly thinking, letting his daughter have a love marriage, and with a Hindu, no less. Her stomach knotted. She was a mistake. She dropped someone's assignment on the ground, picked it up, and hoped that nobody would notice.

Murad sighed. Mina looked so sad. A paper airplane soared through the class. Murad appraised the boys at the back. Padmal's cheeks were red with excitement. Murad cleared his throat, pretending not to notice, happy to see Padmal back to his old tricks.

"Alright, children, you are dismissed," he said. "Omar and Aisha, I would like to speak to you." Noorjahan had been so stubborn last night, insisting that she didn't need help. But Omar lived nearby and could protect Aisha.

The color drained from Aisha's face as she grabbed her bag and approached Murad's desk. Omar strolled up and leaned on the corner.

"Omar, can you please walk Aisha home after school."

"But sir, I am not always going home directly."

"What do you have to do after class that is so important?"

Omar was quiet. He shoved his hands into his pockets.

"If something comes up, let me know, Omar. I will rearrange my schedule to walk Aisha home."

Omar frowned and nodded.

"Omar, you are to make sure that Aisha arrives home safely, understand?"

Aisha stared at him, blinking back tears.

"Very well, then, be on your way." They started to walk toward the door. "And Omar, be kind to her or I'll have a word with your mother myself."

"Yes, sir."

Murad watched the two set off up the hill, and then organized the papers on his desk. Aisha's notebook was on top. He flipped through her work for the week. There were new pictures—the men with knives had fangs. In one, Padmal's ear flew away as a bird. How had this happened? How had their home turned into a place that their children feared?

5

AISHA

THE FIRST COUPLE times Aisha walked home with Omar, things were uneventful, though she was terrified that her mother would see her with him. Then one day after school her luck changed. On their way home, her mother appeared around the bend. There was nothing she could do; they were in plain view. Everything slowed, her limbs felt as if they were detached from her body.

Her mother spoke softly to her. "We are going home now." They walked in silence that did not break when Aisha took off her shoes or started her homework.

"Get the bowls for dinner," her mother said. "I told you to stay away from boys."

Aisha bit her lip. The teacher had set it all up. How could she explain it to her mother?

"Quickly." Her mother did not look up from the stove as she spoke.

Aisha's hands shook as she grabbed the bowls, setting them on the counter. She'd forgotten to take off her dupatta. She took it off and hung it by the door.

"Where is your new dupatta?" her mother asked.

Aisha froze. She stared at the ground.

"What is wrong? Have you lost it or something? Bring it to me, Aisha."

Aisha took down the yellow one, then the turquoise one. Underneath, hung the white dupatta. She pulled it down, exposing the stain, and carried it with the others to her mother. She was going to be skinned alive. She dropped them all on the ground.

Her mother grabbed her by the ear. "Don't you ever drop your things so carelessly. Pick them up."

Aisha grabbed them and handed them to her mother, who carefully unfolded the full length of the white dupatta, exposing the stain in the center.

"Don't you ever lie to me again."

Aisha froze.

Noorjahan grabbed the hand broom and struck her. Aisha cried, unable to control her sobs. "Be quiet." The broom hit her again, squarely on the back. Aisha shrieked. She could not swallow the sounds. Her breath was knocked out of her. Tears stung her cheeks. The blows were sharp and hot. Like flames.

The broom pounding against her back turned into the popping sound of fire, to the night her grandparents were lost forever.

"Grandmother! Grandfather!" Aisha had yelled, gagging from the smoke. Every hair in her body reached to burrow back into her skin, to find any cover from the singeing flames. Her fingers dug into earth. Her grandmother looked right at her, dripping her terror into Aisha's eyes. She lost sight of her grandfather. The fire spread into the wind, consuming the buckets that her grandparents had been using to dump water on it. The fire jumped the trench Noorjahan had been digging.

And then she heard her father. "Run." His voice came through the beat of the flames. "Run, Aisha! Run." And she ran from the heat and flames.

But now she could not run from her mother.

"I hate you," screamed Aisha. The final blow knocked the wind from her chest, leaving splinters welting up her back. Noorjahan grabbed her coat, put on her shoes, and left the house without even glancing back.

Aisha did not move at first. Even the slightest movement caused pain. Slowly, she got up. She'd been a bad girl. No wonder her father had left them. A splinter stuck to her calf. It was right on her birthmark, lodging in the border of her scar. She pulled it out.

Ignoring the sting of her skin and the ache in her bones, she sat down to finish her homework. The numbers spun on the page. The words blurred together. Had she been so bad that her mother would leave her just as her father had? Aisha wiped tears from her cheek.

Her mother returned with herbs.

"Lie down on the mat," Noorjahan said. Aisha lay down and melted under the warm touch of her mother as she spread ointment across her welts.

She did not resist when her mother used a needle to remove the splinters. Aisha inhaled the sweetness of the oil as her mother rubbed the pain from her shoulder. Her skin tingled with the warmth of her mother's touch.

The next morning, her mother was in the kitchen packing food and boiling tea. Lentils steamed on the counter. Aisha didn't feel hungry, but took the bowl and ate quietly.

"Dress warm today. We're going to get some herbs from the warm pools."

Her mother had forgiven her. The pools were her favorite place, not so much the hike to get there, which was straight uphill, but

Aisha loved the warm water that bubbled up from the earth and the small frogs that lived in the ponds.

Aisha dressed in layers, starting with long shirts and a vest. She pulled on her mittens and tugged her wool hat down over her ears.

Her mother led them past the orchard and up the mountain to a small trail that connected to the mountain pass. When Aisha looked back, she could see smoke rising from the shops downtown and the sprinkle of light on the valley that stretched beyond their village. On the muddy path patches of ice formed. Aisha stepped into her mother's footprints. Small white clouds gathered on the mountain-tops to the south. As they climbed higher, Aisha could see the army camp that stretched along the border. She could just make out the villages of Daryastan, across the border. Aisha wrapped her jacket around her waist and stuffed her mittens in her pocket.

They took the smaller fork in the trailhead and the first pond came into view, with green reeds growing all around. Sometimes, her mother let her wade in the steaming water, the hot mud between her toes. They hiked past the first pool and around a grove of trees, stunted by the harsh mountain climate, and then arrived at three small ponds. Her mother lay a thick blanket on the ground. "You must be hungry."

Aisha nodded and her mother handed her a small tin with collards. She ate them with bread and drank greedily from the canteen.

"Look over there." Her mother pointed to a boulder at the other side of the pond; growing on top were the winter cherries that they'd come for. The broad leaves were full of lantern-like blossoms that held a small red cherry in the center.

Aisha squealed. "I'll get it." She ran around to the winter cherries, harvesting the young leaves and some of the pods and digging a few of the roots from the largest plant.

Her mother took the bundle of herbs from her and removed her shoes. "Shall we?"

Aisha nodded and walked to the edge of the water. It was so hot that goose bumps rose up her legs. She stepped back and folded her pants above her knees. Leaning over, she scooped up a small frog, which hopped back in the water, floating for a moment before it swam away. Aisha reached for her mother's hand, warm with spring water.

6

MURAD

MURAD LEFT THE schoolhouse tired and set off toward home. He'd had difficulty sleeping the last few nights. His thoughts spiraled. There was the leak in the roof, three young men went missing in the next village, Alim had been stopped by the border patrol, Haseena kept pressuring him to teach at the private school, and now, Noorjahan. As hard as he tried to wipe her from his thoughts, she overpowered everything. Every color reminded him of her. The scents in the air, the plants and trees, the dirt itself, all seemed to be leading back to her.

The day was crisp and clear, and the warmth of the sun held the promise of spring. Murad went to the market for some fresh bread. Bunches of spinach and lettuce were stacked in mounds, the first of the peaches still sour and green. A small crowd trickled through what was left of the vegetables. Some vendors had left for the day, the metal doors pulled down, the street by their stall swept clean. Murad was in luck; there was still fresh bread. He inhaled the scent, but the line was impossible. So he walked to the far side of the market where the crowds were thin. An older woman he didn't recognize sat on the ground next to piles of chard. Haseena didn't prefer chard and rarely bought it. Murad purchased three bunches, handing the woman three dihabs, and walked toward an old man who had a few flat breads on a blanket with only one woman in line. He was stunned by his luck. It was Noorjahan.

"I'll take them all," she said, buying the last of the bread.

"Please, leave me at least one," he said, walking up to her side.

The breadwalla shook his head at Murad. "The lady arrived first."

"Don't worry"—Noorjahan leaned in so that only Murad could hear her—"I will share with you."

The breadwalla shoved all the bread in a bag and handed it to Noorjahan, who then headed up a small path away from the market. Should he follow her? *I will share with you.* It was an invitation. As he descended over the hill, Noorjahan came into view.

"Did you come for your bread?"

Murad nodded sheepishly. "It's no problem. You keep it all." He glanced around, ensuring that they were well hidden, and reached toward her bag. "Let me carry this for you."

She handed it to him. "Just don't eat them all." They followed the trail down into a ravine.

"It is good that Aisha is walking home with Omar now."

"She shouldn't be alone with Omar."

"She's just a little girl. I spoke to him myself. In a few years, when she is older, we'll figure something else out."

"Girls are never too young. Men are never too old. This is a timeless law." Noorjahan started walking up the hill. The silence stretched between them until Noor spoke again. "You've had these headaches since you were a young man." The way she said it was more of a statement rather than a question.

"Yes, but it could be worse."

"Or better."

"I've tried everything." He stumbled over a rock in the path.

She paused until he regained his balance, and then pointed to a boulder that was flat on the top, just off the path. "Do you want to sit?"

He nodded and followed her. Noorjahan shimmied up the rock with ease. His knuckles stung where he'd scraped them against the rock. Murad sat beside her. "You're a very strong woman."

Noorjahan pulled out her leather pouch and took out some powder in a bag, handing it to Murad. "Put this in your tea in the morning. It should last you a few weeks."

"What is it?"

"Medicine to strengthen your blood. The herbs and the powder will cure you, but you must also focus on your breath. You breathe too shallow."

"My breath quickens when I see you." He placed a hand on her back. She did not move away.

Her face tilted toward him, golden in the light. He leaned in and kissed her cheek. His hand ran down the length of her spine. He blinked twice to convince himself that this wasn't a dream. She didn't disappear.

7

AISHA

ON EXAM DAY, Aisha's stomach ached as she walked to school with her mother. Spring flowers burst along the trail. God could not save her. Inside the classroom, all the children's fathers stood proudly at the back: men with thick-soled boots, white caps, and close-trimmed beards. Even Omar's yellow-snow grandfather was there. Her father wasn't there, nor was Baba Chacha. She slid into her seat, hoping that nobody would notice.

Mina poked her in the back. "Your mom is here." Noorjahan stood away from the men at the back, quiet. Everyone would laugh at Aisha.

The teacher called each child up to the front of the class, along-side their father. When Murad called Aisha, she did not move. She did not speak. God himself could not get her out of the chair. She wanted to disappear.

Noorjahan came and stood next to her. Everyone was silent. She put out her hand. Tears filled Noor's eyes. "Stand tall. Stand proud, Aisha."

Murad called Aisha's name again. Heat flooded her cheeks. She stood up and took her mother's hand.

Aisha did not look at Mina or the men at the back of the classroom. She stood tall beside her mother. They walked up to the front of the class. Murad handed her scores to Noorjahan.

"Congratulations. Aisha placed first in her standard."

Aisha looked up at Noorjahan. Her mother swelled with pride. The tears in Aisha's eyes spilled over. Applause thundered through the room.

Aisha didn't go to the market with Omar after school to get groceries as she was supposed to. She wanted to run home and celebrate with her mother.

"Wait, what are you doing? We're supposed to go the market," Omar called behind her. Every Wednesday after school, they went together to do the grocery shopping. Aisha couldn't understand why her mother changed her mind about her walking with Omar. "Slow down. Your mom is going to be upset if you don't get the shopping done. What will you have to eat?"

Aisha ignored him. What did he know of her mother? She'd want to celebrate.

"You don't even talk, and the teacher gave you the highest marks." Omar kicked a rock off the trail as he caught up to her. "It's only because the schoolteacher likes your mother. Did you see how he looked at her?"

Aisha sped up, leaving Omar in the dust. He was such a jerk. He couldn't stand that she was smarter than him. She didn't need to listen to this garbage. She ran as fast as she could toward home.

Reaching the gate to their driveway, Aisha exhaled in relief. She knew her mother wouldn't be angry that she hadn't done the shopping. Aisha would harvest some vegetables from the yard, and they had plenty of lentils. She imagined her mother's joy when she arrived to find Aisha cooking. The fire would be lit, rice bubbling, flour and water mixed in a bowl, coriander chopped, and water jugs filled.

She went around to the back of her house and washed her hands. Something banged inside. Was her mother home early? Maybe she'd just imagined the sound. Careful not to crush any leaves, Aisha tip-toed up to the window and stood on her toes to peer through. She saw the fish hanging on strings and the bags of spices. Then she saw them.

Every part of her wanted to scream, to erase the image. But she could not move. The schoolteacher was on top of her mother. Her arms were around his neck. He lowered his head and kissed her mother.

Aisha backed away from the window careful not to be seen. She bolted down the path toward the river. Tears blinded her, but she ran faster, refusing to look back.

This was why her father had left. How could he stay with a wife like this?

part 2

POPPIES

AGE 17
1983

Poshkarbal

8

AISHA

AISHA NEVER TOLD her mother what she'd seen. She understood why her father had left and why her mother was shunned. It was a silent burden that she grew strong enough to carry.

All the boys resented Aisha for being the star student, placing first in her class year after year. Murad and her mother always talked to her about going to college. Separate conversations that Aisha knew they secretly aligned during those nights her mother was away "working."

Noorjahan had been gone the last two weeks, visiting a neighboring village to train the midwives. It was the first time that Aisha was afraid to be alone. Last week, someone had thrown a flaming glass bottle through a window in Mina's house. Glass shattered everywhere, but nobody was hurt. Omar told her everything—even though it was on her grandparents' property. He said it was because Mina's father was organizing for independence, and that the paramilitary had probably done it but that they'd framed some boys from Daryastan instead, claiming that they'd targeted him because he was Hindu.

Baba Chacha did not report the crime to the authorities, but still the soldiers came. They grabbed some poor boys from Daryastan who were probably looking for work due to floods in their village, and charged them as adults.

Every thud that Aisha heard during the night, she was sure was a soldier. She was waiting for someone to hurl a flaming bottle through their window, but Omar kept telling her that she didn't need to worry. She wasn't mixed like Mina. And her mother would be back soon.

Today Mina came back to school, but Padmal was missing. They'd been out all week. Mina sat with Aisha in the back of the classroom alongside the two other girls whose families let them continue their schooling. Mina was tall and slender like her mother, with auburn hair that looked wild and unbrushed. Her long and angular face was punctuated by her pointed chin. The front of the classroom was filled with the new students, more than half were girls. One of the little girls didn't speak. Aisha often spent lunchtime with her, reading to her, healing the eight-year-old inside herself who hadn't spoken her whole first year in school.

Murad wore the same thick glasses, a dark blue sweater, and gray pants. His shoulders hunched forward as if he were trying to make himself small. Murad called roll, skipping Padmal's name, and then said, "Mina Khar," her mother's maiden name. Why was her last name changed?

"Who would like to begin the poetry recitation?" Murad asked. What did her mother see in him? This worn, frail man, who'd shake with fear if her father returned. Aisha imagined her father lifting the schoolteacher by the neck and throwing him out of their lives forever.

Aisha raised her hand. The schoolteacher looked past her, waiting for another volunteer. Hadn't he learned by now? She was the star student, and nobody wanted to go before or after her. Aisha stood tall in her fitted burgundy kurta that her mother claimed was too tight and drew too much attention. Aisha felt Omar's eyes on her as she stood before the class, her bracelets clanging together as she tucked a loose piece of hair behind her ear. Aisha chose a poem by a woman poet who divorced, who followed her heart, who was haunted by love. She wondered if the schoolteacher would realize that the rest of the students would know that she was talking about his affair with her mother.

"My friend, this youth is loss
I lost all day on the way
Why were we born?
Why did we not die?"

She did not look at Murad or the kids in her class but imagined her mother, saying the words as she went off to meet him.

"The way of the world is a meaningless storm." Her mom was caught in the wind, dust blowing into her eyes. The whispers of the villagers like daggers surrounded her.

Aisha finished the poem and returned to her seat. Murad did not comment on her choice and went dully on to the next student. Finally, lunchtime came, and Mina and the other girls were on the sunny side of the poplar tree. They never wanted Aisha around. She'd grown used to reading and studying alone at lunchtime, but she couldn't just walk by Mina without saying something.

She wanted to ask about Padmal, but also knew that there were things not to be spoken of. Mina caught her eye as she approached. Aisha squatted down next to them. "I'm so glad you weren't hurt." She squeezed Mina's arm.

Mina rubbed her palm against her eye. "I can't believe they are gone." She inhaled deeply. "I know I shouldn't talk about it, but how can I pretend that my father and Padmal never existed?" Ever since the flaming bottle burst through the window, Mina's life had exploded. First, her father went into hiding. He returned for a few days and then left with Padmal. She'd thought it was just temporary. The military searched their entire house. She'd been shaking in her grandmother's arms. But yesterday, when Mina had asked when her dad and Padmal would return, her grandmother had said, *You don't have a father or brother.* Her mother hadn't left her room for three days. She cried whenever Mina came in. *The less you know the better.* Mina wanted to know where on the mainland they went. Wanted the information to singe her, carve her up like her family. She should have walked on that broken glass from the window. Let the shards embed in her feet, so that she could remember that there was a before—a time when her family was whole.

Tears dripped down Mina's cheeks. Aisha patted her back. "They'll come back soon. This won't be for too long."

Mina shook her head. "It's not like that. It's a new life we are all starting. That's what my mom said. That we will be safe now." Aisha handed Mina her canteen, and she drank from it.

Aisha came home to find her mother had returned and Mina's mother was over. She was shocked to see Suha Auntie, who rarely, if ever, came to visit. Suha Auntie was tall and had Mina's same pointed chin, but her cheeks were full and round and rosy. Her turquoise shirt was covered in a fuchsia shawl.

Aisha wrapped her arms around her mother, relieved that she had returned home safe. Her mother smelled sweet like coconut oil.

"Hello, darling," Suha Auntie said, setting her tea down. Her eyes looked puffy.

"How was school?" Noorjahan asked before she started coughing uncontrollably.

Aisha put her schoolbag in the corner and thought of the poem that she'd read as she handed her mother some water. Her mom took a few sips, but the cough didn't let up. Aisha turned to Suha Auntie, "I'm so sorry for everything."

Her aunt's eyes filled with tears. "This must be God's will. I wish we'd have gone when Padmal was attacked. Then we could still be together. I never should have waited so long."

Noorjahan placed a hand over Suha's. "Let's just pray that Padmal is safe on the mainland. Going with him would only put them in more danger. You must be strong for Mina."

Her aunt dabbed her eyes with the edge of her sleeve. "I don't know how you do it, Noor. All alone, for all these years."

"It's best not to look back." Noorjahan squeezed her hand.

"Can you imagine this is what independence has done to our people? That we kill each other over religion. How can people be so cruel? They hate me for loving a Hindu man. All these migrants keep coming over the border and bring all their problems. I may never see my son or husband again. I can't go on like this."

Noorjahan sat back. "This isn't about religion or migration. Those boys were set up by the soldiers."

Did her aunt not know that her husband was involved in the independence movement? How could she blame this on young boys looking for work?

"Why don't you come for dinner next week, and bring Mina? There is plenty of space. You can spend the night." Noorjahan began coughing again.

"Are you okay, Mom? Have some more water."

Noorjahan shook her head, unable to speak. Aisha pushed the glass of water toward her. Noorjahan wiped her eyes. "It's nothing."

"I am sorry to bother you with all of this. You just came home and I'm dumping all my problems on you."

Noorjahan shook her head. "It brings me joy to see you. Please consider my home yours. Know that you can always stay here."

Suha Auntie stood up to go. "You have built so much for Aisha. It's not easy how you manage. May God watch over you. Please get some rest."

9

MURAD

MURAD TOOK UP drinking to justify his absence. Over the years, his visits with Noorjahan increased. They met at her house and in a shed at the edge of his brother's land. As Aisha grew older, they needed to be more careful.

It was Friday night, and he was ready to leave for his brother's house. The clock ticked, water ran in the bathroom, and Murad cracked walnuts, leaving piles of discarded shells overflowing from a steel bowl on the table.

"Can you walk me over to Mina's house? I want to bring her mother some food." Haseena pulled a blue silk scarf over the shoulders of her brown woolen cloak.

"Why not bring it tomorrow in the afternoon? It's not safe for you to be out so late."

"But if you come with me, I will be safe. It's such a tragedy what is happening to their family. I found a way to send some letters to her husband and Padmal."

Murad's throat constricted. "Is your brother taking the letters?"

She nodded. "I am only trying to help. I can't even imagine Alim being taken from me. We're so fortunate to be together."

His throat went dry. Mina had not said a word when he'd skipped over Padmal's name. Murad leaned over and kissed his wife. She met his warmth, pushing into him. He'd not felt her like this in so long. He ran his fingers over her hair and then slid his hand under the soft skin of her chin, kissing her forehead.

"You are right. It's better I go tomorrow. Tell your brother hello for me." Haseena had hoped that what happened to Mina's family would shock some sense into Murad. That he'd appreciate his wife, his son. That being together was enough. But she'd never been enough for him. Always going to his brother's. He was a fool to think that she didn't know what filth he was up to. Why did he bring such shame upon them? How could she even enter the mosque knowing what her husband did?

Haseena pulled away. "You better get going before it's too late."

"Yes, I'd like to go before the rain." His eye twitched as he stood up. On his way out, he passed Alim in the family room doing homework.

"Father, can you help me with my math?" Alim could not figure out the problem. Each time he tried, his mind went blank. The harder he tried, the more the figures danced on the page.

"What is the problem?" Murad sat on the pillow next to his son. Maybe he should stay home, but he hadn't seen Noorjahan in over two weeks.

"I cannot solve for x." Alim slid his glasses up his nose. The frustration in his dad's voice made him nervous. He was such a disappointment to him.

"Read the problem aloud." Alim stuttered over the words, then lost his place and had to start over. Alim's hair fell over his eyes, his mother insisting that they not cut it too short. He was nearly as tall as Murad. "What does x represent, Alim?"

"The apples."

"So how do you set up the equation?"

Alim pushed so hard on the pencil that the tip broke. Why did his father keep asking him all these questions? If he knew how to solve it, he wouldn't ask for help. He tried again. "Is this right?" Alim looked up at his father, eager for approval.

"You got it."

"Thanks, Dad." Alim put his homework away. Relieved to be done with the problem. "Say hi to Uncle for me."

Murad nodded and set out into the night.

The narrow path at the edge of his brother's land was muddy. Clouds filled the night sky ready to burst. Murad paused before opening the door. It had been weeks since he'd seen Noorjahan. She'd told him that she'd be in the village for a week, but after ten days had passed, she had not shown up. He'd waited for hours at their meeting spot, fighting the urge to go by her house and see if she were alright. The next day when he asked Aisha about Noor, she'd scowled at him and said, "What's it to you?" Then today, she read that poem about a divorced woman seeking love again. It was as if she knew.

A shaft of light from a kerosene lamp illuminated Noorjahan, lying on a thick blanket that covered the dusty ground. Her eyes were shut, and the tips of her lips were curled up in a smile as if she might be dreaming of him, of all the ways he pleasured her. She was safe. She was here. She was his. Every moment with her was a gift, stolen bits of joy peppering his life.

He crouched next to her, kissing her. Noorjahan had lost weight and moved with a new slowness. Still, her lips were full and tasted sweet against his. She coughed, and it rattled her chest. He moved away from her. The winter flu had killed thirteen people in the village.

"You are late," she said.

Late? She had no idea what he went through to get here. She hadn't even shown up last week. "Are you okay?"

"Don't worry. I'm not contagious, just cold. Warm me up."

Murad nestled in next to her, inhaling her scent of narcissus and cardamom. Her belly was warm through the layers of fabric. He slipped his hand under her shirt, her curves familiar and still surprising. She would be wet for him.

"You have too many clothes on." He sat on top of her, pulling off one layer at a time until her skin was against his.

The wind whistled through the cracks of the wooden planks of the shed. The clouds that had loomed in the sky broke into rain, bursting over the metal roof.

Noorjahan opened beneath him. He slid into her softness. He kissed the curve of her neck. Her breath was his. Her hands clasped his shoulders, pulling him in deeper. She fit perfectly against him, he filled her, and everything released inside him.

The wind whipped outside, and his mind drifted toward sleep. Noorjahan ran her fingers gently across his chest, making every part of him tingle. "There is something I must ask you, Murad."

"Yes, what is it, my love?"

She kissed up his chest until her lips were against his ear. "You must help Aisha keep our land. It is hers and hers alone. Promise me, Murad."

Tightness spread across his chest. She was sick. "Let me call the doctor." Why had he ignored it? He should have insisted as soon as he heard her cough.

She smiled at him a bit. "The doctors don't treat this. You know that. I'm not contagious anymore. It's past that stage."

"Is that why you didn't see me last week? What about Aisha?"

"I went away for a couple of weeks so I wouldn't infect anyone. She doesn't know yet. I mean, she must suspect, but I'm not ready." Her voice trailed off.

This couldn't be happening. He'd asked her to stop going near the deadly flu. She'd promised him that she would be safe. If not for him, then why not for Aisha? Why hadn't he forced her to stop treating people? She always said the winter cherries would protect her. What rubbish.

"Let me call the doctor. At least think of Aisha." But he knew that no doctor would come. He shouldn't be close to her, to the sickness. But he held her as if she were the only thing that moored him to the earth.

She stiffened in his arms. "You always think there is some kind of damn choice. Just because I'm not afraid to see the truth doesn't mean that I'm choosing this. You think I want this? You think anyone wants this?"

His stomach tightened. She was wrong. She would fight this.

"Can you just go to the doctor?"

"For what? So they can tell me what I already know? So they can tell you that you need to stay away? So they can take Aisha away? The coughing flu doesn't spread how they think. You'll be fine. So will Aisha. You've been taking your herbs, right?"

"If they work, why aren't you taking them?"

"Do you want me to say it?"

He fought against her words. It was not too late. "You must have faith that you will recover." He pulled her toward him.

"I have faith. This is all faith. Would I be here with you otherwise?"

He kissed the top of her head. "What about the broth you make?" She always gave him a boiled down mixture of celery, coriander, and parsnips when he didn't feel well. She fed it to the families with infected relatives. It protected them—the young ones, at least.

"Will you help Aisha?"

"It goes without saying."

"I don't know, maybe I am asking too much."

"You could never ask too much of me."

"God forgive me for what happened to my parents. Let their death be for something. Promise me that you'll help Aisha."

"You can't blame yourself for what happened to your parents." What did Noorjahan mean? He felt a sudden wave of nausea. The fire had been an accident. Those were terrible rumors that villagers spread.

"I'm going to ask you something impossible." She lay back down, pulling the blanket back over them both. "Treat her as if she were your daughter. Help her with the land, please."

"Yes, love. I promise. I will help Aisha."

"Good, then. I have papers for you to sign."

Murad stiffened. "What papers?"

"After my parents died, I transferred the land into my name. But Babak will get the land. I'm still his wife. You know that women don't have these rights."

What did this have to do with him? What on earth was she suggesting?

"I'll leave them for you at the school to sign."

"Don't worry so much," he said. "You will get through this."

"I'm just taking care of what needs to be done."

He pulled her close, absorbing her warmth into his skin. She was overreacting. Noorjahan wasn't always right. Even she could be wrong.

10

AISHA

"WHERE WERE YOU?" Noorjahan asked Aisha.

"I stayed after school to help." She'd stayed late over at Omar's house, playing with his little sisters, helping his mother with dinner. What did her mother care where she was? Aisha never asked her mom where she went or whom she was with. Her mother had just disappeared for two weeks, saying that she needed to go help at a nearby village. The schoolteacher pestering her the whole time Noor was away.

"Come, sit down. I have something for you." Noorjahan set a felt cloth on the table.

Aisha felt a twinge of guilt. Her mother looked frail. The fabric of her yellow salwar hung as if it were two sizes too big. The trip to the village had aged her. Aisha wished her mother would stop treating the sickness. It was such a risk. But her mother insisted that the winter cherries that she gathered from the springs inoculated the women and children in their village against it. This spring, it was mostly the elders who seemed to be dying.

Noorjahan tapped her fingernails on the table, drawing Aisha's attention to the dark bundle of material. She unwrapped it with care, revealing an ornate silver knife with an eight-inch blade. "This is for you."

Aisha didn't want to take the knife, but the tone of her mother's voice made her grab it.

"It's for protection. You must keep it with you. I will show you something, but you must not speak of it."

Aisha nodded and swallowed hard. Their language was one of silence, of things left unsaid. There was only one place Noorjahan could be taking her: to the spot of the fire. Where her grandparents died. Finally, her mother was going to explain what happened that day. There had been a fight before the fire. Aisha was sure of it. Her father yelling in the field. But he was gone when her grandparents poured buckets of water on the flames. Before the wind started blowing and her grandparents became trapped by the flames. The gaps in her memory were filled with smoke. But she remembered her grandmother's eyes—how they spoke to her, as if she had said, *You, my child, are spared.* Her grandmother prayed for Aisha's protection as she died.

"Wear your heavy cloak." Noorjahan hoisted herself up with effort, and Aisha followed her out of the house. The sun was low in the sky—there were a few hours of daylight left. Aisha slowed down as they approached the barren, burnt piece of land, but her mother paid no heed and continued up the mountain. They were headed toward the poppy field, climbing up the mountain that reached like daggers into the sky.

Aisha was out of breath as they followed the narrow trail. As a child, she had snuck up to the fields, in summer, blooming petals of red and orange, like a liquid sunset, rushed around her. She couldn't remember when she'd first found the poppy field, but she'd always known not to speak of it. As if which secrets to keep were coded into her genetic makeup from birth.

"Never come up here without your knife, Aisha."

Your knife. The blade was warm and heavy. The poppy field

opened before them, a moonscape surrounded by dust and boulders, littered with the carcasses of summer's harvest. Fallen stalks bursting with seeds. They were hidden between the peaks of two mountains. "When did you first plant these?" Many people in the village grew poppies in their gardens, using the seeds for their bread. But nobody could claim to the police this field was for baking. Smoking, drinking, weapons, these were all part of men's worlds and yet, here she was with her mother.

Noorjahan walked along the edge of the large field toward the shed. "Come over here, Aisha." Noor handed Aisha a shovel and a paper bag. "These are my seeds. My strains. You must learn everything."

She looked in the bag at the tiny seeds—both her future and where she came from. The shed stank of resin and mildew. It hadn't been painted or weatherized and stood exposed to the elements. She walked with her mother to the field, where her mother used a hoe to make small rows.

"As long as you keep this patch growing, you will be able to afford to go to school. I will introduce you to the man who purchases from us. You will sell to him—only him, no one else, no matter what price they offer. Do not get wrapped up in any goonda business. Understand?"

Aisha nodded. There was no escaping that this field fueled her education. Her mother did it for her.

"He will help you with the harvest and teach you how to do it properly."

Aisha wanted to say that she didn't need help, but what did she know of any of this. She spread the seeds into the furrows of earth, gently covering them with dirt. They worked silently. Aisha careful with the seeds so that the wind didn't whip them away. Her mother nodded approvingly from time to time and then doubled over coughing.

"Hopefully, we don't get any more snow this spring. The timing of when you plant is most important," Noor said as if she hadn't just been gasping for air. "We can finish tomorrow. Let's get home before dark. Aisha half jogged back to the shed, wiping the tools with a cloth. By the time she finished, her mother had already descended the hill. Aisha ran to catch up. Together, they jumped over boulders, heading down the mountain toward home.

11

AISHA

AISHA RUSHED HOME from school, wanting to get to the fields as soon as possible. Reaching her house, covered in sweat, she found it empty. Of course, her mother was with Murad. She snorted in disgust. Her mother didn't even bother to show up and help her plant the fields.

The house was a mess. Might as well get the laundry out of the way. Aisha collected the dirty clothes and headed down to the river on a muddy path. The rain, her mother had said, was good for the poppies. *Plant before a rain, but after the snow passes.* A log fell across the river. The sun glinted through the trees, casting a few patches of sun. She sat at the edge of the water on a smooth rock. A young man, about her age, skipped stones nearby. She studied his thin frame, recognizing the schoolteacher's son. She couldn't remember his name.

He skipped a stone. One-two-three-four-five-six-seven-eight: the pebble reached half the length of the river before sinking down. He noticed her and smiled. Alim had come up to the river to get away from his parents' fighting. The sound of water cleared his head. He hadn't realized that he'd come so far, and certainly hadn't thought he'd run into his father's star student, Aisha. His dad always compared her to him. How much smarter she was. How she'd get into a university in the city, while his own son would likely have no other option but to work as a laborer. He took her in. Full lips and eyes that absorbed him. Her eyebrows seemed to be arched in question. Alim couldn't help taking in the curve of her hip and the way her shirt was snug against her breasts. He tossed a stone across the river in hopes that she would notice him.

The boy puffed out his scrawny chest as he tossed the rock. His glasses were replicas of Murad's. Aisha looked away from his goofy grin. At the edge of the river, right next to her, glimmered a perfect, round stone. Her first urge was to fling it into the river to see if she might skip it farther than him and reach the other side. But she was too old for such games, so she dried it on a cloth. The stone turned from black to gray.

The boy upturned stones with the toe of his boot. His dark pants were too big on him, and his glasses kept sliding down his nose. Even through the glasses, his eyes were soft brown and full of light.

She set the stone next to the garments that were wrung dry and continued using her weight to rub the dirt from the cloth. He came toward her and squatted down beside her. "Hi, I'm Alim." His voice cracked. He took off his glasses and wiped them on his shirt.

"I'm Aisha." She handed him the stone.

"I know. You're in my dad's class. We're the same age."

Up close, he didn't look much like Murad. Alim's nose arched with a definition his father's lacked. He flung the stone into the water. She counted the skips, as they grew closer and closer together. Twelve. The rock nearly made it to the other side before it sank to the river bottom. A fish jumped out of the water.

"One day, I'll make it all the way across," Alim said.

"Me too." She washed the clothes—the dirt giving way to the water.

———

The next day after school, Aisha arrived home and opened the door, half expecting to find it empty. In bed, Noor's eyes blazed with fever. Aisha rushed over to her side. "Can I bring you some water?"

Her mother nodded.

"Let me get you some herbs." But she really needed the doctor.

"You have to go to the poppy fields and get the rest of the seeds planted."

"I'm going to stay with you."

"What for? To sit and watch me be sick? Bring me the water pipe." Her mother's voice was steel.

Aisha brought her the pipe. Her mother mixed opium resin with tobacco, smoked it, and started to cough.

Aisha took the pipe from her. "You shouldn't be smoking with that cough."

Noorjahan sipped some water. "It's the pain." Her mother never admitted to any pain. "The Gujar is thin and has a gap between his front teeth. He will meet you the first of June, and then you will decide on when he comes back to collect the harvest. He will help you with the first harvest. Do not negotiate. The price is fixed. You are only to sell to him, remember. But give him a little extra for the help."

These were keys to a business that Aisha did not want to inherit.

Aisha slipped the knife into her boot; the tip grazed her birthmark. She imagined the cut, a new border sliced through their land.

"I want to get the doctor, Mom."

"You think I want to die with some strange man in the house? The last of the seeds need to get in the ground before the rain tonight."

Die. She'd said it. Aisha wanted to grab the word and hurl it into the sky so it might cover the sun, so it might rain back down on them, laughing that her mother was wrong.

"Everything I've done is for you." Her mother broke into a cough.

"Everything is for me? What about Murad? Do you have any idea what people say?"

Her mother reached for the water, taking small sips. Noorjahan stared at her; the bits of her green eyes fleeing into Aisha's for refuge. "Maybe it's time for you to learn not to care so much about what other people say. Unless it's your own daughter."

Guilt pitted her gut.

"Go take care of things. I've heard enough from you."

Aisha slammed the door. Walking up the trail, the wind whipped against her. Tears stung her eyes as she reached the field. Her mother planted this field to pay for her education.

The air blew cold, though no rain fell. The clouds above them were full like the belly of a pregnant fish. Aisha longed to squeeze the fat lower edge of the cloud and watch the rain come out.

The wind whipped as she worked, and the soil was wet from the rain earlier in the week. Some of the seeds got lost in a sudden gust of wind. Aisha was relieved her mother wasn't there to see her failure. Her thighs ached, unused to squatting for such long periods of time. A cold sweat broke out on her back. She'd finished the last of the planting when the sky started to mist. The temperature dropped. Her ears were so cold. Putting away the tools quickly, she headed back home.

"Did you finish?" her mother asked as soon as she stepped in. The fever must've spiked because sweat drenched her mother.

"Everything is in the ground." Rain started to pelt the roof.

"You want some tea, Mom?"

Her mother shook her head. Still, Aisha served her a bitter blend of roots to reduce the fever.

Aisha did not go to school the next day or the day that followed. Her mother was a horrible patient: spilling the tea, refusing the tincture, and scratching the hives on her arms until they bled.

The fever raged. Noorjahan's bones pushed up through the yellow leather of her skin. Even her gums receded, causing her teeth to jut out. Rot leaked from her gut. Her lips had turned from red to white, and a film covered her serpentine eyes.

Her mother refused to let her get the doctor. Aisha thought of sneaking away, but her mother was too sick to be left alone.

"Take me outside, Aisha."

"It is too late. Use the chamber pot for your business. You will catch cold outside." The wind whistled into the cracks of the house.

"Who said anything about the bathroom? We must go outside."

"We can go in the morning. Have some nice broth." She stroked her mother's arm.

"Do you not see me? The bones I've become? Bones have no need for soup."

"This isn't fair." Aisha began to cry. "You promised the winter cherry protected you from the flu."

Noorjahan sat up. "I ran out. It was a small child, I thought it would be okay."

"What about me? Weren't you thinking of me? How am I going to live without you? You can't leave me." Aisha began to sob.

Noorjahan took her hand. "You have what you need. I promise." Her eyes filled with tears.

"Did you think about the risk to me? Am I going to catch it? Why did you let me near you?"

"I'm not contagious anymore." Her mother looked away. Her lips sagged down with the weight of an old woman, but she wasn't even forty yet.

"That's why you left. You were sick, not training midwives."

Noorjahan nodded. Aisha was quiet.

"Come, take me outside; I want to show you something." Aisha did not move. Noorjahan stood up.

"Let me help you." It was too late. Her mother was already standing. Aisha dropped her sweater on the ground and went to grab her mother's elbow. "You need to wait, otherwise you're going to fall."

Her mother ignored her and headed straight into the blistering cold of night. Aisha put her jacket and shoes on and went after her mother into the dark. The belly of the cloud overhead was sure to burst with snow. Noor stared at it. "It better not snow. If it sticks to the ground, the seeds will have a hard time." She shook her head and then headed straight through the orchard, taking the trail, overgrown with weeds, to the burnt plot.

"This is where my mother left me. You never get over losing your mother. Mama, I'm coming." She dropped to her knees and squeezed the earth in her hand. Tears dripping down her cheeks. "I'm so sorry. I almost died here long ago. Every day watching you grow was a gift. I never took it for granted."

"I love you." Aisha pulled Noorjahan in closer for warmth.

"God give me peace." Her body rested against Aisha as the thick belly of the cloud overhead birthed snow. The snowflakes coated their hair but melted on the ground, dissolving in a final gift to Noorjahan. "Leave me here. Let the earth hold my pain."

Aisha crouched down next to her mother.

Noorjahan sobbed until her body shook with the cough. "I don't want you to remember me like this."

"I love you, Mom." Aisha wanted to say *don't leave me*, then take her mother back into the house, put her in bed, and make her well.

"The land is yours now." She dug her fingers into it. "Nobody can control you when you have your own land. This is my gift to you, Daughter."

Aisha rubbed her mother's back. Listening, afraid that if Noorjahan stopped speaking there would be nothing left.

"I'm sorry for all of this, Aisha."

"There is nothing to be sorry for, Mom." Aisha took her mother's hands in hers. "I will remember you on the mountainside. I will remember you when I harvest the apples. I will remember you every night when I cook dinner. I will remember your bag full of herbs and the way that everyone comes to you for healing. How you stitched Padmal's ear back, when you saved Omar's mom, how you brought an infant back to life when the doctor pronounced her dead. I remember you as you are."

Her mother smiled up at her, more child than mother. Aisha took her into her arms, for warmth, for comfort, as a final way to hold on. "Please don't leave me." She could smell her again, not the rot of her death, but the sweet smell of her life—narcissus, cardamom, poppy resin. She nestled her nose into her mother's hair to remember the scent, to duplicate it and teach it to her children.

"I will stay with you until the end." Aisha held her mother until her body grew stiff. Aisha prayed, "We have come from God and unto him we shall return."

12

AISHA

AISHA SLEPT IN a dreamless state. When she awoke in the morning, she tried to keep her mind blank, to forget dragging her mother onto a board and covering her with a cloth. Closing her eyes, she willed the grief to spill out from her skin, but someone knocked at the door and refused to stop. Suddenly, Suha Auntie stood before her. "You haven't been in school."

Aisha burst into tears. "She's gone." Her aunt held her, rocked her, and screamed along with her. When Aisha's voice was rough and no more sounds could come out, her aunt stroked her back until her breath evened out.

"Let me get you some water. Have you had anything to eat?"

Aisha didn't say a thing.

"I'll get the mullah after you eat something."

The house was still full of Noorjahan as if at any moment she'd walk through the door, set down her bag, and hang her cloak on the wall.

Suha Auntie set some food down for her, but Aisha pushed it away.

"Come, eat." She pushed her lips together. Suha Auntie left to get the mullah. Would he come even though she had the flu? A thousand pieces of Noorjahan stared back at Aisha—her slippers in the corner, her bag still filled with herbs, coconut oil that she rubbed in her hair.

When her grandparents died in the fire, Aisha had risen the next morning and cleaned alongside her mother. They stuffed the bags they used to store rice with their belongings. No family or friends came by to pick through the items. Her mother kept only her grandfather's water pipe, everything else, she'd given away to her cousin in the next village, who ensured their belongings were put to good use. She buried them with their wedding rings.

But now things were different. There was a village cemetery where they buried those infected with the coughing flu. No one would take her mother's things out of fear. It took everything inside of her to start packing her mother's things into a bag. She dropped in her cloak still musky with her scent, black leather shoes colored entirely with polish, wool socks stretching to the knee, one stick of scarlet-rose lipstick, the tortoise shell hairbrush.

Each item landed with a terminal thud. Death was hungry. *Eat. Take it all. Do you want me too?* She blinked tears away. *God give me strength.*

The only things she kept of her mother's were her wooden bowl, wedding dupatta, and the jewelry in the felt pouch, heavy with gold that no one wore: Aisha's dowry.

She carried the rice bags out to where she'd left her mother, stacking her earthly belongings around her covered body. The trees in the orchard sprouted with the hint of new life. But under the white cloth, her mom would no longer be recognizable. Soon, nothing would be left. Tears dripped down her cheeks. She'd get a proper headstone for her mom and have it inscribed with: *Angels do live on earth, but always return to God.*

———

Aisha looked out the window. She must have fallen asleep. The mullah was already on the hill. She could see him whispering prayers, silhouetted against the darkening sky. Men were with him—they all wore masks. They would take her mother and bury her with the others. Aisha's body refused to move. Her eyes closed against her will. Everything went blank.

The next day, light came through the windows in columns and Aisha did not return to school. She watched a bird on a pine, pecking into a tree trunk. The sound reverberated inside her as if the bird were nipping down her spine. Her stomach grumbled, a little beast, trying to make her remember hunger.

Dust swirled through the light, making complex patterns. The dust would always be here. But without light, it would be invisible. Most dust came from skin. How long would it take before all the dust from her mother's skin went back to the earth? Every particle of dirt in the house seemed to hold the scent of her mother. The bird drilling against the tree became louder. Aisha wanted to yell, to frighten it into silence.

"Aisha?"

It wasn't the bird. It was Omar, knocking, pounding on the door. Why was he here?

How silly he was, banging on the door, just like that bird. What would it solve? The door was locked. She'd remembered to lock it. This pleased her. The bird flew away, a raven, its wings turned to rainbows in the light.

Everything was silent. Omar left. Finally, she was alone. How cruel it all seemed. The bird. Omar. The dust.

One day turned into the next. Her aunt brought her food and spent the nights with her. The place still smelled like her mother. But the scent was not strong enough to create an image of her mother cooking rice on the stove and replace the memory of a white sheet covering a body, seen through a window. A single image burned into her memory that only her mother alive could dissolve.

The beautiful thing was the dust. It became like a stream, swirling around her. At the river, Aisha watched water rushing over rocks, wanting to lie down at the banks, but it was too cold. She was so tired. She sat on a rock. The sky was inescapably blue. The last of the spring snow had taken her mother, frozen her, made her brittle, and then melted away. The poppies would grow despite the snow. Her mother had assured her.

The bird was back. Banging. Knocking. Aisha sat up and threw the blanket off. It was still light. Suha Auntie had left already. It wasn't morning anymore.

"Aisha, open this door."

It wasn't Omar. It was Murad. "I'm not leaving."

He couldn't see her like this. Had she changed her clothes? She'd forgotten to bathe. She didn't want him to know that she'd been sleeping. She unlocked the door and retreated into the kitchen.

Murad came into the kitchen and set a pot of soup on the counter. Aisha took out two bowls and filled them. The broth smelled of garlic. The room swirled. Murad dipped a roti into the soup. How sad he looked. How old. When had his hair gone gray? It used to be just in his sideburns.

"Come and sit. Have something to eat."

Her stomach rumbled in response. She nodded, agreeing more with her stomach than him. The soup warmed her insides.

"We missed you in school last week. You must return on Monday, Aisha."

She glanced outside. It must be midday. Was it a school day? She'd lost track. Aisha sipped the soup, splattering bits on her forehead.

Murad set his bowl down. "She is in God's hands, now." His voice choked.

Aisha closed her eyes. She couldn't stand to hear him speak of her mother.

"You can't stay here alone."

He had no business worrying about her. "My aunt stays with me at night. I'm grown. All is well."

"Aisha, your aunt wants you to live with her."

Why had her aunt not discussed it with her, then? She didn't need him intervening in her life. What happened between him and her mother was gone. He didn't need to worry about her.

Aisha shook her head. "My aunt is fine with it."

"You can't go on like this."

"I'm seventeen. Does your wife know that you are here?"

Murad looked away. "When are you coming back to school?"

Aisha shrugged.

"If you want to stay on your own, then you must start by taking care of yourself. You only have another term until graduation, and then you will need to apply for university."

What did he know of what she needed? She pushed the soup away.

"Just come to school Monday. We miss you."

"You miss her. I'm not her. She's gone."

13

AISHA

THE NEXT DAY, Aisha returned to school with a clean, burnt pot in hand. If appearing normal would keep Murad out of her life, then she would deliver. The room quieted when she entered, even though the lessons hadn't started. She took her seat, wanting to snarl at them all, as if she were a caged animal.

Mina was the first to lean toward her and say, "I am so sorry, Aisha." The chorus of voices from the other students surrounded her. She wished them quiet. Wished that they would go on as if nothing had changed.

The minutes turned to hours—she could not follow Murad's lecture. When lunch came, Aisha headed out to the poplar tree and pulled out a book to read. She hadn't brought food, and her body expressed no signs of hunger. The words on the page blurred together. The sentences failed to take her away.

A shadow fell over her. She looked up. It was Omar. His face somber and nose casting a shadow across his face under the noonday sun.

"Your mother is with God now." Omar sat down next to her, rolling back his broad shoulders.

It pained her to hear his condolences.

"I brought this for you." He pulled a parcel wrapped in tissue paper from his bag. "I missed you."

Aisha set the gift down next to her, exhausted by the weight.

"Open it," Omar said, placing it in her lap. She looked at Omar, the ridges of his face stern, yet strong. His chest was broad and his arms defined with muscle. She willed her hands to move. Funny how her body responded to her thoughts. She watched her hands open the package.

"Do you like it?"

It was a dupatta, embroidered with silk thread. It was beautiful, an apology for the scarf he'd ruined so many years ago. "Thank you."

Omar held her eyes. The silence filled up around them, warm like a blanket on a winter morning. "My mother would like to invite you for tea this weekend. I know it is not such a good time with this terrible loss, but we thought you might enjoy some comfort, family to be around." He grabbed her arm, his fingers sinking in. Her skin cringed. She fought an urge to pull away.

His words skipped in her head like a movie reel, cut on a moment, jammed, repeating. Tea. Tea. Tea. She leaned back to steady herself, to find her way back into what he was saying.

"You are so beautiful." Omar moved his hand down the length of her arm and took her hand with force. Her fingers froze with his touch.

What was he doing? "I just can't." She tried to pull away, but he held her there.

14

AISHA

AISHA WALKED HOME from school with Omar. He didn't stop at the gate but followed her up the path.

"Want me to turn over your summer vegetable bed? It's almost time to plant."

Aisha shrugged. Her chest tightened.

"Are you okay?" Omar asked.

"I'm fine."

"I better get working. There isn't much light left." Omar walked toward the orchard.

Inside the house, Aisha swept the floor and ground the turmeric into a garlic paste. She was exhausted as if she'd worked for twelve hours in the fields under the sun. Her body wasn't working.

An hour or so later, Omar knocked on the door with a bouquet of chard in hand, his nose red from the cold. "This is for you. It was ready to harvest."

"Thank you." What a sweet gesture. His eyes shifted down the full expanse of her body. He stepped into the house and placed a hand on her shoulder, moving it down the length of her arm.

This could not be happening. Her mind ordered her to step away, sent a signal for her arms to push him, but she froze.

He closed the door behind him.

Don't let him close the door. Her mind issued commands that were impossible to follow. *Throw the greens at him. Drop the chard and run. Omar wouldn't hurt her.*

"Why do you play these games with me?" He leaned in close to her.

She dropped all the chard on the ground.

He stepped on the greens, his boots still on. "That isn't a way to behave. I picked them for you."

She stepped back. *Run.* Her body failed to respond. *Run.*

He pulled her close, her body flush with his. "I just want to help you."

Omar pressed his lips into hers, wet and sour. His awful scent sticking to her. She was just like her mother.

Something crackled from the road. He released her quickly. She stepped back. He glanced nervously out the window.

She stared at the ground, wiping her lips on the back of her hand. Nauseated by his scent.

"I'll see you tomorrow," he said. "I can finish weeding the winter vegetable bed." He slipped out the door, pulling it shut behind him.

Aisha went outside and crouched by the jug of water at the side of the house, scrubbing with soap until her skin was pink and raw, but nothing could cleanse Omar from her skin.

Aisha had trouble staying awake in school. She hadn't slept the night before, consumed with dreams of Omar and her grandmother—they bled into each other.

When they were finally excused for the day, Aisha headed for the door. Fearing that Omar would follow her, she pushed her way out of the classroom alongside the smaller children.

"Aisha, wait," Omar called from behind.

She walked faster, sliding on a patch of ice that brought her to the ground. Everything fell out of her bag. She glanced over her shoulder. Omar gained on her. She pushed herself up despite her throbbing tailbone.

"Are you alright?" Omar picked up her book. She turned away as his scent hit her.

"I don't need your help."

"Let me carry your books, at least." He picked up the rest of the books.

They walked in silence until they arrived at Omar's house. Aisha reached for her books.

"Why don't you come for some tea? My mother would love to have you over." He reached for her elbow, gently this time. Her skin crawled. "Come."

"Don't touch me."

"I won't have a wife of mine speaking this way to me."

"Wife?" Disgust flooded her voice.

"Why do you say it like that?" Every part of her revolted at his touch. At the thought of marrying him.

"I'm not getting married until I finish school."

"I wouldn't marry a woman like you." He dropped her books in her hands.

After dinner, Aisha finished her homework and got into bed. She closed her eyes, but sleep did not take her. Moonlight cast through the window. Her chest tightened at every sound—the whistling of the branches, a thud in the distance, the faint babbling of the river.

It was still dark when footsteps approached. She stiffened. There was a knock at the door. Her throat constricted as she balled up to make herself small, invisible.

"Aisha, open the door."

It was Omar's mother, calling to her. Aisha's stomach tightened. Did she know they kissed?

"Aisha-jee, the baby is coming, please help."

Omar's older sister must be in labor. Aisha went to the door and opened it a crack. Her mother was dead. There was no one to help.

"Aisha, we need your help."

She shook her head. Cold sweat beaded down her spine. She had not assisted a birth since her mother died, and could not imagine being near Omar.

Omar's mother's face crumpled. "There is no time to call the doctor. The baby might die without help."

If the baby or mother died, it would be her fault. Aisha nodded at Omar's mother, who stood in the same spot Omar had with the chard. A green bruise bloomed on her wrist. His fingerprints tattooed on her. She closed her eyes. The baby was pure and deserved to live. Aisha collected her mother's herbs and supplies and followed Omar's mother.

Their house was a simple shack, divided into two parts for sleeping and cooking. She did not look at Omar or the yellow-snow grandfather when she entered, but went straight to Omar's sister, who labored behind sheets hanging in the kitchen. The other women clattered about, heating water. The house was hot with birth. The labor had stalled. Aisha held a hot compress against the woman's back.

She prayed to God to help her remember the ways her mother had taught her. The woman's heartbeat was too slow, but the baby's was steady. Aisha reached inside to check the placement of the head. The baby was ready to descend. Then, she felt the problem: a single foot dangling down.

Omar's voice sounded from across the room. Her heart pounded in her ears. She stepped back, smacking into Omar's mother.

"What is wrong?"

Aisha bit her lip. She focused on the laboring woman, who cried out as a contraction knotted her belly. Her mother delivered a footling once before by grabbing the foot and pushing it back up so the baby came out butt first.

She closed her eyes, blocking out all sounds: the clanking of dishes being washed, the breathing of Omar's mother, the whine of a child woken from sleep. There was just the baby.

"You mustn't come out like this." Adrenaline coursed through her veins as she grabbed the baby's foot firmly and pushed. The mother groaned with pain.

"Push," Aisha said. "You can birth this baby. Your body knows how."

The mother screamed as another contraction gripped her. After it passed, she fed some honey to the mother for extra strength. "Easy now." Aisha channeled the movements of Noorjahan. "Auntie, please fetch the blankets." The baby's butt crowned and with a final push she landed in Aisha's hands like a silverfish. Then, she filled her lungs with air and cried out.

15

MURAD

MURAD SAT IN his study surveying the papers he'd signed for Noor-jahan. He owed so much to Noor. There was only one way he could think of fulfilling his promise to her. He had to ensure that the land would go to Aisha, not Haseena. God forbid if something happened to him. The smell of fried fish and almonds leaked in. Everything in the house looked the same, but with Noor's death, his life was a shell, empty inside.

Murad attempted to read the paper. The pressure in his head returned. Haseena brought his dinner out on a tray. The rotis were thicker than usual, the curry too heavy with spice. After dinner, Murad read until he was sure Alim was asleep, and then he went to find Haseena. As he entered their room, Haseena's song turned into a hum. She brushed her thick hair.

"Haseena," he said, too sweetly. She did not look up. He should wait for a more opportune time, but he couldn't stop himself. "I have been thinking of Alim's future. I have selected a wife for him."

Haseena dropped her brush and glared at Murad. He'd insisted that Alim not marry until after college. Murad wanted her to be an old woman before she had grandchildren. "What absurdity do you speak? You went on and on about how we have to wait. You don't select the wife without me." She sat down, attempting to calm herself. Perhaps he'd come to his senses in a way. Too many boys went off to university and ended up in love marriages without their parents even knowing. Haseena snorted. Neither Alim nor Murad were fit to choose a wife.

"I've secured a large dowry, enough to pay for his college, the wedding and even provide him with land. We will have substantial income." A rich girl. This was a turn that Haseena hadn't anticipated. Murad was always trying to be self-made, refusing to take any of the support her family offered, insisting on teaching in that flea-ridden government school instead of getting a proper job at the private school that paid three times the salary. It was that woman. Haseena knew that he'd go to her house after school, that was why he insisted on teaching at the government school, to be close to her. But all sins come into the light. And God saved their family further humiliation. Praise be to him.

Her face softened. "Is she from the village?" Murad could see her running through the eligible families in her mind, ruling each out and assuming that it must be someone from outside.

"Yes. Alim will marry Aisha."

Everything went cold inside her. Murad wanted to bring his sins home. What kind of grandchildren would spawn from this? She dug her fingers into her palms. "Have you lost your mind? They are not even of the same caste. They have nothing at all." Her husband was inviting his mistress to live with them. Pain shot through her chest. He was going to kill her.

"I'll put a deposit for the walnut dining table next week. Choose whichever you like best."

"As if I care about a dining table!" She'd rather eat off the floor than have those sinners in her house. "She killed her mother."

"Noorjahan died of the flu."

How could he have said her name out loud in their bedroom? The pain shot into her ears. "My heart." Everything went dark.

16

ALIM

WHEN ALIM BECAME engaged, an icy silence came over the house. The worst was the guilt. Alim shouldn't have been so happy. He tried to deny the timing—that his mother's plunge into despair did not coincide with his engagement. His father had said, *We have decided that you will marry Aisha. We.*

In his next breath, Murad demanded that Alim not discuss the engagement with his mother, as it was a delicate subject and her heart was acting up. So Alim said nothing, and the silence choked them.

He'd not planned to go and see Aisha. He usually went to his friend's house, but instead Alim walked through town, up the hills, and found himself near her house, remembering that time they'd met by the river—that warm stone Aisha had placed in his hand. The sun dripping into her eyes, catching the hues of green and blue as if a stream ran through them.

At the last moment he became nervous and almost turned back. She was so beautiful. He forced himself to continue up the path and knocked at the door. Silence. She was not home, or worse, she was and wanted nothing to do with him. Just as he was about to leave, she opened the door. What was he supposed to say to her?

"Aisha." Her name was perfect. It rolled off his tongue.

"Yes?"

"Can I help you?"

Her face clouded over. "Help? I don't need you or your father's help."

Alim was stunned by her anger. He shouldn't have been so forward. It's just that with nobody arranging visits, he'd taken it upon himself to meet her.

"I'm sorry. I didn't mean to anger you. I just thought I could help you with all of this."

She didn't look at him. Here was Alim. Just like Omar, trying to enter her house. "There's nothing for you here."

Alim stepped back. "I could prune the trees."

"It's not the right season. Do you even know how to prune trees? It's time to fertilize them."

He shook his head. He'd already failed her. "I can learn."

She sighed. "I'll show you, but all you are doing is making more work for me."

He followed behind her, scrambling to keep up as they headed to the shed at the edge of the orchard. "Can you grab the wheelbarrow?"

He nodded and kept staring at her: the lock of hair that fell around her cheek, the way she pressed her lips together in concentration. When he reached for the wheelbarrow, he hit a stack of pots that came crashing off a shelf.

She picked up the mess he made and then tossed the fertilizer, gloves, and bags into the wheelbarrow, and balanced a small ladder on top. Alim insisted on carrying it and even at his snail's pace, the ladder fell. She pretended not to notice as he quickly put it back. Her frustration seemed to give way to embarrassment at his incompetence.

She showed no fear on the ladder, standing on the top, explaining how to spot infections and pests. How would he ever remember all of this? "Look at this." She dropped a fuzzy, golden caterpillar down. He did not want to touch it, but how could he look so weak?

"Kill it. It's a tent caterpillar."

"Seriously?"

"Use the shovel and smash it." Her tone was matter-of-fact. "What, you've never killed an insect before? I hadn't realized you are such a city boy living in the village."

"Then come down a bit. You can't be on top of the ladder without me holding it."

"I'll be fine." Still, she descended to appease him.

Alim grabbed the shovel and squished the caterpillar. He looked up at her for approval, but she was busy scraping a fungus off a branch.

After they finished, he walked her back to her house. "I'm sorry that I'm not more help."

"It is fine. You did your best."

"I'll come back soon."

"As you like," she said.

17

AISHA

AISHA TRIED NOT to like Alim, but he started by helping her in the orchards and slowly figured out what pleased her. Peaches, she loved. He took care to bring her the best during the summer.

"Thank you." She took the bag of peaches from his hand.

"Can I help you today?" Alim beamed at her, the collar of his gray shirt folded crisply.

"Do you know how to wash clothes?"

"I help sometimes." Of course, this meant he knew nothing, and she'd have to teach him, which took twice as long. He would memorize each detail of how she liked things and the next time, he'd do it for her. He didn't talk much, which Aisha liked. He let her fill the space when she wanted.

"Then come along." They walked down to the river. He was just a little taller than her, and much skinnier, but he insisted on carrying the clothes and the bucket.

He watched her at first, used to having servants at home. "Let me try." She gave him the soap; it slipped from his fingers. His cheeks flushed. Even basic things were new to him.

"It's okay." Aisha picked up the soap. "There isn't too much to wash today. You must have a lot of homework."

Alim shrugged and opened his bag. "I don't feel much like studying." He pulled out some paper and colored pens and began to draw Aisha.

She became overly aware of the smallest things, the pursing of her lips, the blinking of her eyes, the angle that her head tilted. His hands moved quickly on the paper. She craned to see his work. He made her eyes bluer, lips redder, and hair longer.

He held the drawing out to her. "You can have it."

"Why do I need a picture of myself? Maybe you should keep it."

He handed it to her and took off his glasses. "Can I ask you a question?"

Aisha nodded.

"Why didn't you marry Omar?" He hadn't meant to ask her, but his friend knew Omar's sister, and she said that he'd proposed.

Her cheeks warmed. "What do you mean?"

Alim dug at a rock with his shoe, flipping it over. "I just heard that you spent a lot of time with him."

What had Omar said? Aisha shook her head. "He helped us. That is all." Aisha washed her hands in the river, scrubbing until her fingers stung. She wanted to forget that he'd ever touched her. Erase the stains that he'd left on her.

"Like I help you now?"

"It was different."

"He probably knows how to do more stuff." Omar was twice Alim's size. "Are you lonely?"

Aisha sat on her hands, trying to warm them. "What do you mean?"

"Living by yourself."

"I'm fine. I'm grown."

"Are you happy with me?"

"What kind of question is that?"

"Maybe we should get married sooner."

"Why me?" Aisha couldn't wrap her mind around how Haseena had agreed to their marriage.

Alim turned a slight shade of red. "I loved you the first time I met you, right here at the river."

He'd been skipping rocks back then, too, and here he was, still trying to reach the other side.

18

AISHA

WHEN THE FIRST of June arrived, Aisha went to the poppy fields to meet the Gujar, half believing that he wouldn't be there. But he was already there, waiting by the shack, a woody stock of a man, the type that would bend, not break, in a snowstorm.

He made no small talk, went into the shed and returned with a couple razors. Aisha followed him into the fields on the western-facing slope that had the thickest pods. The Gujar leaned forward and made an incision on a poppy pod with a razor. "Watch closely."

Aisha glanced away in discomfort in being alone with this man. He spat on the ground and then dotted the bulb with tear drop incisions, starting at the top of the bulb's starlike crown. "Don't cut too deep, just release the opium." A milky resin oozed out, freezing into a single drop. "The weather is not good. All the moisture in the air will weaken the potency." He handed a narrow, rusted blade to Aisha.

She plunged the razor so deeply into the crown that resin dripped from her hand to the ground.

"Don't let it contact your skin." He tossed her a soiled rag. "That's your money on the ground."

Aisha tried not to let too much of the filthy rag touch her skin, but it was difficult to remove the sticky, caustic resin without force. It smelled like dirt. Mushrooms just sprouting. Part of her brain turned to honey with the scent. She pressed her fingers to her tongue, licking the bitterness. She pierced the thin top layer of the bulb and nothing leaked out. Stabbing again, a teardrop emerged.

"Leave the biggest ones for seeds."

Aisha wanted to say that she knew that. Her mother had taught her already. She kept her distance from the man, but watched him closely. A drop of sap landed on her skin again. She licked it off. Like a bitter honey, it coated her mouth. The scent of raw potatoes oxidizing in the air. Her lips tingled and her tongue felt thick. Aisha's fingers danced up and down the bulbs, tattooing them with designs, like the hennaed hand of a woman about to be married. Hardly any drops hit her knife, but when they did, she was careful to lick them away. Her tongue became lethargic.

The leaves at the base of the poppies reminded her of cabbage, but the haunting crown at the top of the bulb commanded her respect like royalty. "Usually in a day, the color will turn amber. The moisture and cold makes it go slow. The longer it takes, the less potent, the less money. But this time, I give you the same. Even if it's slow."

They walked to the next row. "When it turns black, collect it. This is enough for today. I'll come back in a week for the first batch."

Walking to the shed, Aisha felt woozy. Her legs weighed more. Her brain glided as if it were dancing to a song playing from the mountaintops.

The Gujar helped her clean the tools and then headed up over the hills, the folds of brown and tan fabric that cascaded around him disappeared.

Heading back down the mountain, Aisha arrived to find Alim in the garden. She waved at him and headed to the sink, hoping that the smell would wash off her fingers, that it wouldn't cling to her skin and become a part of her scent. He came up behind her, tentatively touching her arms. She leaned back into him, surprised with her own desire. Alim pulled her in close to him; his arms becoming her home. "I missed you." His voice was soft in her ear.

She turned to face him. His hands moved to her hips, and she leaned into him, flush against him. He kissed her forehead. Aisha closed her eyes. He kissed her eyelids, breathing her in. His scent sweet and soapy, surrounded her. She did not want him to let go.

His hand slid under her chin and he held her eyes for a moment as if discerning her desire. She leaned in. His breath in hers as he kissed her.

19

ALIM

ALIM SPENT AS much time as he could with Aisha. He loved her world and who he became in it—someone useful and competent, even if clumsy. The more he worked in the orchard, the more time she spent in the mountains. He didn't push her about where she went; there was a firm impasse in her voice when he asked what she was doing.

He took to spending more days with her, staying later. The food that she cooked was fresher, less spiced, and far easier for him to digest. She taught him to cook simple things, laughing when he first cut the chard too thick, and the fibrous stems were difficult to swallow. He learned to mince the stems, chop the onions evenly, but the fish she never let him touch. Leaving became harder. Alim feared the coming fall, which would turn to winter, and the snow would be too thick to reach her. How could he be apart from her?

Everyone in the village watched with gaping eyes, pulling back their curtains to catch Alim coming or going. He hated the quiet whispers and wanted to move their wedding date up so he could be done with the matter and live with his wife, but when he approached his father, Murad told him to wait.

Aisha's name remained banned in their house.

Alim couldn't understand why his father had them engaged if he didn't want them married, not that he wasn't grateful—he loved her. Had his father known that she'd bring him so much joy? He still couldn't understand what had compelled his father. But his parents weren't like them—they froze each other away, living in the same house but sharing nothing. He was the land where they met and fought, a forever changing Line of Control that they pretended was a cease-fire zone. Every decision, interaction, and argument revolved around him as if nothing else moored them together. His absence made his mother furious. His mother's cooking grew saltier, creamier, more difficult to digest, and the silence by which they ate unbearable. What could he say about school? His friends? None of it pleased them, and he couldn't mention Aisha. So he let the silence fill their house and found his warmth in her.

20

AISHA

FOR AISHA, SUMMER was easy and light with Alim. Winter was heavy, with Alim's visits infrequent, and loneliness suffocating her. Alim brought her rose water and cashew sweets for her eighteenth birthday. It was a day she should have spent with her mother, roasting lamb over an open flame.

Even with the chunk that Murad took out of her earnings from the opium, she had enough left over to pay her tuition at a university. She studied hard for the entrance exams. But on the day of the exams, Murad pulled her aside.

"I am surprised to see you here."

Aisha hated when he spoke to her as if he really knew her. And even though she stopped going to school, he'd given her excellent marks.

"You'll be a wife soon. It won't be proper for you to be away at university." Murad had become dependent on the money from the opium. Haseena spent money like water. It would be too risky for Aisha to leave the fields for someone else. Still, it pained him. Noorjahan had wanted so much for her. But he'd delivered the land—at a great cost to his own family and peace of mind. So Aisha's education would need to be compromised.

Heat burst into her ears. How had she been so naïve to think that Murad would support her. She said nothing, took a seat, and focused on the test.

Right after the exams, a big snowstorm hit and didn't stop for seven days, causing schools to close early for winter. Suha Auntie was always after her to come and stay with them. She'd rejected the offer repeatedly, in horror at the thought of living with her grandmother. She, like her mother, would live alone.

Still, Aisha's body ached when she did not see Alim. The walk to the river became longer; her back sore from clearing the snow. After seventeen days, Alim finally arrived. She'd played the moment in her head so many times that she thought it would be awkward, that she'd have forgotten the contours of his body, his scent. But skin remembers. Her skin absorbed into his.

Alim kissed her and then pulled out his exam scores for college, along with a sealed envelope, containing her results.

"Mina sent these for you." The mail hadn't been delivered to Aisha's house because of all the snow.

"I can't believe it." His face lit up. "I got into the university in the capital." Aisha pulled him in and kissed him. The poppies would pay for his schooling, just like they provided Haseena with the money to add another bathroom in their house. There were some things that her husband-to-be did not need to know. In some ways, Alim was sheltered. He didn't even know about their parents' affair.

"Open yours." He put the envelope in her hands. "We could go to university together, live in the capital for a while."

She didn't look at him—if she did, she would cry. Murad's voice played in her head, *You will be a wife.* Her hands shook as she pulled out her scores. They were nearly perfect—she even qualified for school on the mainland with a substantial scholarship.

"I didn't make it." Her voice shook as she folded the paper back up before Alim could see. "What does it matter anyway, we will be married soon."

He kissed the top of her head and held her. Her body shook in his embrace. "I'm sorry. Are you okay?"

"Just cold." Aisha rested her head against Alim.

Aisha wanted a small, simple wedding on her land. Neither her father nor Haseena would be there. Shame emanated from Alim; they didn't speak of Haseena's refusal. Aisha hated that their love did this to him.

The morning of the wedding, Mina did Aisha's hair and makeup, weaving flowers into her hair, even though it would be mostly covered. They laughed in ways they'd never been able to as children.

"Are you nervous?" Mina asked, draping the red silk with golden brocade over Aisha's head.

"Sometimes I think that I might be dreaming. How is it possible to find love like this?" There was nothing more that she wanted than to spend her days with Alim, waking up to him every morning and falling asleep in his arms. It would be hard when he was away at school, but the time would pass quickly, and she had the fields to take care of. Alim thought that Aisha's grandparents were paying for the wedding. That they had a change of heart. The poppy fields became her invisible endless dowry.

"Let me put your earrings on for you," Mina said.

Aisha reached for her mother's jewelry and took out the gold earrings. She closed her eyes as Mina slipped them into her ears. "Okay, now open your eyes."

Aisha blinked at her reflection in the mirror. Her eyes thick with kohl, flecks of green from her grandmother and mother, her widow's peak, and high cheekbones. Mina peered at her over her shoulder, a look of satisfaction on her face.

And then Mina's reflection disappeared—and Aisha's face grew rounder, the flowers gone from her hair.

"Don't be foolish." Noorjahan laughed from the mirror. "You think I'd miss this day?"

Aisha placed her hand over her mouth. Her reflection did not follow her movement. "Is this what you wanted for me?"

"Alim is good to you. I am grateful for this. He treats you with care, Aisha. He doesn't drink. He doesn't blame his weaknesses on you. You'll be comfortable together."

"Dad didn't drink, but you still drove him away."

"Your father didn't drink often. May God watch over him. I'm sorry that I couldn't stay with you longer." Noorjahan began to cry. "If I were there, you'd be going to university. When you have a daughter, let her be the one to carry our dreams. Name her Kawthar."

Aisha's eyes filled with tears. She had let her mother down. She should have fought Murad. But how could she explain it all to Alim, and who would take care of the poppies?

"But these are the choices one must make in life. Don't look back. Don't become bitter."

"I wish you were here, Mom. I don't know how to do this."

"You look beautiful. You have what you need. I'm proud of you."

Aisha wanted to reach through the glass and hug her mother. Seeing her, made the loss so much bigger.

"You have to keep yourself healthy. Don't forget what I taught you—about the herbs and medicine."

There was so much to manage with school, the orchards, and the poppy fields, Aisha mostly had given up on her mother's practice.

"Just heal yourself, my child."

Aisha blinked and her reflection blinked back, obediently mirroring her. Noorjahan was gone. A longing burned into her heart. Her eyes brimmed with tears.

Mina grabbed her hand. "Careful, or you'll ruin your makeup."

Aisha squeezed her fingers back.

"You look stunning," Mina said.

Aisha wiped the tears from her eyes. She hugged Mina close, wanting to hold on to this moment when they felt like sisters. Everything seemed possible.

part 3

REVOLT

Age 28
1994

Poshkarbal

21

AISHA

THERE WAS ONLY one photograph taken from Aisha's wedding. Aisha looked at the camera, and Alim looked at her; the sun lit half of his face. It was taken in her garden, against the side of the house, the photographer long forgotten. The look of adoration on Alim's face said everything. She didn't show the photo to the children or frame it on the wall. It felt too private, too intimate for others to see. She'd never seen love written across a face before she met Alim.

She kept the photograph with her mother's jewelry. She did not look at it often. Every time she picked up the photo, oily residue from her fingers was left behind. Overtime, her desire to remember would corrode the photo of her eighteen-year-old self, fierce, unapologetic, and so sure that everything would work out.

Mostly, it had. Aisha hadn't thought that she could trust love. Would Alim leave like her father? Or worse, stay and slink out at night like Murad.

At twenty-eight, her life was marked between the sleepless nights that came with children, and Haseena's demands, which were a warfare of their own. Aisha fought each day to keep calm. Her stability eroded when she was forced to live with Haseena and Murad. It was temporary—one semester, while Alim taught at the university in the capital city of Charagan. The soldiers built a new camp just outside the village, and Alim would not let her stay alone as she had during the early days of their marriage. She was two months, three weeks, and six days into living with Haseena, more than halfway through the semester. Alim would be home to visit in four days.

Aisha hadn't brought the box with her wedding photo to Haseena's house. The more stuff she brought, the more of a bother it would be to move it back. The semester would pass quickly. She just needed to be patient.

The combination of being isolated with Haseena and the incessant bickering of the children boxed her in. Aisha missed waking up and seeing the orchards, the river carving the land, and the mountains swelling around her. At home the land continued into the sky—she was a part of the universe. Her family, Alim and the two children, were cradled and nourished. There weren't hard edges on the furniture for Fidaa to bash his head on, or porcelain vases that might topple and break. At four, Fidaa still behaved like a toddler, subjecting them all to endless tantrums. At home, when the children cried, she only worried that they might be hurt, not that Haseena would be irritated or that Murad would be awoken. She spent a few days each week back home to keep up with the poppies, but the kids often complained of the long walk, and she had to leave them with Haseena.

She wasn't used to this sort of life, where servants cooked and washed, and even cared for the children. Haseena did not deem Aisha worthy of making household decisions, which translated into Haseena barking orders. She'd stand above the servants, instructing them on the exact way to fold and crease a napkin. Sheets were to be folded and then pressed. This baffled Aisha; what purpose in pressing creases into bedsheets?

The tea kettle whistled downstairs. A shrill cry followed by Haseena's voice. "Aisha, come turn off the kettle."

Aisha shook her head at the absurdity. She hadn't put the kettle on. She wasn't making tea, and if Haseena had asked or demanded that she did, she'd be in the kitchen waiting for the water to boil.

"I'll be right down."

If Alim were here, he'd get the kettle. He always dulled the blade of Haseena, never seeming to tire of the exhausting dance he performed between mother and wife. In the kitchen, the servant chopped onions for dinner and did not look up when Aisha took the kettle off the stove. The servants knew better than to engage in the war between the women. Haseena, the general; Aisha, the guerrilla leader. The servants preferred Aisha but could never show it. Haseena would dismiss them without cause.

"Do you want me to prepare tea?" Aisha called from the kitchen.

"No need to make tea," Haseena yelled back.

Aisha laughed quietly. Her best defense against Haseena was humor (second only to distance).

And though Aisha had heard Haseena perfectly well, she decided to prepare a pot of tea. Why not? The water had already been boiled.

22

ALIM

ALIM SAT IN the back of the bus unable to get a proper view. Still, he knew the six-hour ride back home to Poshkarbal was nearly over. They'd made it this time without having to get off the bus and be searched by the army at a government checkpoint. Last time, they'd arrested a man. The trip back home became increasingly dangerous. They'd passed safely through the freedom fighters' barricades when they went through the part of the city controlled by militant separatists. His stomach lurched as they hit a pothole, making the caged chickens cluck under the feet of the man across the way.

The bus stopped on the south end of Poshkarbal, just down from the market, next to a field where children played cricket. Hopping off the bus, Alim's lungs filled with mountain air, and his spirit, which seemed to coil inside in the city, expanded. Muscles he hadn't realized were tense suddenly relaxed. Alim loved the sounds of the river, the freshness of the air, the vegetables that grew from the earth. How ironic to teach art in a city, where the angles of buildings were his only inspiration. The colors were drab, monochromatic beiges and tans, creams and browns. Even the river flowed in shades of gray. Here in the countryside, the water was translucent over rocks, turquoise in the sun; the sky was magenta at dusk, azure against the white of the mountains, and the greens—could someone ever paint all the shades of green?

If it weren't so late, he would've stopped by the market, but the sun had already dropped behind the mountains, and he didn't want to chance running into soldiers. Alim passed through town quickly, taking a side trail that cut off from the main road, instead of grabbing a rickshaw. He'd missed Aisha so much, painted and repainted her lips in each picture he drew of her. Tomorrow, he'd wake up with his arms around her, her face nestled against his chest, and run his fingers through her hair.

A lone cricket sang, croaking off-key without any backup. He paused when he reached his house—it hadn't held much comfort growing up, but he'd always loved the porch—his father sat out there every evening, taking in the vastness of the land that stretched before them. He knocked on the door and whistled for the children.

The paddle of Kawthar's feet rattled the house. "Dad," she wailed, holding down on the word as if it were a siren. Alim slipped into the house and took off his shoes, riffling through his bag for the teddy bear he'd gotten her. Aisha preferred that he brought them clothes—practical things that they couldn't find in the village, but he could never figure out the right sizes, buying jeans that were too small and shoes that were too big.

Kawthar took the bear and beamed up at her father. "Thank you." She cradled the bear. "This one is a freedom fighter." She lifted the paw, as if the bear were shooting into the distance. Alim resisted the urge to lecture her on the problems of militancy. His poor daughter was born into occupation. It was all she knew.

She brought the bear's nose to hers. "He's just perfect. He's hungry now. Did you bring us any sweets?" She smiled at Alim, her front tooth missing. Her unbrushed, wavy hair hung down her back. Haseena always complained that Aisha let Kawthar run around unkempt.

"What on earth happened to your tooth?"

"I lost it last week eating an apple."

"You lost it?" Alim scrunched up his face. "You must be more careful with your teeth. You're seven, old enough to keep proper track of your teeth."

"It's not lost. It just fell out." She shook her narrow face in exacerbation. Her eyes were her mother's—honey with flecks of green in the light.

"Where's your brother?"

Kawthar shrugged, nestling her bear under her arm. "I got a perfect score on my test. Do you want to see it?"

"Yes, bring it." She ran to grab it.

"Alim, darling." His mother called from upstairs. "Please, come."

He climbed the stairs, passed the framed photos on the wall: Haseena's parents, Murad with his brother, Murad with Alim and his parents, Haseena and Murad cradling baby Kawthar. Aisha and Fidaa were absent from the wall.

Haseena lay in her bed, head propped up on pillows. "Thank God, you've returned home safe."

Alim sat in a chair by her bed. "What's wrong? Are you okay?" He already knew the answer would be pain. Haseena began with her knee, a sudden pain that came and made it impossible to go up the stairs, and then her stomach—so sickly that everything she ate ran through her; in bed her joints became so stiff that she couldn't even turn; but worst of all, what they shouldn't speak of was her heart. How it hurt when Alim was gone.

Haseena took his hand. "Now my pain is already leaving." She beamed up at him with an adoration he'd not experienced as a child. "I've made you smoked eggplant and goat curry."

Kawthar burst into the room, waving her quiz. She hopped on the bed, next to Haseena, something he'd never done as a child.

"Such a clever child." Haseena patted Kawthar's back. "God blessed us with this child."

His mother had always loved Kawthar. She'd looked so much like Alim as a baby, except for her hair, which was much lighter. He'd taken her adoration for granted until their son was born. Haseena refused to hold him when he was little. Alim had tried to blame it on her frailty, but his son looked so much like Aisha that he could barely find traces of himself.

"Can I get you tea, Mom?"

"Don't bother yourself," she said, which Alim interpreted as a yes, but that he should have the servant bring it. "Make sure they make a fresh batch. When Aisha brews it, she leaves the tea too long and it's bitter."

Alim nodded. A familiar tension settled into his stomach. Aisha always fell short in his mother's eyes. Still, he wished that Aisha did less to agitate his mother. He'd thought that the children would have brought them closer, but the children were fissures, erupting between the women he loved.

Alim went downstairs, where his father watched Aisha and Fidaa through the window. Pumpkin vines covered the ground. The sun splashed around Aisha. How he'd missed her, all these weeks, longing to nestle against her.

"Aisha told me that you will be applying to teach at my old school." Murad patted his son on the back. "My legacy lives on."

Heat rose in Alim's face. He'd never said that. The last thing he wanted was to teach in a one-room schoolhouse filled with village brats. At the very least, he'd teach at Kawthar's school, where there were teachers for each standard. "They asked me to apply for a permanent position at the university, teaching art."

"You would enjoy that more." But what would it do to his son's marriage? Murad saw the strain between Aisha and Haseena. All of them living together under one roof wasn't working. And Aisha had the poppies to take care of—so many things his son knew nothing about. Best not to meddle though. "Teaching in the schoolhouse—all those children, so many of them poor. It's not easy. Not everyone is cut out for it."

His dad was saying he was too soft to teach at the government school. Alim shrugged, "There will be lots of applicants for the university position anyhow."

"How are things in the city?" Murad asked.

Alim shook his head, not wanting to burden his father, but how could he lie? The Front controlled two thirds of the city, leaving a third held by Nadistan's army. School was hardly in session. Walking to the grocery store required him to pass two checkpoints. The sound of gunshots exploded in his ears. Two of his students were in the hospital with injuries, shot by soldiers. "The jawans are slaughtering the protestors. How is it here?"

Murad sighed. "I wanted so much for your generation. I thought we would have seen the worst of it growing up under the colonizer, but look how our people turn on each other."

"It's so sad. All these young soldiers from the mainland, signing up for the military just because of the pension."

Murad adjusted his glasses. "They killed a boy in a neighboring village. I worry about Aisha going back and forth alone so much."

"Has she been going often?" She insisted on going home, the one thing he asked her not to do.

"There is so much work for her. If I were stronger, I'd go with her, but the walk is getting to be too much."

Alim looked out the window at Fidaa, sitting in a pile of dirt, pulling weeds from under the vegetables. Fidaa looked up and burst into a grin. "Let's go outside."

"Go ahead, son." He wanted Alim to have some privacy with Aisha, they'd been apart for so long. When Noorjahan had been away—each day lasted an eternity.

Outside, Fidaa held up a worm. "Look! A pink one!"

Aisha's face lit up when Alim came outside. "When did you get here?"

"Just now." He stepped toward her and took her into his arms; her head fit perfectly against his chest. "I missed you."

"It felt so long this time."

"I thought I'd get used to it, but every time I'm apart from you becomes harder."

"How long will you be home for?"

"Just a few days." He'd not mentioned that the visit would be so short. She couldn't help feeling angry about him leaving. He rubbed her back and kissed her cheeks. "This summer we'll have more time together."

The shadow of her breast was visible under her shirt. He wanted to peel off each layer of clothing, but he'd have to wait until the children were asleep. He would enjoy his work, stealing kisses as he searched for her, finding her longing, losing himself in her wetness.

23

AISHA

AISHA LAY IN bed, wishing Fidaa would stop crying before he woke up Haseena.

"Alim," she whispered. "Can you go get him?"

"Of course." He searched the nightstand for his glasses and went into the other room. A few minutes later, the crying stopped and Alim slipped into bed.

"How did you do it?"

"Candy."

Aisha threw a pillow at him.

His face dissolved into a smile. Aisha ruffled his hair. She wasn't used to him without a beard, which made him look nineteen instead of twenty-eight. She rolled over and nuzzled into the soapy scent of his chest, lean and muscular. He'd always been gentle with her, building her trust. When they first married, he did not insist on sex the first night, nor in the days that followed. Night after night passed until she became curious. By waiting, he found her pleasure, uncorked it, let it build and unravel. He made a study of learning the art of her desire.

She kissed up his chest. When had his chest become so hairy? One day it was just there, kind of like the children learning to talk.

She couldn't recall Kawthar's first words. They had come in sprinkles. Then one day, she burst forth with sentences. Fidaa was slower to speak; at age four his sentences were still choppy words clinging to each other. Kawthar was reading books at that age, just as Aisha had. Kawthar had Alim's long face and lean frame. She was born a miniature of him, a perfect replica. When Fidaa was born, Aisha only saw Noorjahan—full lips, high cheekbones, and thick black hair. Haseena punished Fidaa for this, that he lived in reflection of Noorjahan.

Alim curled his arms around Aisha and kissed along her collarbone. Her hunger for him outweighed their time together. She didn't want to complain, but her heart ached with thoughts of him leaving, again.

"I should go work up in the fields, today." Really, she should hire someone, but it was hard to find anyone trustworthy, more and more villagers were becoming informants for the army.

"I want to spend time with you." He had the voice of a poet, deep like the hum of wind blowing through a mountain cave. "Let's take the kids on a picnic or something."

"The worms won't stop attacking the apple trees while we have our picnic." They needed to focus on pest control if they wanted a harvest. But still she felt bad, not telling him the full truth. She hadn't meant to hide the opium from Alim. She'd thought that he'd have figured it out—who could pay for college tuition, remodels, and Haseena's lifestyle with orchards and a teacher's salary? But Aisha managed the finances, as did Murad, so Alim was spared the reality of it. Sometimes, she wondered if he knew and never said anything.

"I'll pack the lunch. Or do you want me to come help you?" He kissed down her neckline. "Or maybe I should take you back to bed."

"Your mom would love that. We'll just stay in bed all day."

Alim kissed her so she had to stop talking. He was hard against her, and she pushed back into him.

"Come on, let's have breakfast. I can take the kids fishing so you can get some work done."

"I just need a few hours in the morning." Her hands rested around his waist. "Could we spend the night back home tonight? I'll cook the fish, but you have to clean it."

"Of course." He just wanted to make her happy.

Aisha wore her purple baseball cap and a yellow cotton shirt. The thin fabric kept the sun from beating down directly on her skin. The poppy field was terraced along the slope of the mountain. Over the years, she'd planted fava beans, cabbage, and greens in some of the beds to nourish the soil, making the crops hardier.

She walked through the bulbs, bulging with sap. She'd planted a small plot early. It had been a gamble, but somehow the snow had spared them and some early spring sun gave her a rare spring poppy crop. No one else would be harvesting now. She'd be able to charge a lot for this. Her freshly sharpened razor blade tattooed the skin with milky resin. The first sap was her favorite—the pungent scent released into the air. A few magenta flowers bloomed in the beds below, amid the sea of green bulbs, hints of color against the arid landscape.

Noorjahan flew out of the crimson petals, which matched her dress, and walked toward Aisha. They were nearly the same age, but Aisha was taller. Her mother hadn't aged.

"I didn't think that it was a good idea to plant fava beans with the poppies, but it works. You even planted the rocky, lower slope. Impressive."

The poppies on the eastern slope of the mountain were doing well despite the wind stunting their height. Aisha reached in her bag and pulled out another razor blade. "Do you want to help? Make yourself useful?"

Noorjahan laughed. "You must hire someone. My days of harvesting opium are over. Look, I know you don't like me butting in and all, but I don't think it's good for the children to live with that woman."

"It's only temporary. And that woman is their grandmother. It will be fine." Defending Haseena nauseated her. Still, if Noorjahan hadn't been with Murad, maybe Haseena wouldn't be such a beast. Had her mother thought of that? Aisha turned back to the poppies, scoring a bulb.

"You certainly do a great job with the poppies. I didn't realize you had it in you."

"What is that supposed to mean?" Aisha faced her mother. Noorjahan could always twist a compliment into an insult.

"See, it's not good for you, either, living with that woman. She gives you a temper."

Aisha laughed. Yes, blame her temper on Haseena! "Do you see how big these are?" She gestured to the poppies below, sure that her mother had never succeeded in a spring harvest.

"You do well for your family." Noor refused to acknowledge the miracle and launched an offensive. "Don't you think you should tell Alim? You've been married ten years. It's not good to keep such things from your husband."

"I don't want to give him more to worry about." Really, she didn't know how to talk about something she'd hidden for so long. Alim criticized the role of the drug lords in the communal violence. She'd been selling to the same Gujar family and knew they wouldn't sell to the soldiers, but most people thought it was only goondas and soldiers involved in the opium trade.

"Things have gotten so bad in our country. I wanted to believe that you would be born into something different, but your children were born with soldiers all around. It's only gotten worse."

"It's better here than in the capital. Alim doesn't talk about it, but I read the newspaper. Students are being killed. Young boys arrested just for organizing for clean elections." Aisha's heart ached for the teenagers, just sixteen or seventeen years old and imprisoned. As soon as they got out, they joined the Front. It was so different now, even boys in college and private schools were joining. "It's in God's hands now."

"Prayer is what we have. I'm glad that you keep the old ways alive, too, even though you go to the Mosque."

"We went to the mosque growing up."

"But not so often."

Since marrying Alim, Aisha went to the mosque weekly, sometimes more. It's the one thing that brought peace to her and Haseena. Friday prayers with Kawthar.

"Just don't forget what I taught you. Pray, take care of the earth, love your children, be honest, not just with Alim, but more importantly with yourself."

"Like you and Murad were honest with Haseena?"

"All these years have passed, and you are still angry with your mother. I thought that having children would change that. Besides, Murad has his own issues. I just wish he hadn't put so much on you."

"I have work to do. If you're not going to help me, don't slow me down."

"Going faster isn't going to change how you feel inside."

Aisha wiped sweat from her forehead. She hoped her children would escape the ghost of Noorjahan.

24

ALIM

ALIM WAITED FOR Aisha to disappear around the bend in the hill. It's not that he didn't trust his wife. He hadn't set out to follow her, but all the things that his mother had been saying got inside his head. She did take after Noorjahan. He'd never mentioned it to Aisha, but he knew what happened with Noorjahan and his father. How Noorjahan had tempted Murad. His poor mother made a fool by her sinful ways. What was Aisha doing while he worked in the city, supporting their family? There could be a man she meets in the mountains, just like her mother had snuck away. He kept a distance so that she would not see him and followed her up past the orchards she had said she so desperately needed to work in. Clearly, the apple trees could defend themselves from the caterpillars while she satisfied herself.

Heat from the spring sun beat down on his back as he climbed over boulders. She could be meeting her lover in a mountain shack. He cringed, imagining one of the goat herders touching her. What was so important that she couldn't stay home for the few, precious days they had together?

Rounding the corner, he saw a small shack and a valley of poppies. Most people grew a few poppies in their gardens for seeds and medicine, but this was the largest opium field he'd ever seen. How could she have hidden this from him? His insides went cold. So, this was where all their money actually came from. He'd assumed it was her grandparents. His father must have known. Is this why he'd agreed to their marriage? Alim played and replayed the last decade of his life.

Sweat dripped down his neck. Aisha had lied to him their entire marriage. He didn't want to see anymore. This was no place for a woman. Slowly, he headed back down to the house, gathered the children up, and went fishing. He wished he'd never returned home.

After fishing, Alim went out into the garden to cut some chard and pulled out a couple of onions. The dahlias bloomed yellow, peach, and crimson. Fidaa came over to him and pulled out an onion of his own. Following Alim's lead, he shook off the dirt. Fidaa was still small at four, but wiry and strong, with thick black hair that Aisha let grow too long and hang in his eyes. He looked so much like Aisha, except for the darkness of his eyes and skin. He never understood how their child could be so dark.

"Let me have the onion." Alim reached for it, but Fidaa pulled away.

"No. Mine." Fidaa balled his fists, about to erupt. Sometimes, he wondered if something were wrong with Fidaa. He rarely spoke and would fixate on the smallest thing, screaming and crying when it was taken away. Maybe it was hereditary. Aisha had been mute as a child. He handed all the onions to Fidaa. "Go put these on the counter."

"My onions. I carry onions. Mine."

Alim exhaled. The child exhausted his patience. He glanced up the trail. Aisha appeared on the horizon, her yellow shirt visible against the darkening sky. Rage simmered inside him. He pulled a few weeds. The rocky soil dissolved quickly from the roots. Aisha disappeared around a turn in the path, and he went inside to the kitchen. The fish were gutted and cleaned, ready for her.

To think that all they created together was a lie. Their house transformed from a one-room cottage to three bedrooms, with plaster walls, plumbing, and marble. The only thing left to build was his studio. A quiet place like his father had, to think, to paint, to become what he dreamed, a practicing artist. All from opium. How could he have been so stupid to believe that they could afford all this?

Alim turned on the radio. The news crackled and hissed through the static. Three villagers were killed by the army up north. Alim reached to change the station, but the announcer began to read the names of boys who'd crossed the border to Daryastan to train as freedom fighters.

None were his students. He switched to music. Sometimes he wished to forget, wanting life to be simple. He diced the onions and then chopped up the chard. Everything would be ready for Aisha.

The faucet outside turned on. He imagined Aisha scrubbing her fingers with the small brush that he'd gotten her. Now it made sense, that funny scent that lingered on her. He'd thought it some kind of fertilizer, but it was resin.

Aisha came in, her cheeks flushed from the evening air. "Hi, love."

"Where were you?"

Aisha took off her turquoise shawl and hung it near the back door. "It smells so good." She didn't answer his question.

Fidaa ran up to her and wrapped himself around her leg. She brushed his hair from his eyes and kissed the top of his head. "Did you catch any fish?"

He shook his head. "Kawthar and Dad did. I made a boat."

"Did you float it down the river?"

He nodded. "The boat crashed. Everyone fell."

"Did they swim away?" Aisha asked.

"They all died."

Fidaa hadn't even been sad when his boat full of imaginary people died. He'd shrugged as if a capsized boat were inevitable, as if humankind was destined to suffer.

Alim didn't want to be hungry when Aisha brought steaming plates to the table, but the greens had the right amount of garlic and lemon, the rice fluffed up, the fish fell apart in his mouth. Fidaa dropped some food on the floor but picked it up without being told. Kawthar pinched Fidaa, who blew food out of his mouth, and somehow, they both ended up crying. Alim took them to get ready for bed and Aisha did the dishes.

The children nestled under his arms as Alim read to them, creating a familiar warmth he so missed from those early days when they first married. He wanted to return to the simplicity of their life together. His stomach knotted; Aisha had been hiding the poppies back then, too.

Fidaa fell asleep before the story was done and Kawthar asked Alim question after question so that she wouldn't have to go to bed. He couldn't blame her though. He, too, didn't want the bedtime story to end.

Aisha stood at the sink, drying the dishes. She couldn't sleep until all the dishes were put away, washing them wasn't good enough. After she finished, she sat on the couch next to Alim, nestling into his side. Alim stiffened. Outside, a distant symphony of crickets called into the night.

"I miss being here so much, Alim." She rubbed his arm gently. He tensed under her touch. "Have you thought at all about the position at the school?"

"There's a position open in the art department at the university." He hadn't meant to tell her like this.

"A permanent one?" Her voice was quiet.

"Yes, with full benefits."

"You love teaching art." Aisha ran her hand across his chest but avoided his eyes. "What an opportunity."

"Where were you today?"

She moved away from him a bit and looked at him. "Are you still going to apply to the government school?"

"I never said I was going to. There's no money in it."

"We can manage. It's good for the children to have you around."

"How do we manage, Aisha? Tell me. What pays for all of this?"

She folded her hands in her lap. Her lips a firm line. "The same way your university fees were paid."

"So, you admit it. Everything is a lie. How did you lie to me all these years?" He couldn't even look at her.

"I never lied, Alim."

"What will my parents think when they find out?"

"They know. Why do you think your mother agreed to the wedding? Your mother has no problem with the money, just with me."

"Of course my mother has issues with you, after what your mother did to our family. I thought you were different."

Aisha didn't move. He'd known all along about Noorjahan and Murad. And he blamed her. He thought it all was Aisha's fault.

"How long have you been doing this?"

"Since before my mom died." There was no apology in her voice. The silence spread between them.

Aisha stood up strong and tall, just as she had all those years ago when she received her perfect marks from Murad. Even then, her grades were better than Alim's. But he would never see that. He would never see how hard she worked.

Alim picked up a book and began reading. By the time he went to bed, Aisha was already asleep.

25

AISHA

AISHA WOKE UP before Alim and prepared breakfast. She'd never meant to hide the poppies from him. At least now he'd understand why she needed to be at home. Her mother was right, the secrets were too much.

When Alim came into the kitchen, he didn't come up behind her and kiss her cheek. "We should spend the night back at my parents' tonight. I can help you move stuff over there before I leave." With all the soldiers surrounding the village, he could not have his family left alone next to an opium field.

"It would be easier if I could stay here with the children." She bit her lip. He still didn't understand. "I don't want to be going back and forth so much."

"It must be difficult to manage your poppies when you are so far away." She clearly didn't care about their children's safety. "Are you selling to the soldiers?"

How dare he accuse her of being an informant. "If you are so worried about danger, don't ask such stupid questions." She served Alim breakfast and went to change for work, her appetite lost.

With less than a week left to harvest, she worked rapidly in the fields. She hadn't asked who the Gujars sold to, but knew that they would never sell to the soldiers. Their uncles and brothers fought in the Front. The less you know, the less risk. Maybe after this crop, she'd burn the fields and end this war between them.

When she returned home, a fresh vegetable curry Alim prepared was on the table, a peace offering.

"You're such a good cook, Dad," Kawthar said. "Why do you have to go? Can't you stay with us longer?"

Alim put some rice and curry in her bowl. "I'll be back soon and then it will be summer break and we will go fishing together."

"I don't like fishing. It's so boring waiting for the fish all the time. Let's go swimming! Teach me how to swim."

"Your mother is a better swimmer than I am. We'll all go for a swim in the river when I return."

"Can we go to the springs instead? The one that Grandma used to take Mom to?"

Kawthar loved the spring, even when she was a baby. She'd spend the day on her blanket after Aisha had bathed her in the warm water.

Alim reached across the table and squeezed Aisha's hand. "Of course, we'll all go together."

26

AISHA

TWOS WERE THE WORST for Aisha. Two days after Alim left, she still smelled his scent everywhere. Two weeks, her skin wanted to shed the memory of his touch. After two months, she became a dull canvas that had never been painted under his fingertips. More than anything, she hated that they'd fought in their short time together. He'd left angry and not trusting her.

Staying with Haseena and hiring out some of the work in the fields had been her way to make peace with Alim. She hired one of Omar's nephews. Ahmed was an honest boy. Aisha had attended his birth—he'd come out in the water sack, completely unbroken as if he were born with gills. When she'd punctured it, the warm fluid had rushed over her, an ocean of its own, but the little boy hadn't cried. She'd been worried about his lungs, but they were clear. It was merely his temperament.

In the sixteen days since Alim had left, there had been three nights of curfew, one bombing, an assassination of one of the puppet government officials, and massive protests in the capital city. Last night, when she'd called, his phone was not working. This was normal, she kept telling herself. The lines were often suspended. They would resume soon enough. But still her mind wandered to the possibility that it was something more, that there could be someone else. That he was mad about the poppies, and this weakened him. She pushed this from her mind.

She'd tried calling Alim from Mina's yesterday, but he hadn't answered. There was no way she could call from the house. Haseena monitored all her conversations, listening from another room. If he'd picked up, she would have told him what happened to Fidaa. Haseena had whipped Fidaa with a belt, accusing him of breaking a dish. Aisha had seen the whole thing. Kawthar had put the plate on his head and when it crashed to the ground she'd tattled on him.

Aisha paced in the kitchen. There was time to go over to Mina's and phone Alim. Perhaps he'd answer. But Mina's niece had been running a fever, and Aisha did not want to expose Fidaa to the illness. Aisha hated leaving Fidaa with Haseena, but it would just be for a couple of hours. He would be fine.

Aisha went upstairs to Haseena's room and knocked lightly on the door. Haseena clucked for her to enter. They had their own language of guttural noises. Haseena saved her words for more worthy people. This was Aisha's language of love for Alim—endurance.

"Could you watch Fidaa for a short while?" Haseena folded a linen cloth in half. Her hair appeared silver in the light. "I promised Mina that I'd bring her some pears. Her niece is sick, so I don't want to expose Fidaa."

Kawthar was playing by the bed. Haseena treated her as her own. When Kawthar was born, she purchased a goat from the Gujars, insisting that Aisha's milk was not satisfying Kawthar.

Haseena cleared her throat. "Why didn't you bring Mina the pears yesterday?"

She was so damn controlling. "I won't be gone long."

"Just make sure Fidaa behaves." She shook her head in disgust. "I've never seen a child cry so much."

"Thank you," Aisha said, forcing the words out. "Kawthar, come with me."

Kawthar dropped her cloth doll and walked toward Aisha.

"Kawthar, stay," Haseena said. "I need your help putting these away." She gestured to the pile of folded linens. Kawthar immediately went back to playing with her doll.

"Come, Kawthar," Aisha said firmly.

Kawthar came to her mother's side, and they left the room together. "No bullying your brother. Take care of him a little bit. Okay?"

"Yes, Mama," Kawthar said in a well-rehearsed play. Her role was to be obedient when her mother was present, but Aisha knew that the second she was gone, she'd go after her brother. Aisha never understood why she treated her brother so poorly after she'd been so loved as a child. She wanted to blame Haseena for how Kawthar treated her brother. But in the end, she was their mother, and any failings of her children were her own.

"Can I go back now?"

"Yes, darling." Aisha kissed her and went downstairs.

Outside, Fidaa played in the garden with a stick. He was born with Noorjahan's face, but his eyes never turned green or blue, they remained clouded with smoke. His skin was darker than anyone else's in the family, something Haseena often criticized, but Aisha loved the way Fidaa's skin glistened after she oiled it. Her beautiful boy.

"Come, Fidaa." He didn't respond, just circled his stick around in the dirt. "Fidaa." She grabbed the stick to get his attention. He looked up at her. "I have to go out for a bit, but Kawthar will take care of you." She gave his fingers a squeeze. "But you must be good. No crying, understand?"

Fidaa nodded and then pointed to a bird flying overhead. Aisha gave him a hug.

It was nearing three o'clock. There was no curfew in the village. The soldiers usually didn't enter the village, but it was still dangerous to be alone close to dusk.

Aisha walked up the hill to Mina's house; well, really it was Omar's. Mina had married Omar six years ago. At first, Aisha had kept her distance, not wanting to be around Omar, but as he was rarely home, she was able to see Mina more. She had never told Mina what happened with Omar.

The house hadn't changed at all over the years. The roof sagged with the memory of snow. Pieces of burlap and plastic tarps were slung across the roof in an attempt to keep the rain out. The corrugated metal fence, dented and bent, only covered half the yard. Aisha stepped over a pile of rubble, knocked, and then opened the door. Mina sat on the floor next to her niece, Laila, who was pale with fever.

"How is she?" Aisha asked, stepping toward the little girl, pressing her palms to her forehead. "She feels so hot. Have you given her anything?"

Mina shook her head. Her pink salwar kameez hung loosely over her frame. Her hair was pulled back in a simple braid.

"I used the last of the aspirin. Let me see if I have another jar." Mina riffled through a drawer but couldn't find any.

"I brought these for you." Aisha handed Mina the bag of bruised pears. "Did she take the herbs?"

Mina nodded. "It helped with the cough, but her fever hasn't broken."

Aisha pulled out some more herbs. "Let me make a tea." She put water on to boil. "Can I use the phone?"

Mina nodded. "Go ahead."

Aisha dialed Alim. There was static, a pause, and then connection. It rang thirteen times before she hung up. Alim did not answer. Where was he? Her stomach tightened. They were under curfew in the capital. He'd have to be home. Unless something had happened. Unless he were hurt. Unless he were with someone.

Aisha poured the boiling water over the herbs. Mina pressed her hand against the child's forehead. "She's burning up. Would you mind watching her while I get some aspirin from the store?"

Aisha glanced at the clock. "I need to get back soon."

"It won't take long."

"Alright, just be quick." She would be late. Haseena would be furious. But what could she do? The child needed medicine.

"Thank you." Mina gathered her things.

"Hurry back," Aisha said as Mina put her shoes on. "Can I help you with the cooking?"

Mina shook her head. "Just relax a little."

As soon as she left, Aisha went to the phone. She dialed Alim, again. It connected, but just rang and rang. In a way, it was better when there was no connection. At least then she knew the lines were down.

The herbs cooled and Aisha brought the warm water to the little girl, who drank it down without complaint. Aisha placed another blanket on her to sweat the germs out. She picked up a broom and swept the floor. Mina was such a poor housekeeper, but it wasn't her fault. What could she do, living with so many people? Poor Mina had not been able to have any children. They never spoke of her infertility, but Aisha often brought her herbs. She was still young; it was possible, if God willed it.

Aisha called Alim again. It rang and rang and rang. Footsteps sounded outside the door. She hung up the phone and breathed a sigh of relief that Mina had returned so quickly. Omar walked in, removed his shoes, and closed the door behind him.

"Good evening," he said, sitting down at the table. The sick child slept soundly.

"Mina went to get aspirin. She'll be back soon." Aisha walked toward the door, circling wide around Omar. "I must be going home."

"Stay, have some tea with me." He patted the pillow next to him. "Come."

Aisha froze. "It is getting late. I need to go."

He locked eyes with her. "I can walk you home when Mina

returns. It is not safe for you to be out alone at this hour. I saw some soldiers on my way here. Come and sit."

Aisha slowly walked over and sat next to him. God, let Mina hurry home.

"Why don't you visit more?" He draped his arm around her. His skin on hers. Every part of her collapsed. "I remember how sweet you used to be."

Omar moved behind her and wrapped both of his arms around her, pressing his hardness into her back. Aisha shut her eyes and clamped her nails into her palms. She could not move. She was seventeen years old again. His hands reached around to her breasts, his breath ragged in her ear.

Aisha threw her elbow into his rib cage. Omar grumbled. The door rattled. He released her and moved quickly away before Mina walked in. Omar sipped his tea. The little girl slept in the corner.

"Thank you so much for staying, Aisha." Mina placed the aspirin on the table. "Has she been sleeping the whole time?"

Aisha nodded. "She fell asleep after taking her herbs."

"Omar will walk you home. It's too far to go alone," Mina said, clearing the tea from the table.

"It's okay."

"Omar, go with her," Mina insisted.

Aisha slid her shoes on. "I'll be fine." She could not meet Mina's eyes. God forgive her.

The sun set red fire in the sky. Aisha pressed her fingers into her palms, piercing the skin. She walked up the path, her stomach knotting. Why had she allowed herself to be alone with Omar? Alim would never forgive her. She prayed to God to carry this burden.

27

AISHA

FIDAA'S CRIES REACHED Aisha before she opened the gate. She should never have gone to Mina's. She could not get the feeling of Omar's hands off her skin. If Alim found out, Haseena would twist it. Her throat went dry. Alim already thought she was a liar.

Aisha followed Fidaa's cries upstairs to Haseena's room. The door was locked.

"Fidaa, darling, calm down," she called to him.

His screams were high-pitched.

"Are you hurt?" A servant passed by. "Please, open the door."

The servant shook his head, quickening his pace. Of course, Haseena was the only one with a key.

"Where have you been?" Haseena walked up the stairs.

Aisha thought of Omar against her. "Mina had to get medicine for her niece. The fever was so high." Fidaa's cries continued like a siren. "Please, what has happened?"

"You've done nothing to train this child." Haseena drew close to Aisha. "Look how poorly you raised your son, screaming like this. The apple doesn't fall far from the tree."

Haseena took out the key and held it between her fingers, making no move to unlock the door. She leaned toward Aisha. "Don't think I don't know what you are up to."

Aisha bit her lip to keep from responding. Haseena turned the key in the lock.

Fidaa screamed inside a large cardboard box. Instead of climbing out, he sat in the corner, defeated. If you told him to stay somewhere, Fidaa always would. He'd soiled himself. Flies swarmed him. His little hands were coated in feces. It leaked out his pants and onto his foot. The smell made her gag. Aisha pulled Fidaa out of the box, stripping off his clothes.

"What a filthy child. He's so dark, I wonder if he's even Alim's." Haseena turned and left the room.

She was a filthy, hateful person. Aisha took Fidaa by the hand to the bathroom. She rinsed his body and rubbed Fidaa's back with soap. "Did anyone feed you?"

Fidaa shook his head.

"Were you in the box the whole time I was gone?"

Fidaa nodded. "Grandma told Fidaa stay inside. Bad boy." Red marks swelled up his arms as if he had been beaten. After she dressed Fidaa, Aisha packed their clothes. They couldn't stay here. She grabbed Fidaa's stuffed rabbit with one paw missing and Kawthar's bear. There wouldn't be any rickshaws so late at night and they would have to carry their bags along the dark trail.

She gathered their things and went to find Murad, reading in his study. "Aisha-jan." He closed the book when she entered. "Fidaa has quieted down. Is he feeling quite alright?"

She bit her lip and pulled Fidaa closer to her. He sat there listening to her child screaming and never checked to see if something was wrong. "We are going home."

"What happened, Aisha?" He ran his fingers along the wool of his vest. "We are family. You must not go."

"It is better this way."

"Please, at least stay until morning. It's not safe on the roads at night."

"I'll be fine." She patted his hand. "Just tell Alim that we have gone home."

"What do you mean? You are leaving for good?"

How could she explain it to him? He wouldn't believe her. Even though he lived and denied it each day. "Yes, we are moving back."

"It's not right."

"None of this is right. I'm not going to stand by and watch Fidaa being abused."

"What has gotten into you, Aisha? How can you say that?" Murad's face drained of color.

She turned to leave, but Haseena stood before her. "What is going on here?"

Aisha ignored her. "Come, Kawthar, we are going home."

"What is this nonsense?" Haseena took a step forward, standing between Aisha and the front door.

"How can you treat your own grandson so cruelly?"

"I took care of the crying little boy, while you were off doing God knows what."

Ignoring Haseena, she turned back toward Murad. "Thank you for everything. We'll see you soon."

He gave her a half nod, his permission for her to leave.

"Come, Kawthar." She handed her a small bag of clothes to carry. The cold night air hit them as they left.

"Mama, did Grandma hurt Fidaa? Is that why we are leaving?" Aisha nodded.

Kawthar took Fidaa's hand in hers as they set out toward home.

28

AISHA

AISHA WIPED DOWN her kitchen counter, inhaling the scent of bread baking. It was Alim's favorite. She hadn't called him since she left his parents' home. She didn't know how to tell him any of this over the phone. Yesterday, he was finally due home. She'd been awake most of the night, wondering if he'd made it, feeling his frustration and anger stretch through the dark.

Kawthar came into the kitchen, holding Fidaa's stuffed rabbit. The missing paw concealed under a shirt it was wearing. "The rabbit lost its paw in a protest. So sad. The soldiers shot him. Mommy, can I help?"

"Come, look at the bread." Aisha cracked open the oven. She pulled out the tray. "Sprinkle the poppy seeds on top."

Kawthar dropped them on the loaf. A few stray seeds skidded and bounced off.

"When are we going back to Grandma's?"

"Your father will take you to visit."

"I don't want to visit. I want to live there. It's closer to school."

"Walking to school makes you strong, Kawthar. You can go with Mina Auntie's nieces."

Kawthar sighed and looked out the window. "I see Daddy!"

Alim's beard had grown back in, and he wore a dark wool sweater. Aisha let out a sigh of relief. Praise be to God, he was safe. Combing her fingers through her hair, Aisha dashed away from the window and pulled an onion from a basket, peeling the layers back. He knocked at the door instead of coming in.

Kawthar opened it. "Daddy." She jumped up and down with excitement. "What did you bring for me?"

Every part of Aisha wanted to run to him. Instead, she grabbed the onion and chopped it in half.

Alim's face was knit in frustration; he dropped his belongings to the ground and pulled out a parcel. Kawthar tore it open. "Cashew sweets. My favorite." She kissed her father and hopped up and down, and then dashed outside to show Fidaa her treasure.

Aisha diced the onion, gripping the layers together.

He came over and put his hand over hers. She put down the knife. His eyes were red, tired, and worn. "Couldn't you have just waited a few more days for me?"

Tears streamed down her face. She reached for the onion again. "I left Fidaa with her."

He moved toward her, smelling of soap and cinnamon.

"What happened?" His voice was so tired. Her tears did not stop as she put her face against his chest, and he stroked her hair.

"I went to Mina's." She skipped over the part about calling him, about the fever, about Omar. Her heart pounded in her ears. Was omission a lie? "When I came home, Fidaa was locked in her room inside a cardboard box. He'd soiled himself. He was hysterical."

"But couldn't he have just crawled out? It was only a box."

Her stomach tightened. He blamed Fidaa. "She told him to stay in there, Alim. Do you understand? She left him there and locked the door." She pulled away.

"Come here, Aisha."

"I can't go back there."

"What do you mean?"

"Alim, I'll do anything for you. I didn't go to university, right? Please don't ask me to do this."

He stepped back from her. "I never asked you not to go to university. You didn't get in."

"Of course I got in. Your father told me not to go. Besides, how would we have paid for your school if I wasn't working?"

"I never even knew about the poppies. You told me that you didn't qualify."

"I placed higher than you. Your dad said it was my duty as your wife. There was nothing I could do."

"You could have told me."

"I finished high school. That was good enough."

"If it was good enough, why are you bringing it up now?"

His words stung. He dismissed her sacrifice.

"I brought this for you." He kissed her forehead and placed a bottle of olive oil on the counter. It was hard to come by in the village, and expensive. "Where is Fidaa?"

"Outside playing."

Alim went outside to Fidaa. Aisha minced the onion until the layers were no longer discernible.

29

ALIM

ALIM WOKE UP, stiff from the cold. Even sleeping, he could not escape the image of the boy in the march. His shirt turning from gray to red. Nothing could erase it. He stared at the ceiling. Aisha had already left the bed. He'd thought that the time away would give him more patience with the children, with his wife, with his mother, but every part of him was brittle.

Two weeks ago, he had been marching with his students through the capital, chanting, *Freedom! We want? Freedom!*

As they marched, gunfire erupted. Alim dropped to the ground. The bullet hit the boy just ahead of him. He stumbled forward a half step, and then fell. Blood trickled onto the sidewalk from his shirt. Alim craned to see if it was one of his students. There was no relief in not recognizing him. He was someone's son, someone's student, someone's brother.

Over the last three days since he'd arrived at Aisha's house, he had not spoken of what happened. He wanted to tell her of the marches, of the army, of the boy that died. But no words came. It was rumored that the Front was going to take over the remaining piece of the capital city.

Alim dressed without bathing and went to the kitchen. water for tea. The children were still sleeping, the sky streak pink. Aisha came into the kitchen and started making breakfast promised his mother that he'd bring Kawthar for a visit. Why did the two women he cared for most have to be at war, when there were children dying in the streets?

Alim sat at the table. Fidaa came in still drunk with sleep and sat in his lap. His frame warm. Alim inhaled his soapy scent. For a moment all he could see was red. A young man dead in the street. A boy who had once sat in his father's lap just like this. He hugged Fidaa to him.

Kawthar came in and brought them their breakfast, and then sat across from them.

"Where are your candies, Kawthar?"

She smiled and shrugged.

"You didn't want to share?"

"Fidaa ate them all."

"I did not." Fidaa jumped out of Alim's lap, nearly spilling his tea. "You didn't even give me one."

"We're going to visit Grandma today," Alim said.

"I'm not going," Kawthar said.

Alim chewed his breakfast slowly, stunned at her response. "But she misses you so much."

Kawthar stared defiantly at Alim. "She hurt Fidaa."

Alim's stomach turned. The bruises. The screams. It had gone too far.

When Alim arrived at his parents', the TV hummed and the scent of onion frying welcomed him. He found his father in his study, brown eyes surrounded by wrinkles, straining to read a novel.

"How's Mom?"

Murad cleared his throat and gestured for Alim to sit next to him on a pillow by the low table. "She is resting. She's not feeling well."

"What's wrong?"

"The doctor says it is her heart."

"Is it serious?" Alim's anger splintered away. She was older now, and so frail.

"She's just upset. Maybe you can calm her down."

Alim nodded. "Does she need anything?"

Murad shrugged. Haseena had been vicious and then hysterical after Aisha left. She blamed Murad for not stopping her. Murad was tired of it all—the screaming children, the wailing of Haseena, the absence of his son. "She just wants you home."

Why was his father pressuring him like this? No matter what he did, it was never good enough. A respectable job, the marriage he chose, grandchildren. Nothing satisfied Murad. He was embittered with age. Alim climbed the stairs and opened the door to his mother's room. One framed photo of Murad was on the wall next to his teaching certificate. The ceiling plaster cracked, marbling down the walls. The air smelled stale and faintly of mothballs. Haseena lay in bed with her eyes closed.

"Alim?" Her voice cracked.

He went to her side. Haseena placed her hand over her heart.

"Are you alright?" Alim jumped to his feet. "Shall I call for the doctor?"

"It's just a little pain." Haseena winced and squeezed his arm. "Where is my darling, Kawthar?"

"She is taking care of Fidaa."

Haseena snorted. "Is that wife of yours running around again?"

"Are you hungry, Mom? Can I bring you something?"

She shook her head. "Listen, when I die, I want Kawthar to have my necklace, the one with the sapphire."

"Mom, please. You are going to be alright. Don't talk this way."

"I just pray that I see Kawthar before I die. Just sit with me a bit, Alim. I am in the hands of God. Only he knows if I will make it."

30

AISHA

AISHA SOLD THE last of the resin to the Gujar. She'd harvested every-thing early. Even the bulbs she would have saved for seed. God gave her rare weeks of summer sun and nights that didn't freeze. He'd paid her well and thanked her. She took the bundles of cash. This would be the last time. She would save this to pay for her children's college tuition.

Alim would be with his mother until evening. She irrigated the field as the late spring sun beat down without any wind. She couldn't stand the disgust on Alim's face when he looked at her. As if he could see the filthy hands of Omar and smell the scent of opium soaked into her skin.

She raked the dry and brittle opium stalks into the center of the field. Looking out across the land, a quilt of greens with the river snaking through the trees—it was clear enough to see the mountains across the valley leading to Daryastan and the desert highlands that gave way to the Middle Kingdom. She walked to the center of the field, lit a match, and dropped it. First it smoked, then crackled, and sparked.

The fire popped and Noorjahan emerged. It was the end of their legacy. Her eyes were sad and her body thick with the fat she'd lost at death. Blue and purple flames spread around Noorjahan, a cape furling into the sky.

"You're burning the fields." She picked up a hoe and pushed some embers back toward the fire.

"I don't want any more lies. I'm done with it." Maybe this was the moment to ask her mother. To understand how she'd gotten to this point. "Why did you plant the opium fields? How did we become part of this?"

Noorjahan pushed more coals into the flames. "Your father wanted to plant them. We fought a lot about it because he planted right by the house and sold to goondas. They robbed us. He didn't understand how it all worked."

"And you did?"

"He was gone, and my parents were dead. I learned what I had to. If not for you, I don't think I would have had the strength to get up each morning. How do you make sense of life after something like that? Even the smallest seed of anger, if fed, can get out of control. Our family was destroyed by anger. I knew education was the way out. What I made as a midwife wasn't enough. So I provided. I never want you to be a prisoner in your own home."

The smoke clouded over them. Aisha hoped that the soldiers wouldn't notice, or that they'd assume it was a controlled burn in her orchard.

Flames hissed, scorching the dirt and swallowing the stalks in hungry gulps. "You could always plant again."

"I'm done."

"You could herd goats," Noorjahan said.

"I saved enough money. Besides, what would I do with wool? Sell embroidered shawls to the soldiers as souvenirs for their wives back home?" The fired burned clean with little smoke, reaching the far edges of the field where the irrigation ditches snuffed it out.

"I'll be fine with what the apple orchard provides."

"What about the children? Will you take them back to that woman?"

"This is a fresh start. No poppies. No Haseena. Alim can decide what he wants to do."

"Look at this fire. You understand how to wield it." Noorjahan looked away, and Aisha hoped she would finally admit to starting the fire, to answer the whispers that had clouded her childhood.

"The Front is going to take the entire city," Noorjahan continued. "The university will close, don't bother fighting Alim on this one."

"You always fought with Dad."

"You always sided with your father, Aisha. It's natural, I suppose. The missing parent always becomes the hero."

"You were my hero, Mom."

"And you don't have to be a hero, Aisha."

At its core the fire was purple, the same color the poppies had been. It was as if decades of flowers burst forth into the flame, making the colors more brilliant, waving a final goodbye. Aisha crossed her arms and watched the last of the flames dissolve, like they'd never existed at all.

Aisha had battered the fish the way Alim preferred and waited for him to return home before frying the fillets.

Fidaa charged into the house, nearly hitting the table. "I'm hungry!" He rubbed his tummy and drummed on his chest.

"Do you want a pear?"

He nodded; a bit of dirt was smeared across his forehead. His cheeks were still round with baby fat, unlike Kawthar, whose face was already long and narrow. The bruises along his arm from where Haseena had grabbed him had turned purple.

Aisha skinned and chopped the pear, handing it to Fidaa in a bowl.

He shoved a piece into his mouth. "You're the best, Mom." He wrapped himself around her leg. Aisha leaned down to kiss the top of his head. "I love Mom more than the moon." He reached his arms toward her. "Up, up."

Aisha picked him up and he nestled his face into her.

"When will Dad come home?" Kawthar dragged her bear, which had the Charagan Liberation Front's badge pinned to it. "Look who's come home!" She held her bear in the air. "We must give him food so he can take it back to camp."

Kawthar had been at Mina's when her nephew returned from the militant camp. "Does he want some pear, Kawthar?"

"No. Meat for our men." She shook her head. "I miss Grandma, but I don't want to see her."

Aisha put her hand on Kawthar's back. "I bet Grandma misses you, too."

"But she's mean to Fidaa."

"You are right, Kawthar, but when people get old, they are like those branches you find in the forest, all bent and gnarled. You try to make them straight and you will break them. She loves you, Kawthar." It wasn't her fault that Haseena loved in splintered, hateful ways.

Kawthar hugged Aisha. "It's okay with you if I go?"

This child, how big her heart was. "Yes, darling."

The door rattled and Alim walked in, greeting the children, but not her. Aisha turned her back to him and heated the pan. The children ran outside to play, leaving silence hanging between them. The fish hissed in the oil. "How is your mother?"

"Sick." Alim's voice was low. "Her heart is weak."

"I am sorry, Alim."

"She needs to see Kawthar. She needs us, Aisha."

Aisha swallowed. "Take Kawthar with you tomorrow, for an afternoon visit." She thought of the purple bruises on Fidaa's arm. "I'll drop her over there for visits while you are away."

"It's not safe for you to be alone. Do you even realize the danger with the opium fields? Think of our children."

"Did you see the bruises on Fidaa's arms?"

Alim winced.

"I burned the poppy fields. It's done now."

Aisha turned to the fish. It was burnt. She grabbed the pan, burning her hand on the hot handle. "It's ruined."

BABAK

BABAK SAW NOORJAHAN'S house as he descended from the mountain. It had always been her house, even when he lived there, and she made sure that it remained so after she died. The house had doubled in size. The garden was manicured. His daughter was earning. He often wondered when he took a puff of opium if it was hers. He asked of her when young freedom fighters from the village returned to the camp after visiting their homes. They came back with fresh stories. One even managed to bring him a photograph of Aisha and her children.

He didn't write. What was he but a burden? He'd not wanted to return. The Front was preparing to seize the capital. It would be a bloodbath. Many wouldn't survive.

They had a few days break from their training, and all the men returned home. He'd gone to see his parents. His mother did not recognize him. She'd forgotten about him—and it was for the best. If she were interrogated, she'd speak of her daughter and sons, living with them, no knowledge of Babak's whereabouts. He'd been afraid to see Aisha, but this could be his last battle, and even though it was selfish, he wanted to see her one last time. And since she was doing so well for herself, perhaps she could spare some money to arm the next wave of the resistance.

The trail was rocky; he was careful not to slip. His Kalashnikov was slung against his back, and his green uniform blended into the night, save for the white badge that identified him as a Charagani freedom fighter.

The soldiers didn't know what was coming. The Front would ambush the army like the winter snow, an avalanche to drive the bastards out of their motherland. Babak hadn't smelled the promise of victory like this before. Their new leader was just a boy, straight out of prison, now leading the Front. Jailed like so many others for organizing in support of clean elections. Most of the new recruits came from prison, joining the cause after being tortured by the government. May God give these boys wings.

The forest was its own kind of home, and to survive in it, Babak had to rupture his memory, forget the warmth of a home-cooked meal. The only heat he felt was the fire thawing his fingertips. The best thing to do was keep moving. The scent of shit lingered when they stayed in one spot too long.

The last time he'd seen Aisha, she'd been seven. It was right after the fire. He'd smoothed her hair and said, "Only God can forgive us for what we have done." It was a clean break, and now he was a new man, praise be to God.

The wind bellowed and his stomach growled. The earth smelled of Noorjahan.

The burnt patch from the fire was still visible as he rounded the bend. Babak clenched his jaw. He'd spent the last two decades running from what he saw in that fire. His anger at Noorjahan had drained and left only guilt. Even now, he didn't trust his hands, could still feel them pressing down around her neck.

Noorjahan's serpentine eyes appeared out of thin air and locked on him. He blinked, and her image disappeared.

Praise be to God, sobriety had freed him from her ghost. He

approached the house. Light seeped out from the shutters and the scent of burnt food filled the air. He stood outside the door. A child laughed inside.

In a flash of blue, Noorjahan's ghost materialized before him. He pinched his cheeks to see if he were dreaming. He'd never seen her sober.

She crossed her arms and pulled her scarlet dupatta tightly under her chin. It made her lips look redder. "Just leave her alone. It's been twenty years. Why come back and torment her now?"

On instinct he grabbed his gun.

She laughed. "What can bullets do to me?"

"I'm going to warn her about the capital city. Do you want her husband to die?"

"I already warned her."

"You're dead. How could you even know?" Babak lowered his gun, unsure of what was real. He wished he'd not returned. He'd fallen into Noorjahan's trap. How silly of him to think she'd stopped haunting him. "Leave me be." Her eyes glowed green in the darkness. She was still young and round. His skin hung in tired folds, and his lips were chapped from years of living in militant camps.

Noorjahan walked slowly toward Babak. "I told her you were living in Daryastan. That you have a new daughter. Why give her more to worry about?"

Babak stomped his foot on the ground. Noorjahan was trying to make him look bad. Babak had God on his side. There was only one purpose for which he lived, and that was to set his people free. Dead or alive, they would drive the occupier out.

He trained his eyes on a tree. She would not control him. He was a fighter. Babak stormed up the path. Cold choked his lungs. Noorjahan grabbed a stick from the ground. No twig would stop him. She was no more than air. He raced into her like a matador. She raised the stick and smacked him swiftly in the gut.

The blows knocked Babak to the ground. He lay in the dirt, winded.

Noorjahan knelt down at his side, smelling sweet like narcissus. He used to always bring her flowers. She loved flowers. Why had he never sprinkled them on her grave? Her scent brought back the way his thumbs had pushed down on her windpipe. His anger bursting. The burning of flesh. Aisha almost getting trapped in the fire. Why had Noor let her near the fire?

He swung his fists in the air. But a ghost could not be hit. "Why did you do this to us?"

"Remember when you used to carve wood? How you brought me two birds carved from a single branch. I thought you'd captured heaven. You said it was us. Why did you marry me, Babak?"

"I loved you." He was a fool to have married Noorjahan, to have believed that love could conquer caste.

When he had told his father that he would marry Noorjahan, his father was silent for three days. "These poor people, son, their problems will swallow you. You think that love is blind to riches, but you are blind to poverty. Mark my words, you will come back to me, begging for the life you had."

Noorjahan moved closer. "But I was never enough."

"I came back to help our daughter. I gave up everything for you, and you took it all."

"You gave up nothing. Your parents took you back as if you'd never married me. You left us. I was never good enough for you, Babak. You couldn't live without your parents' money, insisted we grow poppies and sell it to goondas. They robbed us, Babak. Held a gun to my mother's head."

"You're dead. This isn't real." He wanted to push her away. Instead, he stood up to escape her scent. She smelled of their wedding day. His heart had been light then, full of possibility. "You blamed me for everything, Noor, but the fire was your fault."

Babak remembered smoke rising. The sting on his fingers when he slapped her. She'd driven him to his anger, trying to control everything he did.

She lunged for him. Babak ducked. He wanted to grab her wrists. "It's easier to blame me still, isn't it, Babak? You were too drunk to remember what you did."

"You took me out to the field, Noor."

"I had to take you outside before you woke everyone up. Coming home drunk and angry."

"You didn't have to burn the fields, Noor."

"I didn't burn them. Babak, you left us. I paid for Aisha's food, school supplies, marriage, and life with the poppy fields, while you drank away your parents' money."

The air whipped through the mountains. Something inside him broke; his insides went cold. Babak inhaled the air, sweet like Noorjahan. Let Noor have his thoughts. This was what he wanted to remember, the cream of her skin, the curve of where her neck met her ear, the angle of her chin. The brown of her nipple, the taste of her milk when their child was born.

"If you go in there, tell her why you left. I'm tired of covering for you."

Babak pushed himself up and dusted off his pants. "Do you want me to tell her how the fire started?"

"Can you even remember? I know you remember slapping me."

"It was the only time." He looked down, ashamed, and turned away from Noorjahan. He hadn't meant to hit her, and how could he be sure that it had happened? The memory was a shadow that turned to smoke.

Babak walked to the back door of Aisha's house and knocked.

Alim opened the door. He was as thin as Murad, with the same pointed chin. A baby-faced coward.

"Please, come in," Alim said, nearly too stunned to speak. Aisha's father had returned. He'd heard word of him from his uncle but didn't tell Aisha, as she believed he'd married. Why give her more to worry about. "Thanks be to God that you are alive."

Babak took off his shoes and whistled under his teeth. The place was entirely rebuilt, marble floors, a few large paintings hung from the plaster walls. "Looks like you all have been doing well for yourselves." They had enough money to support the resistance and then some.

"Come in, make yourself at home. Fidaa, come here and say hello to your grandfather."

A lanky boy crawled out from the corner and stood before Babak. He had Noorjahan's face. Babak removed his gun, unloaded it, and handed it to Fidaa. "Take this for me."

Fidaa grabbed the gun and sat with it in the corner of the room, gliding his fingers over the metal. This boy would be a fighter.

Before he could sit down, Aisha walked into the room. Babak blinked twice to erase the image of Noorjahan, but his daughter even had the same darkness in her eyes. A wild bite.

"Aisha." God help them. Noorjahan lived in her.

"Welcome, sit." She did not hug him or express any sort of emotion. Babak wanted it to be like when she was a child, when she reached for him. Loved him. "We just finished eating." Her tone was courteous, distant, as if they were not father and daughter.

Alim moved to take the gun from Fidaa, but he burst into tears, holding it tightly.

Aisha went over to Fidaa. "Let's go to the bathroom."

Fidaa shook his head, crying harder. Aisha let him be and turned back to Babak. Ever since Haseena traumatized him, he'd been having trouble going to the bathroom. "Are you hungry? Can I bring you something?" Seeing him in uniform, Aisha realized her mother had lied again. He wasn't settled in Daryastan. What could she even believe?

Babak's stomach rumbled loudly. "If it isn't any trouble."

"None at all. Is there anyone else with you?"

Babak shook his head. She went into the kitchen. A little girl came forward, holding a bear with a freedom fighter's badge. "Would you like some water?"

Babak nodded and shook the bear's paw. "Nice to meet you, my brother." He smiled at the child; there was something of Noor in her eyes, not the color, but the fullness of her eyebrows. Her hair, the color of sunset, furrowed around her.

"Kawthar," Alim said. "This is your grandfather."

"Mommy said you live in Daryastan with another family." She placed the water on the table.

"You are a very clever girl. Whenever someone asks of me, tell them just that." He took a sip of water and looked toward the window to see if Noor was watching. "Alim, are you teaching in the capital?"

Alim nodded.

Of course Alim would be too much of a coward to fight. Kawthar came back in and sat beside her father. No child deserved to lose a father. He had to warn Alim. "Can you ask your mother for some bread, too, please?"

The child nodded and headed to the kitchen.

"Babak, will you be able to stay for a few days?" Alim asked.

Babak shook his head, and Alim appeared relieved. It was a risk having freedom fighters in your house. One never knew which neighbors could be paid as informants. Babak leaned in toward Alim so that nobody would hear. "We will be taking the capital in the next few weeks."

Surprise registered on Alim's face. "Do you have the force and artillery?"

They did, but no thanks to Alim, who hoarded the earnings from the poppies. "We have God on our side."

Alim inhaled. If the Front took over the entire city, the government would suspend funding for the university.

Babak continued on. "Our brothers and homeland do need support. We give our lives and blood. Someone has to pay for the bullets." Babak looked Alim in his eyes.

Alim's stomach tightened. Babak wanted money. If weapons were ever traced back to his family, they'd be tortured and killed. "We aren't producing poppies anymore." It gave Alim such a sense of relief to be done with this dark secret.

"Then how are you affording all of this?" Rage pierced Babak's voice.

Alim became pale. "Not in front of the children."

Aisha came into the room with a plate full of fish, rice, and lentils. "This looks wonderful, thank you." He dipped his hand in the food. Even the burnt parts tasted good. "You are a better cook than your mother."

Aisha ignored his compliment. "Will you spend the night here?"

Babak shook his head.

Her heart sank. Despite the danger, she wanted him to stay. Wanted to get to know him in some small way.

"I'll take some food to go. Whatever you can spare. And I was hoping you could help. We need to purchase some arms. We are headed up the mountain and will cross back over to Daryastan tonight."

There was a bang at the window. It sounded like a rock, hitting the glass.

"Did you hear that?" Babak looked out the window, but fortunately there were no signs of Noorjahan.

"Hear what?" Alim asked.

"It sounded like a rock."

"A rock?"

"It's our signal," Babak said, trying to pretend he wasn't losing it. "They are calling me. I should be going." Aisha packaged his food. Babak picked the bear up. "Could you pack some for my brother here, too?"

Aisha nodded.

He took the food and whispered, "We don't need much, just a few thousand dihabs."

Shame washed over her. He didn't want to know her, he only wanted money. "I don't have anything. I burned the fields." She could still smell the smoke in her clothes. The cash was under the kitchen cabinet in the same box her mother used. Her father hadn't come to see her, he didn't care about them at all.

He looked toward the cabinet, probably remembering where Noor had kept their savings. "She stole this land from me." Anger rose in Babak. Noorjahan had stripped him of everything. Humiliated him.

"Please, that is enough." Alim was measured and firm. He'd never quite understood how the land remained in Aisha's name and he'd inherited it in their marriage.

"You are the one who benefited." Babak laughed bitterly. Something banged outside. Babak jumped. "Did you hear the rock?"

Aisha shook her head. He retrieved his gun from the floor. "You have a beautiful family. May God bless you all."

"Be careful." He was leaving again.

Babak put on his shoes, preparing to face Noorjahan. But when he left, there were only stars in the sky.

32

AISHA

AISHA CLEARED THE table after her father left, and Alim washed the dishes. Had her father come back to warn them or just for money? She wanted to believe that he had come home to see her. That his love was stronger than greed. "You should take Kawthar to visit your mom for a couple of hours."

"I'm sorry she does this, Aisha."

"We can't change her, but we must protect Fidaa."

He turned toward her and wrapped his arms around her, sliding his hands down her waist. Alim had been afraid that Aisha wouldn't allow Kawthar to see Haseena. "Let me do the dishes."

After finishing the dishes, Alim took her by the hand and brought her into their bedroom. "I wish I could protect him from more. A boy was shot right in front of me, one of our boys killed by a soldier. I didn't do anything."

This was why he'd been so silent. He could have told her earlier. "It's not your fault." She rubbed her fingers into his shoulders, massaging out the tension.

"But he is someone's son. I got swept away in the crowd. I didn't do anything."

"You were there, and you came back to us. That is something."

"Your father is out there putting his life on the line each day."

"And you are here with us." She held his hand in hers. Pushing thoughts of him leaving away. "Why do you think he came back now after so many years?"

"I think he wanted to warn me." Alim wasn't sure that he believed it, but it felt better to think that Babak cared for them. That it wasn't about money. And it made everything so clear. He'd been sure that he was destined to teach art and that his family would be just fine without him. The sacrifice would be worth what they gained. If the Front controlled the capital, there was no telling what the government would do to punish the people. It could be months before he'd be able to return home, and that would be if he was lucky enough to survive. "I'm not going back."

Was he serious? She couldn't allow herself to believe him. "But the term is almost over."

Alim shrugged. "There are so many strikes that there are hardly any classes. What good will it do?"

"What about the university position? That's your dream."

"There will be time for all of that when the children are older." He ran his fingers through her hair. Everything inside her tingled. "Being with you is my dream."

"We can build your studio. You can paint again." He pulled her on top of him, slipping his palms over the small of her back.

part 4

UPRISINGS

Age 44
2010

Poshkarbal

33

AISHA

AISHA SOMETIMES COULDN'T believe that Kawthar came from her. She was self-assured and brilliant. Her children were her greatest joy and infuriated her with their world—something she couldn't understand—computers, social media, and cell phones, which left the floors unswept and dishes piling in the sink. Kawthar was leaving Charagan in six weeks to go to the mainland, assuming that the airport opened and flights resumed. She'd wanted to go abroad for graduate school, but her visa was denied. Aisha knew it was likely because of the organizing for independence Kawthar had done on campus.

The summer had erupted in protests. Under military curfew, the electricity was cut, markets were closed, but somehow people found the news and the death tolls. When the cellular network was on, Twitter provided a funeral in tweets, dead bodies with names. From village to village, millions marched. One of every three people in Charagan took to the streets despite the bullets and the tear gas. Everyone, even mothers and grandmothers, demanding freedom. The army slaughtered innocent children. Young men and women. The curfew stretched, day and night. Everyone had their stockpiles of rice for the months of lockdown. Business ceased. Tourism stopped. Even flights were suspended, except for military ones. An Arab Spring in summer that nobody in the world saw because Wi-Fi was cut.

Aisha and the kids were going to visit Murad, who was quite ill. Alim had gone to his parents' house early in the morning. She called them kids, but they were grown. Fidaa at twenty-one was all muscle. His thick hair grew out like a helmet. Kawthar was twenty-three, nails polished—thin and tall, with wavy brown hair that still had auburn highlights from her youth. She had Aisha's cheekbones, and the kindness of Alim's eyes. She held herself tall, as if she knew she was destined for things far beyond their village. Fidaa hardly spoke to Aisha these days. He dropped out of college during the student strikes, and now worked as a mechanic in town. Aisha knew he had a girlfriend. She'd seen him walking with a girl down by the river. Fidaa wasn't there to wash the laundry, *that* she was sure of. She didn't recognize the girl. So many people lived in Poshkarbal now; it had grown over the years. A nearby village was bulldozed by the army several years back, and the refugees settled in Poshkarbal. There were rumors that the army raped the women before leveling the town. She hoped Fidaa wasn't seeing one of those poor girls, destroyed by soldiers. God help those girls.

Fidaa took Kawthar on his motorbike to Murad's house. Aisha preferred to walk. It gave her time to clear her head. Murad wasn't doing well. They couldn't get him to the hospital because the power kept getting cut, so the hospital was only taking those on the verge of death. How to decide who was close enough to death for treatment? But Murad did not qualify. The doctors weren't sure what was eating away at Murad, but he'd lost so much weight and hardly ate a thing. He was sixty-four, young to be so sick.

Walking through town, Aisha passed a store spray-painted in black: *Go, Nadistan, Go* and *Nadistani Dogs, Go Back.* The same slogans that drove the colonizers out aimed at the new occupiers, their neighbors from across the mountains. Brown men, speaking in native tongues. It was the final gift of the colonizer to turn our people on each other. Funny how history repeats itself, how quickly the oppressed becomes the oppressor. When Charagan wins her freedom, will she turn on her neighbors too? All over the world, throughout the decades, military regimes hijacked people's movements, using the struggle for democracy to leave people hungry.

Haseena and Murad's home had decayed over the years. Paint peeled off the house and the flower beds were filled with weeds. The air inside the house was damp with mildew. Aisha was relieved when Alim opened the door. His eyes were red, and his hair laced with more gray than black. "How is he?"

"Not good."

"Were the doctors able to come and do some tests?"

Alim shook his head.

She'd asked the doctor last time how they might rule out cancer, but the doctor didn't answer, and gave Murad antibiotics, thinking it was some sort of infection. "How's your mother?"

"She's out on the porch. Farooq and the kids are upstairs." Aisha was relieved that Farooq was there too. She loved the boy. As an only child, Alim was close to his cousin Maali. When Maali's husband disappeared a few years back, Alim stepped in as a father figure to Maali's son, Farooq.

Aisha went upstairs. Murad was sitting in bed, hands folded in front of him. Farooq stood next to Kawthar and Fidaa.

"Look at these three." Murad smiled up at Aisha with the joy of a child. He pointed at Farooq. "That one will be a journalist."

Aisha exhaled sharply. She would never wish something so dangerous on Maali. Journalists were routinely targeted by the state. "Not a teacher like you and Alim?"

"Farooq has too much drive. How could he teach the government propaganda? He is the one to write our story." Farooq looked up, his eyes wide with the praise from his great-uncle. "Never be afraid of the truth, son. In the end, this is our only weapon."

"How is your head feeling, Murad?" Aisha attempted to steer him away from such a heavy topic. Why put such a load on a child? Farooq already had lost so much. Why weigh him down with the impossible task of telling the story of such suffering?

Murad reached for Kawthar. "This one is going to be a doctor." His words slurred. His grandson, Fidaa, sat by the window on his phone. What could he say to inspire Fidaa? The boy was already lost to him. Thankfully, Kawthar was going to medical school on the mainland. It gave Murad a sense of peace. He'd not always been the best father, but with the grandchildren, somehow it was easier. He could give them some things they needed. He looked up at Aisha. "Can I talk with you privately?"

Aisha nodded, and Kawthar, Fidaa, and Farooq left.

"I sold my father's land, the piece on the other side of the field." Somehow, he felt his promise to Noorjahan was finally fulfilled. Where he failed Aisha, he could provide for Kawthar.

This was the piece that Alim should have built his home on, but instead he lived with Aisha. "Does Alim know?"

Murad nodded. "It was Haseena's idea. It's for Kawthar. We don't want her to take any loans."

Aisha's eyes filled with tears. She sat down, winded with the news. She'd taken on more deliveries and built up her practice as a midwife, but people who could afford care went to the hospital, leaving Aisha to help the villagers who were poor. Of course, with the electricity off, more and more people came to her to deliver babies at home. She was earning, but not enough to pay Kawthar's rent and tuition. Aisha took Murad's hand in hers.

After Murad fell asleep, Aisha went out to the porch where the kids were. "Farooq, you've grown so much." She couldn't believe how he'd sprouted up over the last few months. Boys did that at fourteen. Though Fidaa had grown much later and only recently filled in. He'd been scrawny as a child and now he was muscled. Her boy was a man.

"Can I see?" Farooq stood on his tippy toes, trying to catch a glimpse of what Fidaa was playing on his phone. Fidaa spent hours on these games, where he lined up falling shapes, always obsessing over things. He'd taken apart and put back together all the doorknobs in the house when he was Farooq's age. Now, he focused on cars, building and fixing. His words never filled in, instead he seemed to form his thoughts through his hands, trying to align something in the objects around him. His hair was dark as Noorjahan's, and though he was only a little taller than Alim, he appeared much bigger, thicker like Babak.

"You messed it up." Fidaa glared at Farooq, who was wearing jeans that were too short from his growth spurt. "Just leave me alone." Fidaa stormed inside.

Aisha turned to Farooq. "He's just mad, don't worry about him." She'd hoped that Fidaa would have been like a brother to Farooq, but he showed far more resentment than interest, begrudging the time that Alim spent with Farooq. Why didn't Fidaa see how much pain Farooq was going through? She could not imagine how Maali survived, not knowing what happened to her husband. His bus was stopped on the way home from work one day, and that was it. Twelve men unaccounted for. They'd gone from prison to prison searching for him. But nothing at all.

"His girlfriend broke up with him," Kawthar said.

"How could any girl even stand him?" Farooq said under his breath, causing Kawthar to laugh.

Alim sat in the chair his father always had, sipping tea next to Haseena, ignoring Farooq's comment. "How could he have broken up when we didn't even know he had a girlfriend? These kids today."

"It's nothing like when we were young," Haseena said. "Things were so much simpler. None of this boyfriend and girlfriend nonsense. You better not go off to school and come back married to some mainlander." Haseena raised her eyebrows at Kawthar.

Aisha felt a pang of guilt. Her mother had been Murad's girl-friend in a way.

"I'm not getting married."

"Good, then you can come back and live with your grandmother, nicely." Haseena smiled. "I'll have to count on your brother for the grandchildren, then. Next time, he better bring any girlfriends to meet me first. We can't have just anyone join the family."

Years ago, the comment would have landed with a sting, targeted at Aisha. But since she'd moved out, a slow truce developed between the women. After Fidaa finished high school, he'd started helping Murad and Haseena. Small things, like bringing them groceries, fixing broken items. He taught Haseena how to use her cell phone and put a new antenna on the roof so she could watch her shows.

Aisha sat down on the other side of Haseena and put some herbs on the table. "These are helping Murad. You can give it to him three times a day for the pain."

Haseena shook the bottle and gave it a sniff. "Will it help my joints too?"

"I'll bring you something else. This one is too strong." Haseena had never asked for herbs before.

34

ALIM

ALIM ARRIVED HOME before the rest of his family. Aisha had stopped to visit with Mina, and Fidaa took Kawthar shopping. She didn't have much time to get everything she needed for school on the mainland, and he prayed that she'd be able to leave, that the airport would open, and that she wouldn't lose her spot at school. Kawthar had been devastated when her visa had been rejected, but she'd settled on going to school on the mainland. God, let her have this at least.

Everything had been closed for the last three weeks with all the strikes. The day after a strike, the streets appeared the same: rickshaws buzzed by, meat hung in chunks at the butcher, mangos and bananas piled high. It left Alim feeling exhausted inside, as if he were unsure which reality were real—the stark monotony or this return to life.

As Alim approached the house, he noticed a man sitting on the stoop. He blinked his eyes. Was it Babak? Fear collided with relief—he was alive. Aisha didn't talk about it, but he saw the way she watched the news when militants were captured. Knowing he was alive couldn't erase the last sixteen years of his absence, but relief coursed through him.

"Praise be to God, you have returned." Alim greeted Babak, who stood up to embrace him. Babak's jeans were worn and his green button-down shirt faded at the elbows. His gray hair was buzzed close, but his beard remained thick and wooly. Dirt caked under his nails. "Please come in. Are you hungry?"

Babak followed him inside and set his backpack down. "Starving." His skin was weathered, but there was strength in his gait.

Alim put water on to boil and pulled out some rice. How long was Babak planning on staying? Was he just passing through? "I can fry you an egg?"

"Yes, please. May I use the restroom?"

"Make yourself at home." Though Alim tried to say it with warmth, his tone came out flat. The sooner Babak left, the better. He didn't want Fidaa influenced by him. Alim had overheard Fidaa talking with Kawthar, saying he wanted to join the Northern Division. Kawthar reminded him that there wasn't much of a militancy left, and most of it was just media hype. But these young boys were so hotheaded and blasted things all over social media.

The water boiled as Aisha arrived home. Babak was still in the bathroom. She smiled up at Alim. "Your parents didn't have to sell the land. This means so much."

He turned toward Aisha, her eyes filled with tears. "They want to give Kawthar every opportunity." He couldn't bring himself to say, the ones that Aisha never had.

"Did you know?"

Alim looked nervously toward Babak's bag. He didn't know how to tell her.

Aisha eyed the bag and shoes by the door. "Do we have a visitor?"

"It's your father." Alim cut straight to the chase.

Aisha laughed. "Nice try."

"I'm serious. He's in the bathroom."

Aisha sat down. "Don't joke with me right now."

Alim didn't know how to convince her or if he should even bother. The water ran in the bathroom sink. Babak came out.

Aisha didn't move. Babak leaned against the wall, crossing his arms. In sixteen years, he hadn't sent a letter or a message that he was alright. There was nothing when the children graduated school. When Babak realized the poppy fields were gone, he hadn't wanted anything more to do with her. If there was no money, why show up. Her hands curled into fists. What did he want from her now? She inhaled, waiting for a flood of relief, but only anger coursed through her. "Is there something I can help you with?"

"I wanted to see my daughter."

Aisha turned away from him. "Murad is far more like a father to me."

"Please, help yourself." Alim gestured to some cashews and date sweets. Why was Aisha provoking the situation? It was best to let the past lay dormant. Alim poured a glass of water for Aisha, placing it down in front of her, hoping she'd take a few sips and calm down.

Babak sat at the table and bit into the candy. "You can't find these anywhere but Poshkarbal."

"Will you stay for dinner? The kids will be home soon. You are always welcome here," Alim said.

"If you will have me." Babak looked to Aisha for approval.

A look of defeat crossed her face. "Will anyone be looking for you?" Her tone lacked warmth, and she did not meet Babak's eyes.

"I'm just a tired old man who finally made his way home." Babak reached for Aisha's hand, but she pulled away.

35

KAWTHAR

KAWTHAR REMEMBERED HER grandfather. The only time she'd met him, he'd been armed and offered to train her bear. She'd never fully believed her mother, that they had just lost track of him and his new family in Daryastan. Civilians were not able to cross the border. She hoped that Fidaa wouldn't get any stupid ideas from Babak. She'd seen Fidaa talking with Omar's nephew when he returned for a brief visit after joining the Northern Division.

Kawthar mounded lamb and rice on her plate. They rarely ate meat, with all the shortages.

"There's going to be a march on Saturday," Kawthar said, attempting to get a conversation started. Her mother hadn't spoken at all during their dinner. "We should all go."

"We keep marching and nothing changes." Fidaa pushed his food around on his plate.

"Don't play with your food, Fidaa." Kawthar felt relief to hear her mother speak, and a familiar rush that she got when her mother scolded Fidaa.

"They rounded up hundreds of boys up north," Alim said. "It's not safe for the men."

"Nowhere is safe for our men," Babak added.

"I'll go with Mom, then." Kawthar beamed at her mother, not able to remember the last time just the two of them had gone out together.

"I want to get you to university all in one piece."

"That is if the airport ever opens."

"It will. Have some faith, Kawthar," Alim said.

Faith alone wouldn't open the airports. Kawthar prayed each night for her safe journey. She felt so bad leaving while Grandpa Murad was sick. But she didn't have much of a choice. If the airports opened, she needed to go. Still, she was terrified of being away from her family. The phone lines had been out for sixty-four days during summer. It dawned on her for the first time that if she left, she may never be able to come back. Kawthar watched her mother eat just a few bites before clearing her plate. Babak finished his food and went to wash his hands. "There's still cake, Grandfather." Kawthar had baked a lemon cake, a new recipe she found on the internet.

"I'm just going to rest for a little."

"You can sleep in Fidaa's room," Alim said. Babak nodded and turned down the hall.

"Where am I going to sleep?" Fidaa still whined like a child.

"In Kawthar's room," Alim said.

"It's not fair. She always gets what she wants." Fidaa sulked off from the table, leaving food on his plate, and joined Babak in his room.

Kawthar cleared the dishes, and her father washed the plates. After brewing tea for the cake, Kawthar knocked on her brother's door. "Come, have some cake."

"We'll be out soon," Babak called. Kawthar pressed her ear to the door, slightly jealous that Fidaa was getting to know their grandfather so quickly.

"Once you go, there is no coming back," Babak said.

"There's nothing left for me here. I can't take this daily humiliation. Checkpoints everywhere we go. Besides, you came back."

"I'm what they call one of the lucky ones. You know what that means for the rest?"

Kawthar's heart pounded in her ears. Was Fidaa really going to do this? She wanted to burst in and yell at him.

"Let's have some cake, Fidaa."

Kawthar backed away from the door; her appetite gone.

Kawthar turned on Fidaa's favorite song, but he still didn't look up from his phone. "What were you talking with Grandpa about?"

"Nothing." Fidaa didn't lie well. Truth was his default, which often came off as rude.

"Come to the march with me Saturday." Kawthar needed a guarantee that he would still be here Saturday.

"It's not going to change anything, Kawthar."

"Sure it will. We have to do something. Guns aren't going to solve it either. Didn't you hear they killed four boys from the Northern Division at the border?"

Fidaa put his phone down. "Those weren't even militants. They were villagers. The soldiers are going to kill us anyway, might as well go down fighting." He picked up Kawthar's bear, holding him as if he were firing a gun.

Kawthar's stomach tightened. "And what will more bloodshed get us?"

"You don't get how it works."

"What do you know?" A wave of nausea passed over her. "Just cause some girl broke up with you doesn't mean you get to run away from home and join the militancy!"

"You're the one who is running away, Kawthar. You are leaving."

She turned up the volume. Fidaa was just jealous that she graduated college. He'd always been jealous of her. "Just don't do anything stupid, Fidaa. Grandma needs you right now."

"Right. They sell their land for you, and you want me to put my life on hold and take care of everyone, while you get to leave."

"I'm doing this for our family, too, Fidaa."

"Whatever you say, Kawthar."

AISHA

AS A CHILD, all Aisha wanted was her father, and now that he'd come home to her, all she saw were the ways he'd failed her.

"But really, do you think they are looking for him?" she asked Alim when they woke up the next morning.

"The militants or the soldiers?"

"Either one." She had no idea how long it had been since he had left the Front. "I just hope he's done fighting. I don't want any guns in the house."

"He didn't have anything on him when he got here."

"He could have stashed it somewhere."

"Let's give him a chance."

"Mom!" Kawthar burst into Aisha's room. "Fidaa's gone."

"What do you mean?" Aisha felt the blood drain from her head. This couldn't be happening.

"His stuff is gone."

Aisha went into his room. Babak sat at his desk. "Where did Fidaa go?"

Babak looked away from her. "He'd made up his mind before I came. I tried to stop him."

"So you knew?" Aisha towered over Babak. "You don't get to show up and take my son away."

"You can't stand between a young man and his dreams."

"You sent him into a nightmare. What did you do?" Aisha put her face up to her father's. "What did you tell him?"

Babak stood up. "Yelling won't bring him back. He'd made up his mind. You should be proud."

"Proud that he might end up like you?" Aisha wanted to grab him and throw him out.

Alim came in and took her hand. "He could still come back. We might find him still."

But Aisha had seen the look in his eyes. If Fidaa returned, it would be like her father had. Broken.

The only reason Aisha picked up the phone was because she'd hoped that Fidaa would be calling. It was Mina. "Are you home? Can we come over for a bit?"

"Fidaa is gone. He left in the middle of the night."

Mina was quiet. Static broke the silence. "May God protect him. I'll be right over."

Aisha wished that she hadn't answered the phone. Kawthar and Alim had gone out looking for Fidaa. But they all knew he was gone. Babak sat on the couch, quietly reading the paper. Hair brushed, beard trimmed, nails cleaned. He'd not said anything since the morning.

Mina knocked on the door; her daughter, Nalja, held her hand. Aisha had thought that Mina wouldn't be able to have children—that God was punishing her or sparing her. But by some miracle, Mina became pregnant at thirty-four. Aisha delivered Nalja, and the birth was simple and smooth—a little girl, perfect in every way, though unlucky, as she was born a girl in the occupied mountains of Charagan.

Mina looked toward Babak. "Praise be to God, you are home, Uncle." Babak stood to greet Mina. "This is my daughter, Nalja." Nalja wore a red sweater over jeans and had a butterfly clip in her auburn hair, which was pulled back into a ponytail. "This is Grandma Suha's brother." Mina nudged Nalja toward Babak, who gave him an awkward hug. In her nine years of life, Nalja probably had never heard of Babak. Her eyes narrowed, appraising him.

"How is your mother?" he asked Mina.

"We don't see Grandma," Nalja said. Mina's mother didn't approve of her marriage to Omar and rarely visited. It was sad how alone Suha Auntie was; she never got over Padmal leaving. How could she? Widowed with a living husband who she loved and who loved her. Mina never spoke of them.

Babak sat back down. Mina leaned in and hugged Aisha. "How are you holding up?"

Aisha didn't respond. What could she say? "Can I get you water or tea?"

Mina shook her head. "Let's go outside for a bit." Nalja took a handful of nuts from the table and ran outside; Mina and Aisha followed.

The sun warmed Aisha's skin. A light breeze promised cold at night. Nalja ran toward a rope swing that hung under a maple tree on the trail that led to the river.

Mina and Aisha went over to her garden, thick with chard, peppers, and cilantro. "How do you get so much to grow?" Mina asked, pinching off a bit of cilantro.

"It's my art form. Alim has his canvases, but I love to see my life change along with the land."

"Apparently, all I'm creating is weeds." Mina laughed. "Be careful; don't get too high," she yelled at Nalja, whose feet pumped her into the sky.

"She's so beautiful. I can't believe how fast they grow, and now with Kawthar leaving and Fidaa . . ." Aisha swallowed the painful lump in her throat. She was soon to be alone.

Mina put an arm around her. "He'll come back and visit soon."

"I'm afraid of what he's going to become." Aisha closed her eyes, trying to dissolve images of Fidaa shooting from the bushes, planting landmines in fields, of his picture flashing on the news while his body was carried in a funeral procession. "There's no good way for this to end."

"Your father came back." Mina spoke with gentleness.

"I wish he hadn't."

"I couldn't even find Padmal when I tried. You can't blame your father for Fidaa going. He was talking about joining the Northern Division with Omar, too."

"Why didn't you tell me?"

"You couldn't have stopped him."

"But I didn't get to try."

Nalja jumped off the swing, arcing up toward the sky and landed on her feet. "At least we have this one, still." Nalja was like a daughter to Aisha. "You'll have to send her over more now."

Mina squeezed Aisha's hand. "And you can send Babak to us anytime. This too shall pass, and we will become stronger from it."

37

ALIM

ALIM GRIPPED THE bars of his motorcycle, and Aisha pressed her chest against his back. She hadn't wanted to leave the house or her bed, but he'd convinced her to come on a picnic, choosing an outfit for her. Alim secretly prepared and packed all her favorite things: goat curry, pomegranate chicken, roghani, and carrot halva. In the three weeks since Fidaa left, she'd become depressed, taking codeine and sleeping all day. Alim heard from a friend that Fidaa was safe and in the mountains training. Regret filled Alim for all he'd missed with his son. Nothing would ever be the same.

The cars ahead were stopped at a military checkpoint. When Alim got to the front, he pulled out his ID card and handed it to the soldier.

"Where are you going?" the soldier asked.

"Up to the mountain for a walk," Alim said. Aisha's breath was even and calm behind him, while Alim's fingers sweated on the handlebars.

"Why don't you just take a walk around here?" the military officer asked.

Alim knew better than to appear exasperated. "We wanted to see the flowers blooming, and spend time at the river."

"Oh, so you like nature. Please step off the bike." Aisha scooted forward to keep the motorcycle from tipping over.

"What's in the bag?"

"Just some snacks." Alim didn't look at Aisha. Couldn't stand for her to see the humiliation on his face.

The soldier's dirty hands reached into Alim's bag, exposing each surprise he'd prepared for Aisha.

"Your wife must be a good cook. You don't mind if I take some? Here we are defending you and we are so far from our own wives. I miss home-cooked food." The soldier confiscated the chicken and goat curry. Alim bit the inside of his cheek.

They were left with bread, halva, and walnuts. The soldier pushed the barrel of his gun against Alim's back and told them to move along. The muscles on Alim's neck tensed. They could kill him, but the newspapers would only report: *militant killed near the border.*

The sun splashed across Aisha's skin as she and Alim sat on a picnic blanket on a hill. Clouds covered the crest of the mountain in the distance. The river was opaque with mud from the rains, and poplars darted up like arrows sprung toward heaven.

Alim closed his eyes. "I want to paint this. With brushstrokes, I could hide what is really happening."

"You could paint locusts. Just make the army locusts."

He ate the bread, dry and unsatisfying without curry. "I could paint a flood. Show that one day water will flood out the army."

Or Nadistan's army would break the levees to flood the people of Charagan, and then seize more of their land. "The beauty of the water is that it knows no borders; it flows across the nations. Paint the rivers."

"I've lost my will to paint." Alim hadn't painted since Fidaa left. His canvases sat blank.

"They've taken everything." Aisha gestured toward the river. The fish were mostly gone—the army ate them all in one season, forgetting to leave the pregnant ones to reproduce. Aisha ate a piece of halva, the sweetness caught in her throat. She offered Alim a bite; he nibbled from her hands. From up here, she could almost believe in peace.

"I hope the airport opens next week so we can take Kawthar to school."

"You'll have to take Kawthar, Alim. I'll stay and help your mom." Murad hadn't eaten in three days. Aisha kept urging Alim to go and visit, but it was so hard for him to see his dad like this.

"We don't know if we'll even be able to leave. There could be more strikes and protests."

"You must have faith." Aisha reached over and squeezed his hand.

38

BABAK

BABAK LAY ON the ground, naked. The short soldier with the thin lips dropped the iron roller on his pelvis. Did a piece of bone chip off? The soldiers gripped the roller on both sides, applying their weight as they pushed it up and down his legs. Babak willed his legs to be as soft as dough.

Water on his testicles. They inserted a wire into his penis. The jolt of electricity formed a bridge inside him. Babak bit his lip, tasted blood. Nothing, nothing. He was nothing.

Babak sat up covered in sweat. He was home. The beating at the door continued. Aisha shook him. "Dad, there are soldiers outside." Her voice was low. Had they come for him?

Babak pulled on a shirt and followed Aisha. He'd shaven his beard, cleaned the dirt from under his fingernails. He was nothing but a quiet old village man. He'd never been to any militant camp, hadn't picked up a gun, never felt the prickle of electricity explode in his mind.

Alim was by the door. Babak stood by the table, placing himself between the door and the women. Kawthar sat next to Aisha on the couch, clutching her childhood teddy bear.

The soldier asked Alim to step outside. Babak watched from the window. There were seven soldiers; they shone a light on Alim and had him stand with his hands raised, legs spread as they searched him. And then three men followed Alim into their house. Babak sat down on the sofa between Aisha and Kawthar.

"Is this your son?" The soldier held a picture of Fidaa. Aisha stood.

"Yes, he has run off. He got some girl pregnant."

The soldier pulled out a stick, he raised it and smacked it down against the ground. "What are you hiding in here?"

"Nothing, look for yourself. But you have woken us up." The soldiers moved through the house, rifling through drawers. Throwing things on the ground. Shame filled Babak. His daughter was trying to protect him. She spoke to the soldiers. He focused on his breathing, sitting next to Kawthar. Her hand in his. The teddy bear had fallen to the ground.

39

FAROOQ

FAROOQ HADN'T SEEN his mother cry like this. Murad wasn't drinking water. His mother sat by her uncle, begging him to drink. Farooq was relieved when Kawthar took him outside and they drank fresh lemonade as dusk settled in around them. They folded paper into airplanes and watched the clouds turn purple in the night.

"What's that?" Farooq lowered his voice and grabbed Kawthar's arm. Someone had jumped over the back fence and was hiding behind a tree. Kawthar pulled Farooq closer to the ground.

"I think it's Fidaa."

Farooq had heard that Fidaa had run off with some girl because he'd gotten her pregnant and his parents wouldn't accept a child out of wedlock. Kawthar whistled and waved to him. Fidaa dropped something behind the tree. Farooq wasn't sure, but it looked like a gun. Had Fidaa actually joined the militants? There wasn't a baby or girlfriend in sight. Fidaa wore jeans and a black T-shirt. He was all muscle.

Kawthar ran toward him and jumped on him, nearly knocking him over with a hug. "Come on, let's go in before too many people see us," she whispered. "Soldiers came looking for you a couple nights ago."

Farooq gave Fidaa a quick hug and they headed inside. Seeing him, Aisha Auntie ran down the stairs, kissed his cheeks, hugged him, and refused to let go.

"I'm fine, Mom." He wriggled out of her grasp.

She held his arm. "Come, have something to eat."

Haseena came down the stairs and grabbed Fidaa and began sobbing. "Thanks be to God that you have come. Your grandfather has been asking for you." She rubbed her tears away. "How did you know to come now? God is great. You answered his call."

Fidaa hugged his grandmother. "It's in God's hands now."

Alim Uncle came down the stairs, relief and concern peppering his face. He embraced Fidaa. "Did anyone see you arrive?"

Fidaa shook his head.

"They are looking for you. You can't stay long. Go to your grand-father. Farooq and Kawthar, go too. Murad is asking for you all."

The room was dark and smelled of sickness. Eyes closed, Murad breathed as if each inhale pained him. Fidaa sat on a chair in the corner of the room. Farooq's shoulders tightened as he knelt at the side of the bed, holding Murad's hands, cold fingers wrinkled like aged dates. Murad taught him to play chess, read him poems, and reminded him that justice didn't happen over-night, you must practice and learn, and commit yourself to it. He'd always included Farooq as if he were his grandson instead of his brother's grandson.

"My children," Murad said, tightening his grip on Farooq. "Fidaa and Kawthar, come."

Fidaa knelt beside Farooq. Kawthar stood by their side. "After I die, you must visit my grave and tell me when freedom has come." He inhaled as if his breath alone contained the whole world.

"It's coming soon, I promise," Fidaa whispered.

Murad opened his eyes. "Freedom won't come with guns, my son. Kawthar—" He reached for her.

"Freedom won't come by running away, either," Fidaa said under his breath. Kawthar pinched him in the back.

"Fidaa, it's not too late, son. Come back and stay with your grandmother."

Fidaa looked out the window at the stars starting to form.

"Do you see Noorjahan out there?" Murad asked. "She's waiting."

"Only stars," Fidaa said.

Murad squeezed Farooq's hand. "My camera is yours, Farooq. See if you can capture our people with it. What it is that makes us beautiful."

"Kawthar, the airport is open." His eyes filled with tears. "Go tomorrow, just come back; we are waiting here for you." He pulled Farooq in close so that only he could hear him. "Do not be fooled by the power of a gun. True power comes from the heart, my boy."

Farooq began to pray. Fidaa reached for Farooq. His hard edge dissolved; he was a boy again. Their hearts beat into their fingertips, wanting Murad to stay with them.

part 5

ABROGATION

Age 53
August 2019

Poshkarbal

40

AISHA

POSHKARBAL BECAME A town of widows. Young girls were hidden in cellars at home while the men were gone: mostly dead, or living abroad. There were more graves than people left. The two-story houses at the center of town were boarded-up and marked with bullet holes. The government school where Aisha had gone was an artillery warehouse.

Alim was visiting Kawthar when the Nadistani army cut power and all access to Charagan. It had been two months since she'd seen him. The army sealed Poshkarbal's borders and pumped more soldiers in. They suspended cell phones and landlines. No internet or phone rooms were left. Social media gone. Bank accounts were frozen; no mail came or left. Taxes were neither issued nor paid. It was as if the entire village disappeared. On the mainland, Nadistan dissolved the article in the constitution guaranteeing autonomy to Charagan. News traveled from village to village on handprinted papers, read and reread. Land could now be owned by foreigners.

For over a year, Aisha had been forced to work, harvesting flowers that were rumored to be used for the army's religious pooja ceremonies. Jasmine, oleander, marigolds. They needed the money when

Alim lost his job teaching, accused of being an agitator. The women
who worked in the fields didn't get their houses raided and were allowed to go to work during lockdowns, like this one. They were the
only villagers not hassled for attending prayer services at the mosque,
their fingers stained with the flowers the soldiers were said to use in
their own religious traditions. The prayers of the occupier would be
tainted, wilted flower petals falling back to earth, sending the scent of
suffering to their ancestors.

This morning in the flower fields, the air was crisp and the mountains stoic. Blankets of yellow and orange flowers stretched to the sky.
Women in turquoise, magenta, peach, and paisley fabric stooped over
rows of flowers. The army hut buzzed with static from a transistor
radio. Only they had Wi-Fi or cell service. After work, Aisha would
go by the mosque—a treasured time where the women could pray
together.

The work was strenuous and monotonous. Sun beat through the
back of Aisha's yellow cotton kurta as she crouched down. Her thighs
chafed together, gritty with sweat. An army vehicle gunned in the distance. The tulips in the field were striped like tigers—pink and white,
orange and yellow. Cut flowers that smelled of death.

A few yards away, a soldier with a gap between his front teeth
kept looking at Aisha. Somewhere, this young soldier had a mother
of his own who he sent money to, who cried over his empty bed and
prayed for his return. These boys were younger than Fidaa, who
was thirty and should be bringing his children to school instead of
hiding in militant camps.

The soldier circled around her. Aisha moved to the left so that
some of the larger tulips obscured her from his gaze. He was skinny,
his khaki uniform anchored to his hip with a belt. Everything slowed
and quieted as he approached Aisha. He was close enough that his
scent leaked around her, smoke and sweat ripe with onions.

"Where is the girl?"

Aisha froze. Sweat streamed down her neck. She reached to the ground to steady herself. Had they seen her niece, Nalja, leave her house yesterday? If only Nalja had taken the back trail.

"My husband and my children are gone." Aisha was relieved that Alim was away and wouldn't be taken in. Some men, like Farooq's father, didn't ever return. She prayed that they wouldn't come to the house and that her father would be spared. Sometimes he started shaking when he saw soldiers. Aisha stood up. The soldier's face was tracked with scars, pimples cut under a razor—the clean shave, the mark of the army. This was a boy. Young boys listened to their elders. She was a grandmother at fifty-three. This law governed the universe. She willed her knees to stop shaking.

The soldier stepped closer to Aisha. "Listen, I saw a girl at your house. Where is she?"

She would never give them Nalja. Aisha crossed her arms and shook her head. "As God as my witness, I have no children left in my house. Look what your army has done to our home." She threw her hand into the air, gesturing to the sea of flowers.

Let him kill her right here: she would bleed back into the earth. "We used to grow food; we used to eat from this land. Now you've taken the laws that protect our land. Do you think you own our land?"

The soldier gritted his teeth. "Bring me the girl."

Aisha planted her feet on the ground. Her house was empty. There was no girl.

He grabbed his gun in both hands. "Where is the girl?" She stared down the empty hollow of the gun barrel.

He stomped his black boot. Dust rose. Who would give a child in tantrum a loaded gun to fire? Such was the state of war, the heinous side of democracy. Aisha was silent. He looked like an infant, still wet from its mother's womb, experiencing its first tinge of hunger: the cry of the unsatisfied. This man longed to feel big. How did young men become so desperately lonely?

He raised the gun above her head and then smashed it against her head. Pain. Warm blood dripped down her neck, splattering onto his boots, landing on the pistils of a flower.

"Where's the girl, bitch?"

Aisha picked up the bloodied flower and held it out to the soldier. She willed herself to forget Nalja. Erased her laughter, wiped away her schoolbooks still back at the house.

Aisha stepped closer to the soldier and smeared the blood from the flower across his forehead. If he wanted blood, he could have it.

The soldier screamed and everything went dark.

41

AISHA

AISHA PRAYED THAT the other women working in the flower fields got word to Mina that the soldiers were looking for Nalja. God let her be hidden safely. How was Babak surviving? Hopefully, Mina would send someone to check on him. Two days had passed since the soldiers had taken Aisha. Held in a dark room that smelled of urine, her sleepless nights filled with prayers for Nalja.

Aisha loved Nalja as if she were her own daughter. Maybe she tried to stuff Nalja in the space Kawthar and Fidaa created when they left nine years ago. Nalja was just a child then, but now, at eighteen, she was a firecracker. Aisha had taught her how to make Noor's healing tinctures, and lamb curry, grinding spice mixtures by hand. Guilt coursed through her. How had she been so selfish, allowing Nalja to visit her during curfew?

Aisha thought that the small trail through the woods connecting their homes was safe. That soldiers weren't watching her house because she worked in the fields. That they wouldn't want anything with an old woman living up the mountain. She had been a fool. Sitting there cooking, listening to Nalja rattle on while soldiers waited outside, probably watching them through the window. The last time she'd visited, Nalja had shelled walnuts, eating one for every three she cracked.

"How will we have any left?" Aisha asked.

Nalja laughed; her face lit with beauty. She was a woman at eighteen; God help her.

"Do you miss Kawthar, Maasi? I can't believe you couldn't go see her with Alim Uncle."

Kawthar had been home only once since she had her daughter, who was now two. "I'm so proud of Kawthar." Aisha didn't have a birth certificate, so when her ID card expired, the new laws didn't allow her to renew it. Since her grandparents had died in the fire and she and her mother were both only children, there was no way for her to verify her maternity. They were in the process of using the deed to her land as verification of nationality, but for now, her status was orphaned and she couldn't travel outside Charagan. And then the village was seized.

"I could go and live with Kawthar and go to school and help her with the baby," Nalja said, running her fingers through her auburn hair that fell around her face.

"Soon it will be safe to travel, and I will get my papers and we will go together and Alim will return with us." Aisha patted Nalja's arm, reassuring her. The strikes would end and there would be possibilities for Nalja.

"Mom should have sent me to the mainland earlier."

Mina should have gotten Nalja out when they still had the chance. But there were riots and killings of Muslims on the mainland, and that somehow seemed worse than soldiers and checkpoints. "We all thought there was more time."

"None of us could've known that we'd be living like this."

But Aisha should have known. She'd already made that mistake when she was young and married and she hadn't gone to college. She should have fought for what her mother had created for her, she should have fought more for Nalja. Education was their inheritance.

At least things would be different for Lubaaba, Kawthar's daughter. "We'll find a way out, Nalja."

Nalja dropped another walnut in her mouth.

"Shouldn't you be studying?" Aisha pulled out one of Alim's textbooks that he'd saved. They'd stored them in the shed by the orchard under tools when the government recalled them. "You'll still need to pass your entrance exams for college. The time will come."

Nalja continued to procrastinate. "I wish Mom weren't so difficult. Dad keeps begging her to let him come home. Why is she so hard on him, Maasi?"

Aisha pressed her fingernails into the palms of her hand. Omar had insisted that Mina and Nalja move back into his house, even after he'd gone off with another woman. He'd sworn that it was over, but it was all lies. "It's not your mother's fault. Where do you think your father goes?" Aisha bit her lip; she should swallow the truth.

"What do you mean?"

She'd been silent too long. "Your father wasn't working when he was away. He was with another woman."

This was when she'd scared Nalja away. Had Aisha bitten her tongue, Nalja wouldn't have run off in a hurry, and the soldiers wouldn't have seen her.

A bamboo stick struck Aisha's mandible. She tasted blood. Something popped out of her mouth. "Where is your daughter?"

"My daughter." Aisha gulped fabric and gagged. Warm blood trickled down her arm. "She has her father's eyes." The stick hit her again. There wasn't much of Aisha in her daughter.

Kawthar grew distant from Aisha over the years. She seemed to blame Aisha for not visiting her. But Murad had died right before Kawthar left, and Aisha needed to help Haseena. Aisha hadn't known that the laws would change and that she wouldn't be able to renew her ID card and visit Kawthar. Aisha couldn't even go when Kawthar gave birth to Lubaaba. She'd only seen Lubaaba that one time, when she was two. Lubaaba's hand fit snuggly in hers. Aisha had a pet kitten for her when she came. Lubaaba and the kitten sat curled in each other. Round baby cheeks with Alim's cleft in her chin. The sweet smell of Lubaaba's shampoo forever etched in Aisha's memory.

42

AISHA

IF IT WERE darker, Aisha wouldn't have to see them. "You do not touch a soldier," said the short one with a golden bottom tooth.

Aisha arched away from him as he pulled off her dupatta. The soldiers blocked the door. Aisha braced herself against the wall, pressing the yellow fabric from her sleeve against her temple. Yellow and red make orange, but her blood proved stronger than fabric. Everything was red.

She held her breath and willed herself to become the wall. A shadow. She searched back through the layers of herself until her memories carried her away. She reached for Alim. He smiled back, a boy, skipping rocks across the river. Alim as a man, his eyes memorizing the way her muscles engaged. Alim's last phone call before the phone lines were suspended: "We'll be together, my love."

"Tell Kawthar that I'll have my papers soon. That I'm sorry."

You are not sorry yet." A crack to her sacrum.

The skinny soldier from the flower field entered the room with a bamboo stick: just like the one they used to beat her with when the soldiers came looking for Fidaa. It used to frighten her, but as long as soldiers asked for Fidaa, it gave her hope he was alive.

Aisha saved the Facebook videos of Fidaa on a computer that never went online. In the video, Fidaa wore full camo gear, his gun visible behind the commander, a handsome boy a few years younger than Fidaa. Sometimes they played cricket, or read passages of poetry, other times they ended with a song. Fidaa never spoke, but he was often in the background. The videos stopped three years ago when the commander was killed. Aisha had seen a clip of Fidaa at the commander's home, hugging his father at one of the hundred funeral processions for him. And then nothing more from Fidaa except for the T-shirts that the young villagers made with his silhouette.

Every time there was a knock on the door, her heart constricted in hopes that it could be Fidaa, and fear that it could be news that would shatter her. Their home sang of his absence. His cologne was still on his desk; pants hung in his closet; a book with a bookmark, marking the last page he touched. Babak moved into Kawthar's room after she went to college. Fidaa's room awaited his return.

When a soldier asks you a question. You answer. Understand?" Raw onions leaked from his breath.

Aisha's head fell back against the plaster wall. He grabbed her, his skin against her, his mouth pressed into hers.

She folded her hands in front of her heart, thumbs crossed in an X, pressing into her rib cage. Her fists were the final barriers between them. As if the gesture could close her. She willed herself so small that he could not enter her. As if her body were not hers, but perhaps a scrap like Styrofoam, floating in the lake. There was nothing sentient in her.

———

Three days later, Aisha was still slumped up against the wall in Building C, the soldiers moving around her. Pain pierced Aisha's leg. A soldier burnt her birthmark with a hot iron rod. It was red like her grandparents' bones had been in the fire. He burnt up her thighs, a trail of burns. A high-pitched screaming—like an infant who would not be able to sustain its life—came from her, but she could not feel her mouth moving.

"I see that I'll have to loosen your tongue." The soldier clamped her mouth open. The muscle in the back of her throat felt like it would explode. The tongue was the strongest muscle in the body. He dropped liquid on her tongue, spit foamed up. The pain pulsed through her cranium until her skull seemed to part like tectonic plates. God, let there be an earthquake.

They were digging into her brain. The pain of her mother beating her. Her heart bursting when her mother died.

A soldier she had not seen before ripped her hands apart and bound them with rope. She did not whimper or beg as he tore a hole through her undergarments. Aisha could not block out the sound of the soldier's zipper. Her throat closed.

"That way we don't have to see your ugly, old hole."

No pain. Bound hands crushed. Just pressure. Her eyes burned with sticky heat, like tears spilling over.

43

GOPAL

GOPAL URINATED AGAINST his tree—a maple that reached its branches toward the sky. His throat prickled, thirsty for a beer. He preferred pissing on the tree to using the latrine. They called it a toilet, but it was two boards over a hole under a tin roof. Their shit froze over in the winter, but the smell never went away. Seventy-eight soldiers were never meant to all relieve themselves in the same spot. But it wasn't the stench that kept him out. It was the centipede that made its home under the board. He prayed to Lord Shiva every time he lowered his ass that it would not bite him.

In this godforsaken land, the giant centipedes were more venomous than snakes. A creature small enough to climb into your ear or mouth left open in sleep. Back home, his eyes were trained to see the muddy brown of the cobra in the rice paddies.

Gopal killed one when he was fourteen. With his schoolbag on his shoulder, he grabbed a stick and brought it down on the cobra's body. The hard blow smashed its scales, dark blood seeped out.

Whenever he saw blood, the image of the snake came back to him. He preferred to think of the snake than that old woman bleeding in Building C.

He checked his cell phone, even though he already knew that it was only six o'clock, his shift just starting. There would be no beer until just past eleven when the commander went to sleep. Then Gopal could get his warm beers. Every man had his hiding place, and every soldier his vice.

The commander ran the camp as if he were Rambo. Every day he pointed toward the border with Daryastan and howled, *Shoot those insurgents dead. I don't want to see one live body coming through that border.* But in his fourteen months in the village, Gopal had not seen a single insurgent from Daryastan—dead or alive. Everyone he shot, interrogated, detained, and frisked was from Charagan. He learned to hate the natives too. These villagers weren't grateful for the army's protection that cursed him to this land.

The smell from his uniform overpowered the cool night air. He'd not been able to get the scent of burnt flesh out of his uniform. He could still see the white of the village woman's eyes when Ashok forced himself into her. He shuddered, unable to keep the image out of his mind. That goddamn woman left her burnt scent on him like some bitch in heat.

Gopal sat in his chair and stared at the starless sky. He thought of his girlfriend back home. The softness of her breasts. He reached into the stickiness of his pants, his cock hard and fast in his hands.

Footsteps came down the path. Gopal looked up. It was Ashok. They often were placed on the night shift together. Sometimes they played cards, sometimes they drank, and once they spoke about what they would do when they were discharged. But Gopal never really thought he would make it out. It seemed impossible that he could ever go back to his life. He liked who he'd become. If anyone fucked with him, he'd crack his gun right over their head.

"Stand up, you lazy bastard. I can hardly see your black ass in the night," Ashok said, his eyes red from smoke. Ashok was late, and as always, Gopal would say nothing. Ashok always tried to humiliate him. Last time they'd taken a piss at the same time, Ashok had said, "Better watch out when you're in the river that the fish don't bite that off, thinking it's a shriveled worm."

Gopal wiped his cum onto his pants. His uniform was done for the week. Each uniform was labeled with the soldier's number, not name. Gopal knew that if he were shot, another soldier would inherit his number and uniform.

"Stinking bastard," Ashok said. "You blackies can't get any. So, when you had your chance the other night, you couldn't get it up." Ashok exposed his yellow teeth with one prized golden cap and pulled a chair up next to Gopal.

He wished Ashok would just shut up.

"See what came today." Ashok took out an envelope with roses and kittens on it and pulled out a picture of a woman with a bow-legged child that had Ashok's wide-set eyes. "My wife."

The woman was beautiful. Her breasts, like two doves, trying to peak out from under her shirt, almost made him hard again. He'd joined the army for his girlfriend. She had let him touch her breasts the night before he left. Gopal hadn't realized that her breasts would be so soft, that her nipples would pucker at his touch. She promised him that she'd wait for him. He told her that when he came back, he'd build them a home. Their children would go to school. She was almost as black as him, with pink lips turned up to the sky, teeth as white as the clams he used to gather from the bottom of the river back home. She could not write and did not send photos.

In his village, the girls were much darker. Even so, he was the blackest shade of black. His mother gave up trying to keep him out of the sun. *Find a girl who is light, even if she is poor, so that your children won't be cursed like you*, his mother said.

He'd not told his mother about his girlfriend, but she found out all the same. No one kept quiet in his village. His mother had beaten him as if he were a child.

Two months ago, his childhood friend wrote to him with the

news. The fat old grocery-wallah up the street had taken his girlfriend in and dressed her in new clothes. He already had a wife, but she was the man's pet, kept in a little house near his shop. Gopal imagined the fat rolls of the grocery-wallah's pale back cupped in his girlfriend's hand. Their offspring would be spared Gopal's blackness.

"Don't look at my wife like that." Ashok grabbed the picture from Gopal. "If you need it that bad, why don't you come down to the village with me? We'll get us some nice girls."

Wednesdays were payday. Gopal's check seemed smaller this week. Every check had bites taken out: interest collected on his debt, his tab at the store, savings for his sister's wedding. They were lucky that his sister was born a few shades lighter than him. His mother used creams to peel off her darkness, whitening her over the years. Soon, he'd have enough saved to pay for her wedding. The bank owner's son was the best prospect back home. With his sister's beauty and his savings, Gopal was sure to secure her future.

With what was left of his paycheck, Gopal wanted to send a gift to his mother. Charagan was the pearl of Nadistan, the heartland of handicrafts. Such a shame that there was so much fighting in such a beautiful land. He went to the store that was more like a hut at the edge of the army camp. A feral villager with a long gray beard dyed red with henna ran it. Despite buying from him regularly, Gopal made no conversation, and the man only grunted, marking down the merchandise. The shopkeeper was getting rich off the poor soldiers that came to keep their motherland safe. This man was probably an informant for the militants. There was something about him that made Gopal uneasy, the way he closed his shop several times a day for prayers. How he wore that pious white cap on his head. Gopal held his gun in both hands and turned toward the biscuits.

That is when he saw the girl. Probably the same one that Ashok said the old woman was hiding. She looked about the same age as his sister, seventeen or so. The girl dropped her parcel and then leaned over to pick it up. He imagined coming up behind her. She'd struggle against him, but want him.

Gopal forgot the gift that he wanted to buy for his mother. Instead, he picked up a Cadbury milk chocolate bar and a book of butterfly stickers for the girl. His sister loved these stickers.

The girl was making her way to pay for her goods. Gopal stood between her and the shopkeeper. She stepped back.

"Can I help you?" asked the shopkeeper.

"I'll take these." Gopal placed the items on the counter littered with yellowed newspapers, dusty magazines, and plastic toys.

"It will be eighty-seven dihabs."

Gopal pulled out one hundred dihabs, paid the shopkeeper, collected his change, and then took a pen from the counter to draw a picture on the back of the stickers for the girl. He'd always been good at drawing. Sometimes he dreamed of painting the mountains around them. But the only thing a soldier was to paint in the valley was the snow with his urine.

For the girl he drew a bird. Not the kind from here, but the bright-colored ones from back home. He had nothing to color it with, so he gave it a branch. Under the perch he drew a heart—a lovely heart with his name under it: Gopal.

Waiting for the girl outside the shop, he held her gifts in one hand and his gun in the other. The shopkeeper's eyes were on him as she emerged, pulling her scarf over her mouth. That heart-shaped, pouting mouth. Gopal walked alongside her. She quickened her step, her muscles tensing. He imagined her tightening around him. This was the woman for him. He liked the angles of her face, not too pretty, so he wouldn't have to worry as much about other men.

"These are for you." He held out the gifts. She did not look at them, but quickened her pace, making her breasts jiggle. "Come take it. You must like chocolate." He took a couple of giant steps and stood in front of her, holding the gifts between them. She took them, walked around him, and dropped them on the ground. A fiery temper. Gopal watched her disappear, saying a prayer to Ganesh that she would be his.

44

AISHA

AISHA WAS FINALLY released at night, barely able to walk. One of the boys from the village found her, slung her over his shoulder, and brought her home. The boy pretended he'd never seen a thing, but he or Babak must have called Mina, because she arrived shortly.

The first few days back home bled together. The itch from her wounds was unbearable. She rubbed parts of the birthmark on her calf right off. The south part of Nadistan scraped off. But no matter how much she clawed, the scar remained just like a border.

It was a day or two before Aisha found the hole in her mouth. Her tongue traced the bloodied gum for hours before she believed it. They'd knocked her bottom front tooth out. Her hair would grow back, the skin would heal, but the hole in her mouth would always be there.

The burn marks stretched up her thigh, purple, blistering scars. Her navel was still the smooth white of almond meat. The soldiers had not burned her there. Aisha took out an old scarf that looked moth-eaten, like her childhood dupatta. That first day of school, it was so clean and crisp: full of promise. Aisha wrapped the old dupatta between her legs, then around her waist, tighter and tighter, bandaging her wounds.

It took forty-seven steps to walk to the table. The phone was there. The line still cut. Alim waited on the other end—Alim as a boy offering to help her with the wash. The way he woke her with kisses in the morning. The absence that filled their relationship after Fidaa joined the militants. Alim's last call to her from Kawthar's house before the army sealed the borders to Poshkarbal and cut all telecommunications. Her tongue traced the gaping hole in her mouth. She could not stop the sounds from coming back: zipping and unzipping, the tear of fabric.

She picked up her cell phone. No service. She wished she could go back in time and leave him a message. Give her husband some hope. But hope was a curse when the truth was this terrible.

Tears ran down her face. She put the phone down. Grateful there was no connection.

Aisha lay on her bed, the darkness that covered her bruises a relief. Her father didn't ask her anything and rarely spoke.

When Mina came over, she opened the shutters. Light streamed in.

"How is Nalja?" Aisha asked. "The soldiers . . ." Aisha coughed uncontrollably.

Mina knelt beside her. "Are you alright?"

Aisha shrugged when the fit ended. She sat up in bed. "The soldiers were asking about Nalja."

"She wanted to come today. She's hardly left the house at all over the last three weeks. Just gone to the store a few times. It's no way to live."

"It's better than ending up like this."

Mina winced and squeezed Aisha's hand. "Omar is living with us again. It's safer to have a man in the house."

Omar. Nausea overwhelmed Aisha. Omar came up behind her. The soldier pushed into her. "There's no keeping the soldiers away. You must keep Nalja hidden."

"How long can we keep her stuck inside?"

"You have to get her out of here, Mina."

"Omar says there's checkpoints everywhere. Even if we got her to the city, then what? Soldiers are everywhere. Who knows if the airport is even open. Let me clean you up a little."

Aisha was silent as Mina bathed her with a sponge. "Bite down on this." Mina placed a cloth into Aisha's mouth. Mina did not flinch when she pulled off the thin gauze dupatta from between Aisha's legs. With it came a layer of skin and scab. Mina cleaned the wound with alcohol. The fire was back, burning Aisha from the inside out. She bit the cloth.

Flames licked up her legs, searching for her heart. This must be why God demanded that they cover their skin: to protect them from fire. Pain burst into her ears. She was seven again. Fire surrounded her. Smoke filled her lungs. Her grandmother lost in the flames. The bucket she'd been using to dump water from the canal started to burn. The wind intensified. Aisha ran to her mother, who was digging a trench to protect her house.

She grabbed her mother's arm and pointed, unable to hear her own words over the roar of the flames.

Her grandmother reached for her mother. A wall of fire separated them.

"Keep your eyes open. Stay with me," Mina said.

Aisha wanted to explain to Mina that there were ghosts all around her. But instead, she nodded. There was something firm in Mina's voice that let her know she must obey. Her body was drenched in sweat, soaking the sheets. Her grandmother prayed for her protection. Aisha's heart held the prayer, finding strength to heal herself.

Mina massaged her feet. Her skin tingled.

"How do these soldiers live with themselves," Mina said. "God knows no human can live with these sins."

Soldiers: the broad nose, the blow to her head, and that room. The dryness of her flesh as they crammed into her. The dark one who burned her.

The story of the soldiers beating her spread from village to village, even though there were no newspapers, internet, or phone lines. There was no talk of the rape. Only Mina saw the scars. Women knew when to be silent.

But when Aisha turned her ear to the fields, she heard the story of a woman they called freedom. She stood up to a soldier. When he beat her with a gun, she dripped her blood in his eyes. He was blinded by her blood and fled from the army. The rest of the soldiers were so scared, they left too. The story traveled on the wing tips of the birds, beyond the fields to other villages. And a story was born about a woman so powerful that one drop of her blood caused the army to leave her village. They call her Freedom.

45

GOPAL

WHEN GOPAL WAS not on duty, he searched for the girl. He thought of reporting her neighbor as a militant so that he might be stationed closer by. When the mail came, he no longer rushed down with the other soldiers in hopes of receiving news from home. His future was here, in the hands of that girl. Instead of buying his daily pack of cigarettes, he saved his money. She might have refused his first gift, but there would be no denying his next. Gold.

The days inched by without the relief of cigarettes. Gopal saved some cash, took the rest from his savings, and then went to Ashok for the gold. Ashok was part of a special group that raided militant villages. He didn't talk much about it, but sometimes, he'd show Gopal the things he took with him—a watch, thumb drive, camera, ring. Last week, he'd stabbed a man to death, said that he'd been buried with the rest of them in a ditch.

Ashok was asleep in his bed. The room was rank with his farts. Gopal nudged him awake with his gun.

"What do you want, fat fuck?" Ashok asked. He was the fat one though. Gopal was all muscle.

"Gold. I need to buy some gold."

"What do you need gold for, yaar?"

"My sister's birthday. I need a bracelet." The perfect gift, she would know that he was serious. Gopal prayed that Ashok would never notice the village girl wearing the bracelet.

"I thought you were broke?" Ashok's sour breath wafted up. "How much do you have?"

"Twenty-eight hundred dihabs back in my room." It was far more than Gopal's cigarette and liquor allowance. This gift would bite into his sister's money. But he must show the girl that he could provide for her.

"Shit, yaar." Ashok was still lying on his side, his hair slicked to his head. He got up and scratched his balls. "Give me a minute."

Gopal stepped outside onto the balcony. Would this harsh land become his home? In his village there were the monsoons and then the dry months. The heat never wavered. During the winter in Charagan, Gopal thought he would die from the cold. He could never raise his children on this freezing mountain surrounded by jihadists. He'd finish his time here and leave with his wife. They'd go back to the south, not to his village, somewhere new.

Gopal looked to the mountain. Several army vehicles were parked on the road below, and a soldier's socks hung from the balcony. Ashok came out to join him. "Which one do you like?" Ashok asked, holding out the jewelry. One was a solid gold bracelet, sturdy and thick like a snake. The other was a thin, delicate necklace with a splinter of a diamond in it.

"This one," Gopal said, taking the bracelet in his hand.

"Between friends, I give discounts." He patted him on the back. "Bring me twenty-five hundred dihabs."

"Thanks, man. I'll bring you the money later. Where did you get all this gold, yaar?"

Ashok slid his hands over his hair. "What do you care?"

Gopal shrugged, wondering if it was from the man he'd killed. His wife's. He shuddered, remembering the pleading of the village woman. These villagers were just waiting for a moment to ambush them.

"My wife didn't answer my call last night." Ashok chewed the end of a toothpick. "After all I do for her. She doesn't understand what we go through." He grabbed Gopal's shoulder. "Do you ever wonder why we are even here?"

Gopal looked up at the mountain. He hadn't heard Ashok talk like this. Gopal rubbed his hand over his eyes, erasing the images of the women—the old one in the field, the wife of the dead man whose gold was in his hand. "There's nothing to wonder about."

The next day, Gopal set out for the girl's house. He'd oiled and brushed his hair, dusted off his boots, tightened his belt an extra notch, and put just a hint of Calvin Klein Eternity on his wrist. It was hard to get any kind of cologne up here, so even the dab was measured. He stopped by Ashok's room to pay him for the bracelet, knocking several times. Lazy bastard was probably still sleeping. Gopal opened the door.

Time stopped. A bolder crushed the breath from his diaphragm. Ashok lay dead on the floor, dressed in full uniform, gun in his mouth, eyes open, staring back at Gopal. There was a note on the table.

Tell my parents it was an accident. Tell my wife that I love her.

Gopal stepped away from the body, crashing into a chair. Accident. Three soldiers had died this year in *accidents*, one just days before. He fought the urge to gag. Ashok stared at him. Blood seeped toward Gopal. What would they tell his wife? His child? Gopal's heart beat faster and faster.

Should he report this? He closed his eyes and shoved the money he had brought for Ashok back into his pocket, backed out of the room, and shut the door. It was an accident, a terrible, terrible accident. Something he shouldn't have seen. He took off down the hill toward the girl's house.

Gopal needed to believe that at 6:15 p.m., Ashok would stroll up. They would shoot the shit. Drink some beers. But it would never be like that again. He needed the girl, now more than ever. She was all he had left.

He couldn't wipe Ashok from his mind as he walked toward her house. The sulfuric scent of his blood. The vacant stare.

Arriving near her home, Gopal waited for the girl just up the path, but she did not arrive. Maybe she was home. He knocked on the door three times before some old woman he didn't recognize cracked it open.

"Open the door," Gopal said.

The woman stepped out. Her eyes sunk back into her head. Her skin was thin and marked with blue veins. "Yes?"

Gopal looked past her into the dim room with a dirt floor. The TV blared and the scent of curried tomatoes filled the house. "I would like a word with you about your granddaughter."

The woman propped herself up against the doorframe.

Gopal shifted back and forth in his boots. He felt her staring at the blackness of his skin. "Is her father here? I would like to talk with him about her future." He held the gun in front of him.

The woman blocked the door. He craned to get a view, searching for traces of the girl—her house slippers by the door, scarves hung on the wall, and the stack of books on the case must be hers. The woman cracked her knuckles.

"When will her father be home?"

"He is away."

"Then I will come back to talk to him tomorrow about your granddaughter."

The woman hunched forward. "There's no need to come back. There is nothing to discuss." She wanted to spit on him. She did not bother to correct him—that Nalja was her daughter. What on earth did he think? That they'd give Nalja to him? She'd rather scrape his eyes out and let him kill her than let him near her daughter.

Gopal set his gun on the ground and took out a parcel from his bag with some coffee and sweets. He handed it to the girl's grandmother. "I heard that next month new girls will be selected to attend to the needs of the soldiers. Usually, they do not take girls from such good families as yours. But times are difficult. One never knows who will be taken." Gopal had no idea how the girls in the brothel were chosen, assuming they were poor, fatherless girls just like back home. His words had the desired effect, though. The woman's face crumbled from a stern impasse to fear. "Any woman promised to a soldier of course will be left alone."

Mina fought to keep from vomiting. Her heart spasmed. They had no time left.

"I will return to meet with her father tomorrow."

"Don't waste your time coming back. There is nothing to discuss."

The gold was heavy in his pocket as he walked back up the hill. He wished that there were somewhere else to go. Back home the men spent hours playing cards in sand eddies by the riverbanks. When they tired of this, they rode their motorbikes into town. It wasn't that he couldn't leave the village, there was just nowhere to go. Daggers of snow caged them in. The roads crumbled and washed away with rains. And what was there beyond the next bend, but another worn village with old women spitting at him from under their shawls.

Gopal put on his sunglasses and headed back to the barracks. It was quieter than usual. The men off duty usually clustered on the porch. He didn't want to talk to anyone and headed up the stairs toward his room.

"Gopal, a word please," the commander called to him.

As he followed the commander around the building and into his stark, white office, all he could think of was the vacant look in Ashok's eyes. Blood seeping into the floor.

"Have a seat." Every paper on the commander's desk was stacked perfectly in place. Gopal sat in a metal chair across from the commander, clicking the heel of his boot against the ground. "I have some bad news. Have you heard what happened?"

Gopal shook his head. He focused on the commander's mug. He'd not seen Ashok. There was no blood. No old woman.

"Ashok died in an accident." The commander pushed the mug to the side of the table.

There was only the girl. No village back home. No girlfriend with the grocery-wallah. Nothing to remember or forget. He would have a new life, washed clean from the dust of Charagan.

"Ashok was cleaning his weapon when it inadvertently went off."

Inadvertently. Gopal blinked away the image of blood spilling from Ashok's mouth. It was an accident. There was no note. He never bought the gold from Ashok. They had never been in Building C together. All of that was behind him. It was all an accident.

"Please give my condolences to the family." Gopal stood up. "Anything else, Commander?"

"I'm sorry, Gopal. I know you were close."

Gopal gave a nod and walked out the door into the light of day.

46

AISHA

AISHA'S HOUSE SLIPPERS sat at the foot of her bed along with a worn copy of the Quran. She had on two sweaters, but still the cold leaked in. Someone knocked on the back door. Aisha looked up and saw Nalja and Mina through the window. Relief and fury surged through her at once. Nalja shouldn't be out.

Babak answered the door. Nalja burst into the house, greeted Babak, and hugged Aisha.

Aisha froze under Nalja's touch. No skin would ever be welcomed against hers. Mina nodded and seemed to understand, gently pulling Nalja off Aisha.

"What have they done to you, Maasi?" Nalja surveyed her ruin. An image where all the negative space became filled with things too painful to see.

The sounds of zippers. The grip of fingers. The scent of flesh burning.

"It is over now, Nalja. Leave it be."

"Those bastards have taken our land and children," Babak boomed from the kitchen.

Nalja's eyes filled with tears. "I wish it were over. I think the only way out is death. Why don't they just kill us and get it over with?"

Aisha looked up at Nalja, the girl in her ironed into this hard woman.

"I have to go, Maasi."

"Yes, it is time, Nalja. We should have sent you away before."

Nalja started to cry, hiccupped, and then swallowed. Aisha reached for her hand, an impulse left from before, when touch had been a comfort. They both needed to believe in the possibility of warmth. That life was stronger than this.

Nalja cried even harder. She couldn't believe what they'd done to Aisha. The bruises, the blood, the swelling. Aisha Maasi's face was nearly unrecognizable. "A soldier wants to marry me."

Aisha's heart stopped. She could not breathe.

Mina explained, "He asked to meet with Omar tomorrow."

Aisha bit her lip. Not even Omar would agree to this. "Nalja, could you help me by folding the linens in Fidaa's bedroom?"

"Of course, Maasi."

When the door closed, Mina turned back to Aisha. "Omar doesn't think we can make it out."

"I'd rather die trying than stay."

"How can we get her out? Where will she go?"

"We'll go to a neighboring village. I know a doctor there. He will help us get to the city. Once the airports open, I'll send her to college on the mainland. Just while all this passes."

Mina sat on the pillow next to Aisha. "Omar wants to take her."

Aisha's head spun. Why had Mina let him back into the house? "Where? To his other wife?" Aisha fought the urge to throw her tea against the wall. Instead, she held the cup tighter. "Say something, so I can understand."

Mina said nothing.

The sound of zippers unzipping. Aisha pushed the tea away. The silence spread out between them.

"He is watching our house, Aisha." Nalja needed to leave tonight. It was their only chance.

"Who?"

"The soldier. He said that they would take her as a prostitute if he didn't marry her." Mina pushed her fist into to her lips, biting down on her own flesh. "He is the dark one that works in the fields."

The news washed over Aisha, thick like the fog that came from the mountains and hung over their village. And Aisha saw the white of his teeth as he burned her. He had snuffed out the flame before she burned to death.

"We'll leave tonight during the shift change."

"She'll be killed if they find her, Aisha. We all will."

"Death is better than this. Come back tonight. We can all leave together. It'll be safest from here."

47

AISHA

AISHA PUT ON her chador, concealing the white streaks in her hair, but some things fabric failed to hide, like the gaping hole in her mouth. The pain subsided some as she moved about, busying herself, packing tins of food, containers of water, and layers of clothes. Fidaa had left with a bag just like this. She went into his room and sat on his bed. When they built his room, he was too scared to sleep alone and slept with Kawthar in hers. Kawthar never teased him about it. His sneakers were worn and dirty in the closet, the smell long since evaporated. A pair of Adidas pants he'd bought but not taken with him, worn only a few times, hung in the closet. She'd wanted everything to be as it was, so that when he returned, he might remember who he was, that his childhood might melt away the pain he'd endured.

Aisha imagined the army coming into their home. Soldiers claiming his shirts, wearing his worn sneakers, sending his pants to a cousin back home. The bits of Fidaa she'd saved for him, consumed by their greed. Anger hardened to hate in these men.

She took out all the cell phones and computers and handed everything to Nalja to wipe clean. Leave no trace. Alim wouldn't be able to reach her when she made it to the doctor's village. She'd have to

find him on social media. It would work out with God's help. She
breathed in, imagining the sound of his voice, his arms wrapped
around her. Pain shot through her jaw as she clenched her teeth. But
how would she face him after her ruin?

Aisha packed her cash and the jewelry and a few snapshots of the
children and the picture from her wedding day. Alim's face still lit
with adoration. The sun hung low in the sky; the guards would soon
change. She willed her muscles strong, and focused only on their safe
passage out. Since the village was seized, sixteen had made it out, four
had died trying. If Noorjahan were listening, Aisha begged her to
shield them with invisibility as they climbed the mountain.

Aisha looked down at Poshkarbal. The poplar trees, dotting
around the black ink river. The mosque was visible, like a small
crown on the horizon. She prayed to God that they melted into the
night. And though her mother did not appear, she felt Noorjahan,
taking the aches from her legs and giving her strength to forge on.

Her house would be visible from the switchback. The flower
fields would have turned into a sea. They were high enough to see
the orchards, to see the river, to see the tin roof of the school. If she
looked back, there would be her whole life staring back at her. Instead, she looked ahead at the mountains. It would be slow going, all
uphill, a one-way path. Mina was not with them; Babak and Nalja
trailed behind her. Mina had stayed to wait for Omar.

Aisha paused to catch her breath just as gunfire erupted. She
couldn't tell which direction it had come from. She prayed that they
wouldn't get hit. Lowering herself toward the ground, she tried to
figure out where the shots came from. Another round was fired.

"Follow me," Babak whispered, crouching past her. "Keep low."
The shots continued around them. Aisha prayed. Babak slipped off
the path, leading them through low brush. They stopped behind a
rock, lying flat on the ground. Dirt under their fingers. Their breath

too loud. The gunfire grew fainter and then disappeared altogether. She squeezed Nalja's hand.

"Paramilitary," Babak said. "I saw them run down the mountainside. We are safe now."

How had Babak seen all this? Thorns dug into her calf. She pulled a few burrs out of her pants. "Let's take the smaller trail—it will be longer, but less risky."

Nalja sat up, crying. "I didn't think we'd make it."

Babak stomped his foot on the ground and then wheezed.

"Everything alright?" Aisha asked.

"I'm fine." He walked slowly, starting up the path, clutching his jacket. "They hit me."

Aisha inhaled. Babak had taken the bullet to protect them. May God forgive her for being so angry at him and spare his life. "There is a cave, just a bit up the trail," Aisha said, leading them toward it.

The narrow mouth was difficult to pass through; it took her father several minutes to contort his body through the opening. They walked deep into the cave where they would be well hidden and safe. They needed to rest.

Her father drank the broth she'd brought, and she mixed in some herbs, which seemed to stop his wheezing. They were going to make it over the mountain. Slow like turtles, hobbling on either side of Nalja, who had already fallen fast asleep. It was nearly morning, and the village was hours away. They should sleep during the day, so they could travel at night. The dark would protect them.

"Noorjahan." Babak reached for Aisha.

The pain must be terrible. "It's me, Aisha."

Babak spoke and wheezed. "You look so much like her. She gets angry when I visit you."

Had he forgotten that they lived together? She needed to see how bad his injury was. "Let me see where you're hurt."

He pulled up the shirt, wet with blood. The wound had coagulated. She pressed her fingers gently against his stomach, feeling for a bullet. Her father doubled over in pain. It was much too deep for Aisha to extract.

Her father hissed as she cleaned the wound. The doctor would have to remove the bullet. She poured her dad some more cough syrup with codeine and then took a swig herself. "Let us sleep."

Babak fell into a deep sleep, and Nalja did not stir. Aisha drank more cough syrup, hoping to numb the ache in her pelvis. May God take this pain.

A light flickered in the cave.

Noorjahan lit a fire. "Come, warm yourself."

Aisha sat up and walked over to the fire, studying the perfect ring of rocks surrounding it. She held out her palms.

Noorjahan sat across from Aisha, her face mostly covered in shadows.

"Will you protect us?"

"Of course. That is why I'm here, but I can't stay long. I don't want him to see me."

She pointed at Babak, a look of tenderness crossing her face. Aisha felt like an intruder on their intimacy.

"I'm afraid he's not going to make it." Aisha choked on a sob, rising. "I shouldn't have blamed him for Fidaa leaving. I just couldn't . . ."

"He's been through worse. Just keep giving him the codeine."

Aisha pressed her palms against her eyes. "Even if we make it, how are we going to survive in the city? I lost our land. Everything you fought for."

"Don't be afraid." Noorjahan placed her hand on Aisha's back. "Remember the old ways I taught you. Bring them to the people. Heal them with what you have learned. The land will return to us. Praise be to God."

"I won't even be able to find the herbs out there."

"Don't worry so much. You will find new spots to forage. Rest now. Tomorrow night, go slow and move without fear."

The cave became dark; Noorjahan's fire extinguished, but the pit was there, a perfect ring filled with ash. The ground was cold against her body. Aisha finally fell asleep. When the pressure on her bladder became more than she could manage, she went outside. It was already late afternoon. More time had passed than she'd thought. She ate some flat bread and waited for night. When she poked her head out of the cave, stars shone brightly in the sky.

"Time to get up." Aisha packed up while Nalja fed Babak. As they emerged from the cave, Babak leaned on Nalja, who carried his weight.

48

BABAK

BABAK FOLLOWED AISHA through the darkness. Maybe he should have rolled over and died when the bullet hit him. Was it the instinct for self-preservation that kept him going or was there an actual purpose left to his life? He was merely a burden.

His great-niece, Nalja, bore his weight across the mountains as if it were nothing. The only way to block the pain was to talk. "Do you remember your grandmother?"

Nalja swallowed. Grandma Suha died when she was thirteen. Babak Uncle carried her body during the funeral procession. Nalja wished that she were stronger, so she could carry him through these mountains and get him to the doctor before it was too late. "God rest her soul. Remember her almond nests?" They were Babak Uncle's favorite. A sweet almond cardamon crust, filled with honey-glazed ground nuts.

"You have a grandfather, too, but you were too young when he left."

Nalja knew her grandfather had died of the winter flu before she was born. The same sickness that had taken Noorjahan. Nalja nodded as Babak leaned into her to step over a branch that had fallen. At this pace, they wouldn't make it to the village for another day or two. She sighed, wishing her uncle would stop talking and preserve his energy.

"He died on the mainland. I found his son, your uncle Padmal, on Facebook."

Nalja knew better than to argue with Babak when he became delusion. She'd never heard of anyone in the family named Padmal, and certainly didn't have an uncle. Her mother was an only child. Last year, he'd been seeing Noorjahan and locked himself in the bathroom for a full night.

"Padmal's ear was chopped off and Noorjahan sewed it back on. She was a healer, you know. Noorjahan." Babak's voice became soft when he said her name.

When Babak talked of the past, ghosts consumed him.

"And now his child has forsaken us. Do you realize that your uncle refused to admit that he was from Charagan? He kept saying over and over how his father was Hindu; his father an orphan; that he never lost an ear! What stupidity. I explained how the ear was sewn back on."

"Did you call him on Facebook, Uncle?" Nalja bit her lip. Uncle had been calling all kinds of people online before the village was seized. They'd had to disable his account. Hopefully, he hadn't called this poor man.

"The jawans froze my account. We've been cut off for months. This was before, Nalja. When Aisha was smaller than you." The pain was clearly too much for him. "Remember when Fidaa came back to us?" Nalja knew her cousin more through his absence. Aisha Auntie would be glued to the news whenever militants were found or shot. The entire house froze until they could find an image and make sure it wasn't Fidaa. They hadn't heard or seen a trace of him since the Northern Division commander's funeral.

Pain surged through Babak. It was his fault that Fidaa left. What had he said to the boy? Hadn't his example been enough to deter him? He clutched his stomach. At least the bullet hit him instead of his daughter. Maybe he was still good for something.

They walked for hours through the mountains, finding shelter by day. He pretended not to be hungry, knowing he was taking food out of his daughter and niece's mouths. The pain became too great. He grit his teeth until he tasted blood. Nothing would break him.

Dad, what would you like to eat when we go to the city?"
As if he deserved to be called *Dad*. As if he had not abandoned her. When he left her as a child and moved to Nadistan, he had not slept, consumed with guilt. But he could not have stayed in Poshkarbal. Not after his fingers took on a life of their own and tried to strangle Noorjahan. He knew then that his daughter would not be safe with him either. The worry had consumed him until he dulled it with whiskey. Pain and whiskey were made for each other, and his body was the medium where they danced until he could almost forget where he came from.

"I have failed you." His heart pounded in his ears.

"No, you haven't. You protected us from the gunfire."

They had finally arrived safely in a village where they could stop and rest. There was a doctor who would help him. Aisha had worked with the doctor over the years. They had made it here alive, praise be to God. The azan sounded, cardamom simmered, and bread baked. The doctor was saying something, but Babak couldn't understand. Aisha squeezed his fingers. The pain plunged his gut. He gripped Aisha's hand.

What was he telling her? It was important. Pain exploded in his head. He bit his tongue. Tasted blood. And the bullet was out. The doctor sutured the wound, stitching him back together. Thread pierced skin.

He gripped tightly to his daughter's hand. It was all he had.

———

The doctor arranged for their passage to the summer capital city of Charagan, where his friend who was also the brother of one of the women who Aisha had delivered children for lived. They had two capitals, because the winter capital was less cold, but the summer capital more beautiful, and the two locations afforded the government officials a second life where they could live with their lovers away from the watchful eyes of their wives. Babak hadn't been back to the capital for twenty years. He'd been part of the unit that seized the city. They'd converted a corridor of shops downtown into the Front's headquarters. But after the puppet government took back the capital, he never returned.

The doctor drove them by car to a friend of his who was hauling lotus roots into the capital. Aisha, Nalja, and Babak were packed with the cargo and covered in blankets. Babak tried to sleep, but every bump they hit in the road sent heavy roots crashing around him. He held his breath at each stop, waiting for soldiers to find them. After several hours, they stopped, and the trunk opened. Babak did not move. Every muscle remained still.

"Come out, quickly," the driver said. They exited the truck and looked down on the city. They thanked the driver and gathered their things.

Babak started to ask Aisha where they were going, but she silenced him and shook her head. Nalja took him by the elbow. They boarded a bus overflowing with people. He peered out the window.

The military encampment on the mountain was barely visible through the smog. Soldiers stood like lampposts lighting the city. Near the center of town, Aisha pulled them off the bus. She asked an older woman for directions. He knew this city. Why didn't she ask him? The woman gave Aisha elaborate directions—left then a right, head down the stairs, go by the riverfront—on and on she went.

They walked in circles until Aisha stopped in front of a pashmina warehouse with a yellow sign with letters peeling off. They walked up the narrow steps and went inside. Aisha gave the shopkeeper a photo of his baby niece with his sister-in-law. The shopkeeper took the photo and tears filled his eyes.

"They are doing okay? I haven't heard in months," the shopkeeper said.

"The baby is growing well. The delivery wasn't easy. They are all healthy and alive, thanks be to God."

He wiped his tears away. "Come." He took them into a back room, among mounds of moldy smelling fabric.

"Praise be to God. A miracle that you have arrived safely," the man said. "The doctor called and said that you were coming, but I didn't know that you also knew my brother. That you delivered his child." He placed the photo to his heart and closed his eyes and inhaled. "I will treasure this photo. We have a flat for you and will take you there."

Aisha handed him a bundle of cash. "Thank you for your kindness."

"It is nothing. We have some work for you too, with a local doctor."

"We are grateful to you," Aisha said.

They finished their tea and then followed the man through the narrow city streets to their new home, a small concrete flat on a sloping hill. When they opened the door, hardly any light streamed in at all.

part 6

PANDEMIC

Age 54
Spring 2020

49

BABAK

BABAK NEEDED TO buy socks: the woolen kind that did not bunch at the top. He hated the tightness of the sock around his calf. In time, the elastic would fail, and the sock would fall limp to his ankles, bunching at the heel. His toes were cold and locked in place, causing pain to shoot up his legs.

Main Street overflowed. Everyone walked on top of each other, elbows brushing, rickshaws honking, and motorcycles nearly hitting pedestrians. Stacks of DVDs and thick metal watches were displayed on blankets strewn across the sidewalk. Toward the middle of the block the sockwallas stood between the undershirts and pants vendor. Babak had already purchased socks from eight different places downtown. Each sock failed within hours, either compromising his circulation, or just shrugging down his leg. It pained him to waste the little money they had, but he needed socks. Standing before the mound of socks, he tried to convince the merchant to sell him a single one.

"If it is a good sock, I will buy more." Babak slowly counted on his fingers until he reached six. "Yes, I will come back for six pairs, plus the mate."

"Sir, I cannot sell you one sock. You must take the pair." The young man's hair rolled in a wave. He was lean, with dark eyes and crooked teeth.

"But how will I know if it is good? I have already purchased . . ." Again, he counted on his fingers. "Eight pairs of socks—none of them usable. What will warm my feet?"

The boy riffled through the mound of socks. "Here, grandfather, take the pair."

Babak unfolded them and returned a sock.

"What will I do with one sock?"

"Have some pride in your product. I told you, if it is good, I will be back for it. Are you telling me that it is worthless?"

"Don't worry," said the vendor. "I will keep it here for you. I hope your foot finds some comfort." The young man's eyes crinkled in a smile.

"How much do I owe you?"

"Nothing."

Babak put his wallet in his pocket. He had his allowance of dihabs that Aisha gave him. She worked delivering babies and selling herbal tinctures to the nearby villagers. He didn't like the herbs she tried to force him to take—he knew it was Noorjahan's influence. Still, she slipped it into his tea or water, insisting that the virus was among them and that he needed protection.

Babak veered off the busy street and headed toward the river. The houseboats crumbled into the sewage-colored water. It was hard to imagine that this was the same city he'd visited in his youth before he married Noor. The boats once padded in velvet, swaying on the banks, were covered in green moss, the planks bloated and falling apart.

Babak sat on a bench, facing the water. On the second story of the house across the street, he could still see the watermarks from the flood. Was it six or seven years ago? He'd watched the videos on Twitter of the dam bursting and flooding the city. The military evacuated their troops and left the people to die. Charagannians didn't need guns or soldiers; they had boats and good hearts and saved one another.

A stray dog sunned in an open pit littered with trash. Babak removed his shoe, exposing a bare foot. Better to sweat into a shoe than have a sock fall into it. He slipped the newly purchased sock on and put his shoe back on. The sock was too tight at the top. He'd been swindled again. The sockwalla sold him a dud. Pain shot through his toe. Everything around him dissolved.

The soldiers dipped his toe into a bucket of icy water, then turned up the electricity. They always started with the toe, the same two soldiers. Electricity shot from his genitals to his spine. Babak counted to one hundred, then backward. At seventeen, the electricity was back in his toe—the current against his bone.

"Lie down."

The rope burned into his ankle as he moved. Losing his balance, he fell to the ground. "Tell us the names of your militant brothers."

Pain burst into his temples, a scratch of light in the universe.

Are you alright?"

Babak opened his eyes.

He had escaped the soldiers again. Thanks be to God. A young man wearing blue jeans and a leather jacket stood before him, hair greased back. Something about him was familiar. So many people in the city reminded him of someone back home, but after four months living in the city, they still hadn't found anyone else from Poshkarbal.

"What's it to you?" Babak asked. The boy was too clean, probably an informant.

"You didn't sound so good."

"The past rarely sounds pleasant." The boy shifted to watch the soldiers from his periphery. Babak did not bother looking behind him. He knew they were there, every few feet, another soldier. Each bit of barbed wire, every tin hut, concealed a jawan. "Do you have a cigarette?"

"Certainly. I'm Farooq," he said, pulling out a cigarette and lighting it for Babak.

"You must be more careful. You'll be taken in, howling like that. You sounded like a bloody dog in heat."

Babak laughed. "It couldn't have sounded that good." There was no desire left in him. It had all been ironed out.

"They were starting to come toward you." Farooq moved his head indiscernibly to the left. Sure enough, there were soldiers posted behind the tree. The boy had good eyes. "I figured I might be a better awakening for you."

"This cigarette surely is." The boy would help him. He wasn't an informant at all. "Do you know where I can buy some socks? The kind that will fit."

"Socks?"

"Yes, my feet are so cold. I can't move my toes." He stood up, nearly losing his balance.

"Careful, now. Are you able to walk?"

"I was made for walking," Babak said. "My feet led me, half-dead, with a bullet in me. A little numbness surely won't bother me."

Babak removed his shoe and peeled off the lone sock. He dropped it on the ground next to a used rubber. For a moment, they appeared as a pair.

50

AISHA

AISHA NO LONGER went outside to meet the rising sun. Dawn was muted in the city, all the light blocked by the houses. Their concrete flat remained dark. Each morning she called Alim and Kawthar. As soon as social media was restored, she'd found Alim. His profile picture a dahlia blooming in their garden back home. Neither of them could use their video because there wasn't enough data. The calls dropped over and over, leaving them with half-finished conversations. The airport still wasn't open. Alim could not return.

Over the last three months, they spoke every day that there was a signal. Sometimes, Lubaaba would sing in the background. Aisha imagined her twirling and swirling. Then the call dropped and there would be weeks or days without contact. When the airport finally opened, there was talk of a virus in the Middle Kingdom. They built a new hospital in eight days, but it wasn't enough. This was worse than the winter flu that took her mother. Some kind of coughing disease. Aisha urged Alim not to travel with this new flu spreading.

At least Nalja was in college. Her first semester, she had hardly gone due to all the curfews and strikes. When they first arrived in the city, leaving the house had been nearly impossible. The newspapers stopped printing until, finally, local reporters used a hand press, printing a few hundred papers each day that were passed from home to home until the ink wore off.

Ten months had passed since she'd seen Alim, but it felt more like three lifetimes.

Nalja was getting ready to go to school and was in somewhat of a good mood today. "Thank you for the delicious omelet." She cleared her plate, grabbed her camera off the table, and slipped it into her bag. Aisha had refused to buy her one initially, fighting against Nalja choosing journalism as her major. Not that she wasn't proud that Nalja wanted to become a journalist, she just couldn't imagine losing her. It was too dangerous. But when she got into the university and classes resumed, Aisha hoped that school would ease her depression, and the camera sparked her passion.

Aisha poured a bag of lentils into a bowl, sifting through them, removing the occasional pebble. Babak came into the kitchen and sat across from her. His eyes trained on each lentil.

He cleared his throat. "I have to tell you how the fire started."

Aisha's shoulders tightened. He kept going back to when she was seven. The fire. And then he'd scream or yell because the soldiers took him.

"Uncle, do you have an umbrella for me?" Nalja interjected. The sky was heavy with the threat of spring rains.

"The jawans took it from me, thought it was a gun. Can you imagine the stupidity?" He popped a toothpick between his teeth.

"It's in the closet," Aisha said. The soldiers had not taken his umbrella, he'd just forgotten where it was. "You'll be home by four today?"

Babak cleared his throat. "One time, I was stopped by soldiers, and they started questioning me about my beard. They implied that my beard marked me as a militant. I could not help but say, 'You are the one holding the gun!'

"The soldier asked me, 'Really, what is with the beard?'

"I told him, 'The beard, it comes.' It is just like that. The beard comes. I do nothing. It's nature."

Aisha and Najla ignored Babak's interruption.

"I might go to the mosque with some friends for evening prayers," Nalja said, avoiding Aisha's eyes. Her backpack was slung over her shoulder and a royal-blue dupatta pinned around her face.

"It's Friday, have you lost your mind?" The young men pelted stones at the soldiers on Friday evenings in the old city near the mosque. The army fired pellet guns indiscriminately into the crowds. "What kind of journalist can be blind? Stay away from the old city on Fridays."

"What kind of journalist avoids protests, Maasi? I will not live in fear."

"There is a difference between living in fear and stupidity. You are still in school." Aisha grabbed a sharp pebble from the lentils, saving a tooth from cracking. Her tongue ran across the hole in her mouth.

Babak slammed his fist on the table. "These bastards have blinded a whole generation of young men."

"Yes, and even so, they make us so afraid that I can't go and pray on a Friday night." Nalja grabbed the umbrella from the closet.

"Come home and pray. You have the rest of your life to be shot at." Aisha poured the lentils into the pot and added water to soak them.

"You look just like your mother," Babak said, pouring his tea into a saucer to cool. "I had to leave you."

Aisha sighed, hoping to redirect him. "Last week a poor young boy was shot by pellets and blinded. He was just an innocent boy, playing in the park." Aisha hadn't even cried for him. The dead became numbers without names. There weren't enough tears for the thousands of dead. The names that did not circulate online because there was no internet. Photos weren't shared on social media because they could not be uploaded. The death toll was not a headline because the hospitals were forbidden from counting the dead or wounded.

Babak sat up straight.

"To think, I almost lost you." His voice shook. "I was such a monster when I left. Do you remember how I pushed you the day of the fire?"

Aisha pursed her lips together. Here he went again.

"Nalja, you better go. You'll be late," Aisha said. A hazy piece of memory came back. She bit her father's leg. Her mother gasped for air. How had she forgotten this?

"I couldn't trust myself after the fire." He cracked his knuckles. "It wasn't your mother's fault." He started to cry.

"Who started the fire, Uncle?"

Aisha locked eyes with Nalja. Why was she encouraging him?

"She wanted to protect you and her parents from the goondas." He took a deep breath, suppressing tears.

"That is enough." Aisha stood up. "If you talk about Noorjahan, she'll come for you. Do you want me to call her right now to sort this out?"

Babak's eyes opened wide. He drank his tea out of the saucer, obedient and quiet.

Nalja grabbed her cell phone and dropped it in her purse. She leaned close to Aisha as she headed to the door. "Why are you so cruel to him? It's not kind to scare him like that."

Aisha shook her head and went back into her room. How could she possibly manage them both?

51

NALJA

NALJA LEFT THE house with relief. The sky was full of gray clouds, but the warmth of the sun found its way to her. Walking down the narrow street, she passed a mound of trash on the ground, the fruit stand with wilted cabbage and bowls of imported fruits. She waited at the corner, turning her back to the soldier in his guard station, and caught the bus to school. Some days she counted the number of soldiers she passed, but it was best to ignore jawans and never let them know she was watching, even when they said filthy things to her.

The soldiers were one thing, being followed was another. Since she'd started with her program in journalism, she'd felt a shift in surveillance. The clicks on her phone, footsteps that trailed at just the right distance, the intensity of ears listening to her in every public place—there became fewer and fewer places to speak freely. Even the classroom, her professor explained, was surveyed.

Nalja hadn't heard anything from her parents. She shouldn't have let her mom stay, but Mina had sworn that she would find her. Her mother's profile was time-marked with the stamp: *last active August 2, 2019*, when Nalja still lived in Poshkarbal, before it had been cut off from the world. She'd heard the army burned parts of the village, but there was no news of who had survived or what was left. There'd been a news report on a militant encampment, some place she'd never heard of, but when it flashed on the TV screen, Aisha Auntie had clamped her arm and they stared in frozen horror at the charred carcass of their mosque, the crumbled remnants of the private school, the burnt skeleton of the market. Not a person photographed. Aisha Auntie's hand was a lead weight on hers. When the news report ended, she said nothing and went to bed. They never spoke of what they'd seen.

Nalja kept trying to get word of who survived from their village, hoping that somehow her mother and father had made their way to the city or a neighboring village.

Arriving early to class, Nalja sat off to the left. Not in the mood to talk. Class had been so erratic over the past months. It was boring being shut inside with her aunt and great-uncle, day after day.

Her professor came in wearing a maroon shirt and jeans, Nike knockoffs, and thick black glasses. He often sat at his desk, sparking conversation and dialogue instead of lecturing. His goal was for each of them to find their story—the one that only they could tell. "But to do this," he said again and again, "you must know your voice."

At first Nalja was inspired and then baffled and finally angered, when he kept writing on her assignments, *This is fine work, but this voice here, it's not you.*

As if he knew her voice. What she stood for. He was arrogant, and more so with her as she was a woman. He'd suggested that she start with her family. Interview them. "You must not subscribe to the idea of objectivity—any journalist who says they are neutral simply fears their own bias. Know your bias. Know your truth. Then one can understand one's own voice."

A good-looking guy sat next to him at the front of the class. Nalja caught his eye for a moment and then looked away. His worn leather bag sat on the table. He couldn't be that much older than her. He chatted with the professor, running his fingers through his wavy brown hair. A smattering of students came in.

"How's everyone?" Professor Hasan began.

A few of the students responded. Nalja took out her notebook.

"This is Farooq, our guest for the day." Farooq nodded at the group, leaning back casually in his chair. "As I've mentioned before, reporting on your own conflict is very difficult. Occupation is personal, and as journalists, we are charged with telling the truth. What then is the truth? Is it, I ask you, what you see?"

Farooq jumped in. "I'd say more of how you see versus what you see."

Professor Hasan asked, "Is that why you chose photography?"

"Yes, because I can bring people close to how I see. The camera is such an intimate tool."

"Please show us your work."

The lights dimmed and Farooq began clicking through images. First, he started with protests, funeral processions, mothers crying while holding pictures of their sons, unmarked graves.

"What has been your biggest challenge?" Professor Hasan asked as Farooq clicked through the images.

"As a journalist?"

"Yes."

"There are a few things. There was the time they came to my house and tried to stab me. Thank God my mother wasn't home. I was wearing my leather jacket—and it saved my life. The blade just grazed my skin." Farooq stared out the window. "The attacker was never caught, and it happened just ten days after a newspaper in Australia published my photos of civilian mass graves.

"Taking those photos was crazy. I just saw those mounds of dirt and all I could think of was my father and the ten thousand disappeared men. I cried. I wanted to climb in and hug the bones of the missing men, fathers, just like mine. Then I just started photographing, clicking away as if I could capture the memories that never came from those stolen lives."

The class was completely silent. Photos of unmarked graves flashed before them, mounds of dirt under squat trees. Seemingly harmless dirt, harboring the hearts and spirits of thousands and thousands of disappeared civilians.

"Other things have been hard too." Farooq lifted his head and looked out the window. "I went back to my ancestral village just last month. It was very difficult, and everyone warned me against it. I couldn't tell anyone where I was going."

He started flipping through the pictures. Nalja felt cold inside. What remained of Poshkarbal flashed on the screen. He'd done what she only dreamed of. She wanted to close her eyes and stop the images. The poplar tree by the government school twisted and burnt. A Gujar with his goats, hands folded behind his back, shoulders stooped forward. Barbed wire in front of the barbershop, iridescent, glowing, sparkling in the sun.

Did she know him? She had a vague memory of a scrawny boy called Farooq whose dad had disappeared. Was this Alim's relative? Her lungs choked. It was as if someone had vacuumed the air out of the room. She became nauseous. The lights came up and the room spun. Class wasn't over, but Nalja grabbed her bag, left the school, and became a ghost in the street, no home to return to.

52

BABAK

MOST OF ALL, Babak despised the bridges in the city. The ghost of Noorjahan loved water. There was no way to avoid her when crossing the bridge, because she waited for him below. She was still punishing him. In the end, Noorjahan would win. She had all of eternity to haunt him.

Babak was safe at home and at the mosque. Aisha did not understand why Babak prayed at the mosque five times a day as soon as the curfew lifted. He couldn't tell her that it was because Noorjahan would not follow him there. In order to get to the mosque, Babak had to cross the river. She liked all the bridges, but the foot bridge, with its ornate wood, was her favorite. Anywhere there was water, Noorjahan was bound to be. She came to him right out of a bucket of water when he was a prisoner some twenty-five years ago.

There were two buckets in the prison cell. One overflowed with piss and shit; the other was for drinking and washing. The light was always on. It was either excruciatingly hot, or so cold that he shook. Babak took to counting, trying to decipher a minute, an hour, a day. The intervals by which they came and went. But it was impossible. There were only black boots and the smell of urine.

Two officers entered his cell. "Ready to talk?"

Babak tricked his mind and erased the militant camp from his memory. He knew too much. Knew where the artillery passed through the mountains. Knew who the next target was. Knew which opium lords were on their side, selling opium to the soldiers and supplying arms to the Front. If he had a gun, he'd shoot himself and bring this information back to the earth. Because there were some things that even God did not need to know.

The short one unzipped his pants and pissed just above where Babak slept. His dreams would be drenched in urine. "Get up."

It's not that he didn't want to move. His head flashed with dizziness. Water. They poured it over his head, pulling his legs apart at the ankles until it felt like he would split down the middle.

"Open your eyes," the soldier ordered. Something had ruptured. "Let's clean you up. You filthy bastard." The soldier grabbed him by the back of his head and slammed his face into a bucket of water. Blood rushed to his head as if it wanted to find a way out, back to water. The body was comprised of water: 60 percent. How could the rest resist so much? He willed himself to relax, to die. But his instinct to live was cruel.

And then she appeared. Noorjahan. Not the girl he fell in love with, but the woman, hard as nails and mad. Lips curled up. She grabbed him by the hair at the nape of his neck and pulled him out of the water just in time. So he could gasp for air.

As the soldiers came and left, Noorjahan lived in that bucket. The temperature changed from hot to cold. They did not speak. But when he got close to the edge of death, she pulled him to life.

When Babak became weak with pain and his tongue got loose and he needed to talk, she let him. Filled his mouth with words about her. And the soldiers kicked him harder, not wanting to hear about a dead woman. She invented buried stocks of artillery. She knew of all the slain guerillas and gave them imaginary villages that would yield only rocks in the mountains or the barracks of soldiers. Noorjahan gave his weak tongue things to say. God bless her.

How could he face her now? Babak ran across the bridge at full speed, but Noorjahan must be under it. She hit him in the calf with a stone. Pop, another stone hit him, this time in the back. Noorjahan was stoning him as if he were a soldier.

Smoke came up from the river. She wanted him to peer over the edge so that she could throw a stone right in his face. But the faster he ran, the younger he became. He was running to their house in Posh-karbal.

"Babak, there is a fire in your field!" He sprinted up the path toward the billowing smoke and saw Noorjahan, holding a rake, trying to reach her mother's body, unmoving. God, how could this be? Please, let her move. Let her be alive. Aisha was at her side. What on earth had happened? He'd fought with Noor. He hit her. This he was sure of. The screams of his daughter sobered him. She needed to get away from the fire.

B abak ran to the side of the bridge, jumped on the ledge, threw his arms in the air, and screamed at Noorjahan, "Stop! Stop with all these rocks. Let me be. I am sober now."

A woman, walking by, grabbed him and pulled him off the ledge. He'd wanted to resist her, but her face was so round and soft that he had to obey. She was younger than his daughter. "Come now." She patted his back. "Are you alright?"

He pointed to the river. "She is down there throwing rocks at me."

The woman looked down toward the water. A man in a lungi went by on a motorboat, hauling pieces of concrete. Trash lined the banks. Noorjahan had disappeared. "She is gone, no more rocks Ba-bajee. Tell me where are you going?"

"To the mosque."

She walked him all the way to the mosque. Down the sidewalks covered in barbed wire and across the streets flooded with auto rickshaws. He did not even flinch when he passed the soldiers, each one standing with their rifles aimed. Noorjahan did not like mosques, soldiers, or other women. With this woman he was safe. This moon-faced woman who smelled like washing detergent. He did not want her to leave. But when they arrived at the mosque, she disappeared into the throngs of people. Babak was in time for prayer. God keep him safe. But as he prayed, he heard the sound of pebbles being tossed at the window of the mosque. Noorjahan was getting bold. Even God could not keep her away.

53

NALJA

NALJA SAT IN a café watching the driver of a mini truck loaded with crates of chickens smoke a cigarette. She sipped a cappuccino, barely tasting it. Her stomach rumbled, but she had no interest in the display case full of pastries: cream tarts, vanilla cakes, éclairs. How long did a slice of cake sit in the display before being disposed of?

Farooq, the guest lecturer from class, walked through the parking lot straight toward the café. It was too late for Nalja to bolt. She'd just left his lecture less than an hour ago. Nalja couldn't avoid looking up when he entered the café. He walked up to her, putting his bag on the chair across from her. "Weren't you just in the class?"

Nalja nodded, still uncertain whether they knew each other from Poshkarbal.

"I was so boring, you had to leave?" There wasn't any bitterness in his voice. He was sort of unassuming about the whole thing, as if it were perfectly normal for her to walk out. "Can I get you something?"

"I'm sorry."

"Don't worry about it. I don't like speaking in front of so many people anyways. Do you want another coffee?"

Nalja shook her head.

"Will you watch my bag?"

"Of course."

Farooq came back with an espresso. Nalja didn't trust herself to make small talk. All she wanted to know was who he'd seen in the village. Was anyone left? Maybe he'd said it in class, but she hadn't been able to hear once she saw those photos.

"Are you sure you don't want anything to eat?" Farooq sat down and hung his worn, brown leather jacket on his chair. "I'm Farooq. I didn't catch your name."

"Nalja, nice to meet you." She watched his face closely, but no look of recognition registered. Maybe it wasn't the Farooq she'd met before. Farooq was a common enough name.

"I must be quite boring compared to Dr. Hasan. Do you mind if I sit with you?"

"It's fine, enjoy your drink."

He sipped the espresso. "What do you think about this virus? My mother just had me bring home fifty pounds of rice and lentils."

Nalja shrugged. "What does it matter if it's a virus or curfews? You'll eat the rice."

"Such an optimist, aren't you?"

Nalja couldn't think of anything but her parents. He may know who was left or how to get word. "When exactly were you in Poshkarbal?"

Farooq flinched as she said Poshkarbal, placing his coffee back down. "You know it?"

"Was anyone left?" She could not meet his gaze. A man wearing a plaid shirt, carrying a briefcase, came into the café. He sat at a table on the other side of the café, out of earshot.

"Have you been there?" Farooq's voice was nearly a whisper.

She'd come from that land. Seeing those pictures was like having her innards pulled out and captured in stills, projected across the walls for the class to discuss. "It's my home." Then she laughed, not with joy, but with the bitterness that war brings. "Was my home."

Farooq stood up. "Let's go for a walk."

She grabbed her things, suddenly aware of how much she needed air. Sweat formed along her forehead. "I have to go home soon."

"A short walk, then." Farooq put on his bag, leaving his coffee undrunk. He held the door for her, and they crossed the parking lot, going up the stairs to the footpath by the river. They walked in silence until they reached the maple trees, majestic elders with thick branches that became the sky. Some men were gathered on prayer mats on the grass in front of the ornately carved wooden mosque. Everything appeared so calm and beautiful, the wind rustling through the leaves, roses filled with buds awaiting bloom at the edge of the river, the sound of the azan, floating through the air.

"Which way do you want to go?"

"It's quieter this way." Nalja walked away from downtown. They passed a tea shop, and her favorite leather store, and then sat on a bench overlooking the river, lined with trash. A few boys strolled by on the path, but they were mostly alone.

Farooq pulled out a cigarette. "Okay if I smoke?"

She hated the smell. "Do you mind waiting, it's just my lungs." She became asthmatic in the city.

He put the cigarette back and cracked his knuckles. "What do you like to do?"

"It's quite boring," Nalja said. "I'm always stuck in the house."

"Nothing ever changes."

He had a point. Army men on every corner. She was born into conflict; it was all she knew.

"When were you there?" Nalja asked.

"Just a month back. You're from there? You do look kind of familiar."

Heat rushed into her cheeks, feeling his eyes on her. She wanted to sit in this moment a little longer, wishing their life could be simpler and that he could just be looking at her.

"I was born there. My parents are still there." Her voice broke and she swallowed. "Or they were when I left."

Farooq stuffed his hands in his pocket. "Were you there during the blockade? I left years before all of that." His lips ironed into a straight line as he looked across the river.

Nalja nodded, not trusting her voice.

"How did you get out?"

"How did you get in?" Inherently, she felt trust with him, but she couldn't be too sure. Perhaps she'd already said too much. She never spoke of how they left or where they went.

"After the fire, a lot of the military was transferred, they couldn't keep the village cordoned off."

"What fire?" she asked, even though she knew that it was the one she'd seen on the news.

"They burnt the village. My cousins made it out and found us in the city. I went back a bit later. I don't know why, but I just wanted to see things for myself."

Nalja swallowed. She wanted to pull up pictures of her parents and ask if he'd seen them, but when she reached for her phone, her hands shook.

"It kind of destroyed me, going back to nothing."

Nothing. His words landed with weight inside her. "Was anyone left?" She couldn't ask about her parents. Didn't want to hear what he might say.

He shook his head. "There wasn't much of anything."

"My house, it was up the hill, toward the end of the road to the north, on the way up to the Gujars."

"Near the Maliks' place?"

Nalja's head spun. She reached to steady herself and forced her words out. "Aisha and Alim Malik. Just down the road." She couldn't mention the path that connected their houses, nor how the soldier had seen her and taken her aunt. All that erased when she crossed the mountains. She'd not come from the village of Poshkarbal. A motorcycle backfired from the road, someone honked incessantly, birds chirped in a tree nearby.

"So you know Alim?" Farooq spoke quietly. He pulled out his pack of cigarettes, placed one in his mouth, and then slid the pack back into his pocket.

"He's my uncle, I came here with his wife," Nalja said. Each morning, Nalja prayed that he'd come back home to Aisha safely, they had been apart for nearly a year.

He clasped his hands together. "Aisha Malik is living here? How is she? Is she okay?"

Doubt swelled inside her. Could she trust him? Always operate on a need-to-know basis. "She's fine."

Farooq smiled. "I can't believe that she is here. We weren't able to find Alim Uncle. We didn't know if Aisha Auntie had made it after what I'd seen."

The images of Poshkarbal from class flashed in Nalja's mind. Maybe her parents had left before the end.

"Everything was burnt up north. I didn't see anyone. How is Alim?"

"He's living in the mainland. He's trying to come home. How do you know Alim?"

"He's my uncle."

Alim was an only child. Instinctively she'd trusted Farooq, but those photos made her vulnerable. "On your mother or father's side?"

Farooq's eyes traced Nalja. "Are you checking to see if we are related?"

"Something like that."

"My mom is his cousin."

The pit in Nalja's stomach softened. Maybe he could be trusted.

"Aisha is my mom's cousin, so I'm only related to Alim by marriage."

Farooq smiled just a bit. "Well, that is good, then. I think I remember you."

She wiped the palms of her hands on her sweatshirt, suddenly cold. "It's getting late." She stood up.

"Can I give you a ride?"

She nodded and they walked to his motorcycle, and Nalja slid onto the seat behind him. She didn't hold on to the handle under her seat, but wrapped her arms around Farooq, leaning into him as they wove through traffic.

54

AISHA

EVERY TIME HER phone rang, Aisha's hands would sweat, convinced it was Alim. There were three missed calls from him, each of which she returned, only to hear Alim's voicemail filled. She thought of texting him a photo that she'd taken at sunset yesterday, but she'd aged so much.

Alim would be returning to Charagan next week. He'd assured her there wasn't a risk of the virus. That it was only in the Middle Kingdom. Her phone buzzed, but it wasn't Alim. It was a local number, the sister of one of the women in a nearby village who was pregnant.

"Can you please come? Her face is so white. I am getting worried."

"Bring her to the doctor. I won't be able to make it for at least two hours."

"The doctor is sick with a terrible cough."

"I'll come then." Aisha set down the phone and dressed herself quickly. The villagers wouldn't have money to cover more than her taxi fare. Usually she took the bus, but the morning one had already left.

The air was brisk as she walked down to the taxi stand by the lake, negotiating the rate. Without tourists, they had no work. She, too, had her family to feed. Her body relaxed as they drove through the countryside. In six days, she'd see Alim. And then she would have to tell him about the soldiers. Her body would not be able to conceal her ruin. She gripped her bag tightly.

The driver dropped her in the village. Aisha inhaled the cold, sweet air. When she knocked on the door, the woman's sister cried, "Thank you for coming."

She went into the house, greeting the children, husband, and his parents, and then went into a back room. Aisha pulled out her doppler. The heartbeat was strong. Feast or famine. War or peace. Pandemics and plagues. Babies knew how to be born. The mother squeezed Aisha's hand. As she pushed, the amniotic sack, not hair, became visible. The baby was born still swimming. Aisha pierced the bag and the little girl let out a cry. Wrapped in a blanket, she wriggled onto her mother's chest. This was what she lived for.

After managing the afterbirth, the family came in to meet the baby girl. Aisha's stomach rumbled. Time stood still when she delivered babies. She used the restroom and when she returned to the kitchen, the grandmother offered her a plate of chicken, potatoes, spinach, and lentils. She thanked her for the food, prayed, and ate.

The sister came to clear her plate and slid a wad of cash into Aisha's hands. It was more than the taxi fare. Aisha pulled out the herbs that would strengthen the mother's milk supply, and also handed her the herbs that would protect them against the cough. She didn't believe Alim. It was spreading. She gave them enough for the whole family. "God bless you," the sister said. "The village head has come to talk with you. Just a moment, I will get him."

The sarpanch wore a gray sweater with brown pants and wool knit hat. "It is very good to meet you," he said, shaking Aisha's hand. "I pray that you and your family are well."

"Praise be to God we are healthy, and a new baby girl was born today."

"Thank you for coming. The doctor is very sick with a cough. It is very bad. Two people died this week."

"May they return to God in peace."

"I don't want to keep you long, but the families you are working with said that you are giving them herbs to protect them. What is it?"

"When I was little, my mother would take me to collect the winter cherry. I still gather them and make a tonic. It's a simple tincture and it protects the lungs. I've been using it for decades." Aisha pulled out her last two vials. "Take these for your family. Use them twice a day for two weeks."

"How much do I owe you?"

"It's fine, don't worry."

He reached into his pocket and pulled out crumpled dihabs. "Can you cultivate the herbs?"

Aisha had planted some in the village back home and they grew along the riverbanks in the shallow water. "I did one time along the river, but I can't in the city."

"Does it really work?"

Aisha shrugged. "Try and see."

The sarpanch slid the bottles in his pocket. "We are greatly indebted to you."

"It is nothing." They waved goodbye and Aisha climbed into the cab, which had waited for her.

When she arrived home, her phone rang. It was Alim. "Hello," she said. His voice warmed her.

Alim swallowed. "Did you see the news?"

"What do you mean?"

"Nadistan grounded all flights. It's a global health emergency."

Alim sounded so far away. She opened her news browser. Nadistan orders residents to stay home, starting tomorrow. Everything inside her turned cold. "Just come home, Alim."

"I can't."

She shut the news. And held the phone to her ear. She could hear the inhale and exhale of Alim's breath as if she were resting on his chest.

part 7

HOME

Age 56

May 2022

55

BABAK

BABAK NEEDED TAPE. The ghosts were calling. Fidaa meant him no harm. God praise the boy. Fidaa kept Noorjahan away. Babak closed the window and went to look for tape. He grabbed the *Valley Times* and tape, returning to his daughter's room.

He shredded the paper into quarters and taped pieces into the edges of the window. Maybe glue would be better? Glue would fill the cracks, so no ghosts could enter. Unlike Noorjahan, Fidaa used doors. This pleased Babak. He would welcome Fidaa. Someone was tapping on the glass. Babak's fingers were clumsy. The tape did not stick to the window frame.

"Fidaa, help me." But it was too late. Noorjahan's serpentine eyes pierced him through the window. She took him back to the prison cell.

They zapped him. "Who is your commander?" His pants were hot with urine. Finally, a scent more powerful than primrose.

When he begged Noorjahan to leave him to die, she freed him. She just opened the door and they walked out of prison. He knocked the guard unconscious. Noorjahan handed him the Kalashnikov and led him through the forest, all the way back to the guerillas.

He taped the final piece of paper on the window, covering up her eyes. He ripped off his shirt. His skin itched, as if flies swarmed him. Aisha came in.

"Dad, please keep your clothes on."

Aisha was angry with him too. "Do you want the top layer of my skin, as well?" Noorjahan did not stop tapping on the window. "Where is the glue?"

"What have you done to the window?" Aisha asked.

"Your mother is trying to look in. I don't want her to see you here."

"She'll understand. We had to leave the village. Don't worry." Aisha looked so small in the doorframe, just like she did the day of the fire.

She was under the table, then. It was a table low to the ground. Her body barely fit in the space. Noorjahan was in bed with swollen, purple burns. All he could smell was burnt hair and flesh.

He'd seen the billow of smoke and come running back. Nothing could have prepared him for seeing his wife trying to fish the remains of her mother from the fire. Babak yelled at Aisha to get in the house, and then he ran into the fire and pulled Noorjahan away. The flames burned her as she tried to rescue her mother. Flames nearly catching Aisha. He beat the flames with water and cloth, but he could not save Noorjahan's father. He did not stop until he removed their remains.

When he went back into their house, Aisha's face was covered in ash. If the wind had switched direction, Aisha would have died too. How had Noor allowed her near the fire?

Babak shook her by the shoulders. "Aisha could have been hurt. We could have lost her."

She blocked him with her blistered arms.

His thumbs pressed into her neck. Large hands acting on their own accord. Her eyes filled with glassy tears, but it was not terror in her eyes, it was a plea. She wanted to live and protect her daughter.

———

D ad, leave the window be," Aisha said.

 He had to keep Noorjahan out. Aisha would never forgive him.

 Noorjahan coughed and sputtered. Teeth bit into his calf. Aisha's little body wrapped around his leg, forcing him to release his choke hold on Noorjahan. He lifted his leg and gave it a shake, but Aisha held fast. He used both hands to pry her off. Really, it was a shove. That was how he left his daughter: crying against his blow.

 "Dad? Do you hear me?"

 "My anger was too great. I was scared of myself, scared of what I would do to your mother and you."

 "Why were you so angry at her?"

 Finally, Aisha was listening to him. Still, they had to be careful. "Don't talk so loud. You will anger her." It was too late. Stones hit the window. He prayed to God. Noorjahan hurled three more stones against the window. Two missed the glass, bouncing off the wooden shutters. The glass was going to break. There was no way to keep her out. Even glue seemed silly now. How could glue protect them from rocks hurled at glass?

 "Come, let's go into the kitchen and you can have some tea with Nalja," Aisha said.

 Babak looked back at the window. It wouldn't hold long. A series of pebbles bounced off the window. Noorjahan's face appeared through the tape.

 "I was afraid that I would kill her, Aisha. That's why I left. My anger was too big. I was hurting you both. I couldn't stop feeding the anger inside me." His fingertips pushed down on Noorjahan's windpipe.

 Does the body choke when deprived of air?

W ater filled his lungs. His temples pounded. Spit dripped down his throat. He was choking, and then they kicked him in his rib cage. A fist in his nose. "Where is the camp? Who is your commander?" And that is when he began to tell them about Noorjahan. Not the ghost, but the woman.

His fingers pressed into Noorjahan's windpipe. It wasn't a cough. She sputtered. Aisha grabbed his leg and bit his calf. "Don't hurt Mom." His fingers faltered.

Come, Father." Aisha led him into the kitchen.

"Uncle?" Nalja asked. "Can I get you some tea?"

Who could drink tea now? "We have no time for tea. Noorjahan is going to break the window." He paced back and forth in the kitchen. "I tried to kill her."

Nalja sat him down, adding sugar to his tea.

"Who did you try to kill, Uncle?"

"Noorjahan." Babak looked to Aisha, her eyes wide enough to swallow his memory whole. He stepped inside.

56

NALJA

NALJA COULDN'T DO her homework. She washed the dishes while Aisha watched the news, trying to ignore the headlines: a grenade attack, the military getting vaccinated, hospitals overflowing, pellet guns exploding. Dinner had been quiet. She was sickened by what Babak had said about being afraid that he'd kill Noorjahan. So many women around the world were murdered by their lovers each day, but Babak? She couldn't even look at Aisha Auntie. Why was the anger inside these men so big?

Nalja sat on a chair across from Aisha. She wanted to turn off the TV, couldn't stand any more of the news. How could she say anything about Alim Uncle's return after what Babak had just said? Maybe none of it was true at all. He was losing his mind. "I have news," Nalja started.

Aisha said nothing.

"It's about Alim. He is coming to visit for Ramadan. He finally got the required vaccine." For more than a year, the airport in Charagan was closed to civilians. When it opened, residents were required a full vaccine, of which only government officials in Charagan could access. In the mainland, there was more access to vaccines, but still most people couldn't get them. Kawthar was finally able to get one for Alim through her work.

Aisha turned off the TV. "What are you saying? Is Kawthar coming too?"

"He's coming home, Maasi. It's too much of a risk for Kawthar, since she's applying for her visa to go abroad."

"When is he coming?" Aisha couldn't let herself believe it to be true.

"Next week. He didn't want to tell you until everything was booked." Nalja pulled up a photo that Alim Uncle had taken after the single dose vaccine. Alim, thinner than she remembered him, smiled, Lubaaba in his arms, lips puckered, eyes laughing.

Aisha's eyes filled with tears. She did not look away from the phone. "Thanks be to God." Nalja put her arms around her aunt. Finally, she'd been able to give her something.

57

AISHA

THE DAY BEFORE Alim arrived, Aisha woke up to a series of photos he'd texted her. Her phone slowly downloaded the pictures; 2G was so difficult. They came through one at a time: Lubaaba playing in the sand. Kawthar cooking a fish curry. Alim with a mask at the grocery store. Kawthar driving a car. Lubaaba throwing bread for the birds to eat in a park. Alim on a bicycle wearing a silver helmet. What a life they had created without her in their nearly three years apart.

Aisha needed to go to the market to buy some fresh lamb to prepare for Alim's arrival. Nalja and Babak should go with her—an outing would be good for them both. She went into the family room, where Nalja was sitting on the sofa, scrolling on her phone.

"Good morning, Auntie."

"Come to the store with me. I'm making lamb curry."

"Alim Uncle always loved your curry. How was the birth?"

"It was twins. The mother didn't even know. Can you imagine the shock?"

"That's amazing. Was she terrified?"

"Thrilled. What a blessing twins are."

"I heard the village is getting hit hard with the virus. Aren't you afraid?"

Aisha shrugged. "How can I leave the mothers?" She thought of her mother in the snow, her body frail with the winter flu. "All the families I work with are healthy. The head of the village understands the power of our herbs. He wants to start a business with me."

"You really think it's possible? That it could be working?"

"In every village I am working in, I am seeing the same thing. You tell me."

"I wish we could get the vaccines. All the soldiers are vaccinated, and nothing is left for the people. Such an injustice. Are you serious about the business?"

"We've been talking for months. He is offering land and labor. Everything."

"How will you afford the land?"

"Now that people from the mainland can buy land, the sarpanch is very worried that outsiders will come in. So he is thinking to give me some land as shares in the business. Then proceeds will fund the village schools. We are thinking of this in our own way."

"I'm so proud of you, Auntie." Nalja jumped up. "Will we move to the village? I'm close to finishing my course work. I can run marketing for you."

"I thought all of you young people are bored in the village."

"I'm bored here with all the lockdowns, what difference does it really make?"

Babak came in and sat next to Nalja. "Good morning, Uncle. Will you come to the market with us today? We'll need help carrying all the food home."

"Let's go tomorrow."

"Tomorrow, Alim Uncle arrives."

How was it possible that she would see Alim after nearly three years apart? Aisha opened her phone and thumbed through the photos he'd sent, mostly of Kawthar and the baby, but there was one of him at the beach, sun splashing him in light.

"Who is Alim?"

"My husband, remember." Aisha held the picture up for Babak.

"Impossible. You never were married." He refused to believe that Aisha had a husband. This part of his memory was conveniently wiped clean.

Nalja asked, "Remember Fidaa?"

"Praise God for his bravery."

"His father. We are going to see Fidaa's father," Nalja said.

Nalja had arranged for Farooq to pick Alim up at the airport. There were so many checkpoints, it was best to not have too many people in the car. Aisha would soon see her husband, the love of her life. How could she explain what the soldiers had done? Her chest was heavy under the weight. She'd promised to be honest with him, but had never been able to tell him over the phone. Some things needed to be shared in person.

"Are you sure you don't want to come Babak-ji?" Nalja asked, feeling some relief that he wasn't coming. It was hard to be around him after the things he'd said.

He shook his head.

"Auntie and I will go to the market, then."

Aisha grabbed her bag, Nalja opened the door for her, and together they went in search of lamb.

58

AISHA

THE NEXT MORNING, Farooq texted her of Alim's safe arrival as she cooked. Alim was in Charagan. His SIM card wouldn't work. He'd need to re-register. Had he been faithful these nearly three years apart? She pressed her palms against her eyes, trying to still time. There was so much left unsaid on phone calls.

Face-to-face, things could not be hidden. She dressed herself, taking kurtas on and off. Nothing could be done about the wrinkles. Her lashes were still thick, and her lips stained red, but these traces of youthfulness could not cover the gaping hole of her missing tooth. She was glad that her mask would conceal this. She pushed her breasts into a bra that was too small. How much weight had she gained during the lockdown and siege? It was two years, ten months, and twenty-two days since she'd seen Alim.

In the end she dressed simply in a pink silk kurta and beige dupatta. The lamb was still tough on the stove. She added in the soaked garbanzos and a bay leaf.

Nalja sat at the table. "You look beautiful. When did you get the scarf?"

"I've had it awhile."

Before leaving, Aisha took a few swigs of her codeine cough syrup, washed her face, and reapplied her lipstick, even though it would smudge under her mask. She went over to the stove, stirred the curry, and put it on the lowest setting so the lamb would flake apart. Babak would turn it off when it was ready.

Nalja started to put her sneakers on. "Are you ready for this?"

Aisha paused. "Remember when we left the village? Were you ready?"

Nalja shook her head. "I couldn't have been. I wasn't afraid though. That was the strangest part. I needed all my energy to focus."

"Fear gets in the way of so much. You just have to live your life. We can't have all this fear. All this looking back and what-ifs."

Nalja put her arms around her. "We made it so far."

"Sometimes there is no other option than to move through." Seeing Alim should be the most joyous moment of her life, but after all that happened, she was filled with fear.

Sunlight splashed against the brick buildings as they walked through narrow roads. They passed the fruit market, bursting with almonds and walnuts. The first of the cherries and peaches. A courtyard in bloom, roses, crocuses, and tulips. Avoiding the storefronts busy with people, they took a side street and then crossed the river on the footbridge to the old city.

Soldiers stood at every corner, behind every fence, masked, shielded, and armed. Aisha ignored them, pretending it were normal to live like this.

Farooq's house was a two-story brick building with carved windows and doors. Aisha wished she could stay outside in the courtyard under the sun. Tears slid into her mask. A hawk circled above them, its tail a forked silhouette against the blue sky. She knocked on the door.

Farooq's mom, a stout woman with a broad face, greeted them. "Praise God," Maali said, kissing Aisha's and then Nalja's cheeks. "I can't believe he's finally home. Come in."

Maali's hair was dyed a reddish brown, her waist had thickened with age. The house smelled of coffee, and a few pictures of Farooq's father were on the wall. May God bless his soul.

They followed Maali toward the voices down the hall. Aisha could barely breathe when she saw Alim.

He stood to greet her, wearing jeans, slim to his hips, and a black vest over a burgundy shirt. His trimmed beard was streaked with gray. Aisha walked toward him but could not look into his eyes. If she did, she would cry.

He took her hand in his, warm and steady, and led her away. She felt bad for not greeting Farooq, but could not deny her relief in being alone with Alim. He held her in his arms, cocooning her. Her heart beat with his, and for a moment it was all she could hear. He smelled different, soapier. There was something almost lighter about him, as if he had not aged in their time apart. Aisha pushed her knees together, hiding her scars. He removed her mask, folding it carefully and tucking it into his back pocket. Her tongue traced the gaping hole in her mouth.

His hand moved from her hair to her back, making her tingle. Yet she stiffened.

"What is it?" Alim asked.

She leaned her head against his shoulder. He stroked her hair. She thought of staying like this forever, of never speaking, just being warmed by his touch.

She started to pull away, but he held her close. "Where do you want to go?"

Aisha looked into Alim's eyes. "How do we make up for nearly three years?"

"I'm here now."

"But what about all that happened in between?"

"You are my wife. None of the rest matters." Was he saying that there had been others? Her heart tightened.

Tears streamed down her cheeks. What of the past did she have to tell him? "I'm so sorry, Alim."

"You have nothing to be sorry for." She had everything to be sorry for. For who she was. For what she would tell him. She slid out of his arms.

"How is Kawthar?" Aisha asked.

"Kawthar is a bit upset that her visa was denied the last time she applied. She was worried that if she came home, they'd deny her application." He looked away as he said it. She'd spent the last days imaging that Kawthar would come soon with the baby. If the visa came through, her daughter may never return.

"Will her husband be going with her?"

Alim shifted his weight to his other leg. "They split up just after Lubaaba was born. I told you when he left."

"With such a young baby, I thought they would work it out."

"I asked him to leave." Alim looked at the ground as he spoke.

"Does Kawthar still see him?"

Alim shrugged. His left eye twitched involuntarily. He took in a few deep breaths to steady his emotions. He'd not discussed what had happened with anyone. Alim saw the bruises first, and Kawthar made excuses for how clumsy she was. Alim didn't do anything when he saw Kawthar's husband grab her by the hair and slam her into the wall. He waited until the next morning after Kawthar had left for work, and told her husband to go. It's what he feared most, that Kawthar would rekindle things with her husband when he was gone. That being alone would be too much for her. "How is your father doing?"

"He is not keeping so well." It was the first time she'd admitted this out loud. She looked away from Alim and started back to join the others.

He reached for her. And even though her mind told her to spare him, her body refused to obey. His fingers laced between hers and he pulled her against his chest. Alim did not let go.

———

Farooq cleared his throat. "Sorry to interrupt."

Aisha moved away from Alim, embarrassed that they'd been caught. "Farooq, is everything okay?" He looked worried.

"I just. I'm sorry. I don't know how. It's just." All the color had drained from his face.

"Let's sit down," Nalja said, taking Farooq by the hand, sitting a bit too close to him, her hand remaining on his arm. They really seemed quite cozy.

"I just saw this, and I can't not show you. I'm so sorry." Farooq started to cry. Tears dripped down Nalja's face, and he draped his arm around her, seeming to both console and find comfort.

Farooq handed his phone to Alim. Aisha leaned in to see it. "I'm sorry. It's just . . ." He scratched his forehead. "I just saw the video."

The caption on the video read: *Militants Slain at Checkpoint.*

Nalja fought an urge to pull the phone from Alim's hands. To let them not see. Gunshots sounded. A photo of Fidaa with two other young men flashed on the screen. Her body shook involuntarily.

The sound of gunfire erupted. Men screaming. Then, Fidaa. A photograph from five or six years ago, holding up a Kalishnakov behind their spokesperson. Aisha had left everything of Fidaa behind—his rabbit with one paw, his cricket racket never to be swung again.

"May his spirit rest in peace," Farooq said. "God bless his soul. He is a martyr now. I'm sorry. I just didn't want you to see it on the news. I had to show you."

"How will we get the body?" Aisha asked, sure that Alim would know what to do. How to go on. The room spun.

"I'm going to be sick." Aisha's voice came out composed and calm. It wasn't her speaking, but someone else. She ran to the bathroom and everything inside her came out. Still, she wanted to scream. She wanted to claw at the ground. She wanted to pound her fists into the wall.

Images of Fidaa consumed her. The first time he made a run

in cricket; when Kawthar taught him to swim; how he woke in the middle of the night to eat, leaving a trail of crumbs discovered in the morning; how Alim taught him to shave, and he cut himself right away. And the memories she would never have—of welcoming his wife into their house, of seeing his amazement holding his first-born child, of him bringing Aisha treats from the city. The shattered impossible future of what he should have had. His place at the table to always be empty. His sneakers in the closet to be claimed by a soldier. The book he was reading, left behind. The bookmark, long forgotten.

Her tears came out through her pores.

59

ALIM

ALIM FOUND IT hard to move from the sofa. His limbs stiff with grief. There was no body that they could recover. Only the video, watching the news story as if it were a funeral. How impotent he was to protect his family. In the darkness, he reached for Aisha to fill something that died inside him. Parts of themselves gone with Fidaa. Still, his lips found her neck, and the scent of soap on her skin. When images of Fidaa consumed him, sounds of gunfire refused his sleep, he listened to Aisha's breath as she slept. He couldn't imagine being away from her again.

Over the last week, they'd performed the last rights for Fidaa, exhausting themselves with logistics of trying to find his remains. The grief coursed through his veins. How had he failed his son? Fidaa reaching toward him as a child, his hands covered in dirt, insisting on carrying all the onions. So innocent.

His phone vibrated; it was Kawthar. Alim answered the phone and went to find Aisha, and they put her on speaker phone.

"How is my Lubaaba?" Aisha asked.

"Asking for both of you. She misses you so much, Dad." Alim put his arm around Aisha. "How is it that we live this nightmare."

"He's returned to God," Aisha said. "They took his body, but they can't keep him from God." They were quiet for a few moments.

"How are things going with your visa?" Alim asked, breaking the silence.

"Still no decision."

"How will you survive in a foreign country, just the two of you?" Aisha asked.

Kawthar was quiet. "We applied for a visa for Dad, too." Alim felt heat flooding his cheeks. He hardly even remembered filling out the paperwork. Had it been when Poshkarbal was cut off from the world? It was before Aisha called him. Before he knew that she was safe and alive.

Aisha stiffened next to him. "Your father hadn't told me."

"I'm sorry, Mom. I didn't mean . . ."

"So instead of your husband, your father is going."

Alim felt the blood drain from his head. What was Aisha saying? He wished he'd told her more. He wasn't even planning on going.

"I'm sorry, I have to go. Lubaaba just spilled her paints." Kawthar hung up.

"When were you going to tell me?"

"Aisha, I wasn't planning on going. I don't even remember filing for the visa, it was so long ago. We hadn't even found you."

"How do you forget filing for a visa? What else are you forgetting?" Alim took her hand. "Just listen."

"I've heard enough." Aisha stood up and went to the bathroom.

Alim had fallen asleep, exhausted by the emotions of the day and was in a deep sleep when the alarm sounded at four a.m., time for the morning prayer. His body was stiff, unused to sleeping on the ground. After prayer, they returned to the mat to sleep. He slipped his hand around Aisha's waist and pulled her flush against him. His wife.

He reached into the folds of fabric, discovering the softness of her skin. She grabbed his hand and stopped him as his fingers traced a thick scar on her thigh. He fought the urge to push the blankets off and ask what had happened. Instead, he closed his eyes. How could she have been burned like this? It was as if the fire from her childhood came back to consume her.

He took her hands in his, then kissed her fingers gently. She would tell him in time. He rubbed her arms, searching the topography of her body. He found the bits of her from their youth—the small of her back, the pink of her lips, the arch of her neck. He took off her kurta, peeling the cloth off with ease. How long he'd waited to be with her. To feel her. He resisted the urge to hurry, savoring the unfolding.

He kissed her eyelids. Slid off her undershirt. She still had her dupatta on, dangling around her neck. He wound it around her breasts. She ran her fingers through his hair, pulling him closer to her. He moved his hardness up the length of her body, sliding her pants down so that only her panties separated them. Alim kissed the indent between her breasts, the round of her belly, the depression of her belly button, the thickness of her scar.

He slid her panties off, revealing a thin gauze scarf, wrapped like a diaper between her legs. He recoiled, closing his eyes, not wanting to know what had happened. Kissing her again, his hunger was gone. Reaching for the scarf, he attempted to unwrap it, to finish what he'd started, but the worn fabric was safety pinned closed. He fumbled with the clasp. She grabbed his wrist, pushing until he withdrew. He closed his eyes, not wanting to know why she wrapped herself down there.

Somehow, he had failed his wife. He wished he could rewind time and find a way back to her.

"I'm sorry I didn't tell you."

"How could you have hidden the visa from me?"

"That's not what I mean. The visa was all Kawthar's idea. It's nothing, but I should have told you about her husband." Alim slid his fingers between hers.

"He should be going with his wife. It's his duty, not yours."

"Remember when you left my house?"

Aisha's breath deepened. Was he referring to Haseena? "I made peace with your mother. May she rest in peace. Praise be to God."

"This is what I love about you. Your capacity to love. You were right to leave."

"Just tell me what he did." Aisha felt the room start to spin. She couldn't take anymore.

"I saw the bruises first."

Aisha bit down on her lip. Not her daughter, too. God should curse her for what she had said. She wanted to clamp her hands over her ears and not hear another word.

"When I saw him hit her, I didn't do anything. That night I dreamed of your mother. She asked what would happen next. All I could see was his hands around Kawthar's neck. In the morning, after she left, I asked him to leave. To never contact us again. I didn't tell Kawthar what I said."

Aisha started crying. Alim reached for her, and she stiffened. "How can the truth be so ugly?"

Alim stared at the cracked plaster ceiling. The noise from the flat above dripped in: the morning news, the bubbling of water boiling, and the frying of onions.

60

AISHA

BABAK'S FACE BECAME pale. "It is awful what they did to him."

Aisha grabbed some garbanzos to soak.

"You were too young to remember," her father said. "I was afraid I would kill her."

Aisha hunched forward at the sink. She didn't want to hear about the fire. Not today. Why couldn't he just give her peace. Fidaa was dead. She didn't have anything left inside her.

"The fire, Uncle?"

Aisha turned around, wishing Nalja silent. What was wrong with these young people? Could she not give her a moment to grieve the loss of her son without inflicting more pain?

"Do you remember how Noor almost jumped into the fire?" Babak asked Aisha.

Every muscle wound tight in Aisha's belly, constricting her breath. It was the last struggle for air and her insides went limp.

"No," Aisha said, taking a seat at the table between her father and Nalja. "I don't remember." But she was there at the door, watching her parents fight. Her father slapped her mother, and coals came tumbling out of Noorjahan's lantern. Her father walked away. Down the road. Noor wiped blood from her nose and that is when she saw Aisha crouched by the door.

At seven, she hadn't registered the look of humiliation that washed over her mother's face. Aisha looked away, seeing the smallest tail of smoke from the coals. Her mother walked past them, not seeing it at all, grabbed Aisha, and pulled her into the house.

"The coals came from the lantern. They fell when you hit her, Dad." Aisha's voice was steady. Her mother hadn't known. She'd been the only one to see the smoke.

Babak remembered the smoke when he came back. His rage at Noorjahan had sparked the fire. His daughter saw it simmer, but he'd been too drunk to notice until his neighbor told him that their land was burning. By the time he returned, the wind had exploded the fire. Noorjahan's mother was dead.

Run," somewhere in the distance her father yelled. "Run!"

Aisha froze, wanting to drag her mother away from the fire.

"Leave her, my child. Run." And she ran from the sound of the flames, all the way back to the house.

Her father picked at his toenails. It made an odd clicking noise, like tiny little pebbles hitting glass.

"She was ready to die to save her mother."

"But she had you." Babak began to cry. "I blamed Noor all these years, but it was me, my anger. I don't know. When I came back. Your grandmother was dead. Your mother was heading in or trying to get her remains."

"She was trying to save them?" Or had she been trying to kill herself? This part of her memory never made sense. Each detail came back alive, breathing. Her mother's face had been determined. Jaw set like bones after surgery—flush and straight.

"Only Noorjahan knows. But she had you. She lives for you." How had he been so blind. Anger in the home creates war in the world. His own anger aimed at his wife, the creator of life, who brought Aisha into this world. How could he fight for liberation with the blood of his wife on his hand? "You were screaming under the table. Do you remember, Aisha? I was strangling her."

The bite. Her teeth clamped into the hairy calf, her father's legs. The weight of her father's anger pressed down on her as her mother gasped. The rage in her father's eyes. The breaking of three hearts. This time she could save her mother. She ran to her mother, not away. And she bit the bad man, who was her dad, who was hurting her mom. He shook his leg, but she held on, and then he threw her on the ground and slapped her face. The sting pricked her seven-year-old mouth.

"You bit my leg," Babak said. "I slapped you. I was a monster. I had to leave." Babak began to cry. "Do you hear the stones on the window? She's trying to come in right now. I just pray to God that we will be free. God forgive me for my sins."

All she heard was the sound of her father clicking his toenails. There were no stones on the window. A newspaperwallah hollered the headlines. The tick, tick, tick of an auto rickshaw. The scuttling of the neighbor upstairs. The blare of their TV, but there was no ghost hurling rocks at the window.

"Open the window, Dad. She is not there."

His face contorted. "Aisha, do not speak this way. She will expose us to the world. Leave the window shut."

All the wind was gone from Aisha's lungs. The breath that anchored her life, exhausted.

"Don't you see what she is up to? She is trying to open the window." Babak slammed his fist on the table. "Have you not seen what troubles I've gone through to keep it closed?" The window was still coated in glue and newspapers.

"You hold the memory, Aisha. Tell me of the monster I was. Tell me. I will listen." He cried like a child, gasping for air.

And then she heard her father yelling. Her mother crying. Glass breaking. Her mother's eye swollen purple. They sat by the riverbank, Noorjahan icing her bruised face. The parts of her memory Aisha had willed to disappear. She'd always thought her mother was to blame.

Infidelity. Her mother with Murad.

Her feet in the dirt as she watched her parents fight in the field, the booming voices of her parents. Her father shoving her mother. A slap across the face. Coals dropping into dead grass that kindled his anger. A spark of light. Her father a silhouette. Her mother's shame as she pulled Aisha into bed. A purple swollen eye and thumbprint becoming visible as they fell asleep. A moth with no wings grew across her mother's face. Her grandmother yelling, smoke flooding the house. Her mother told her to wait inside, while they went outside to fight the fire. Aisha watching again by the door. Her grandparents on one side of the fire, dumping buckets of water. Her mother on the other side, digging a trench between the fire and house. The wind blowing toward her mother. Sparks catching and turning to flames. The wind quieting. Her mother digging deeper. Her grandparents, starting to control the fire. A huge gust of wind blew in from the south. The fire surrounded her grandparents. Aisha yelled and ran to her mother. Her voice did not rise above the roar of the fire. She pulled on her mother's sleeve, but it was too late. There was no path out for her grandparents.

———

was so stupid. I was so angry." Babak held his hand in the air. "Listen." They were all quiet. "It stopped. I finally stopped it."

"What has stopped, Dad?"

"The stones. Your mother is gone."

She listened for the sound of her mother, but there was only the buzz of the city.

61

FAROOQ

FAROOQ WAS ON his way down Main Street, heading toward his office, when he passed the chief of surveillance, smoking a cigarette outside a corner store. "Hello, Farooq, how are you?"

"All is well," Farooq said. The man looked like a corpse, a bloated piece of bread floating in the river.

"So, you have found a nice girl?"

Farooq's heart sunk. He'd been texting and talking with Nalja. How could he have been so careless with her? The internet had been down, so he hadn't been able to use an encrypted app. He just wanted to hear her voice, let her know he was thinking of her. Comfort her amid Fidaa's loss. He replayed their conversation. They hadn't mentioned Fidaa, their project, anything really.

"That was a lovely poem that you read her last night. You seem to be getting along nicely. First coffee, then nice walks, now poetry. You two have gotten quite close over the years."

Anger prickled up his neck. He was bringing up the first time he'd met Nalja, over two years ago. "Is there something that I can help you with?" Farooq asked. His voice remained calm, despite his urge to flatten the man against the wall.

"Nothing at all, Farooq. You enjoy the rest of your day, now."

Farooq turned from the chief of surveillance, clenched his hands in a fist, and walked up the street. Ever since he'd became a photojournalist, his life was constantly surveyed and threatened. His most intimate space invaded by the occupying forces, exhausting him in so many ways. His desire to whisper privately to a love interest over the phone was so simple.

Farooq turned to the right. He often changed directions to confuse anyone who might be following him. Farooq went up a side street, walking in the opposite direction of his office. He didn't feel like working. Instead, he went to the bookstore up the road. The owner often put aside books that she thought he might like. His stomach grumbled with hunger. He'd gotten up early to pray with his mother and hadn't eaten since. He didn't intentionally fast. But he almost couldn't help but fast, since nothing was open. Usually the owner of the bookstore would pour him tea and they would talk about small things. He was pleased to find the store empty.

"Farooq, come and sit. How are you?" The owner was his mother's age, in her late fifties, but was nothing like his mom. She wore jeans and a kurta that wasn't too long, her hair covered with a shear dupatta as if it were an afterthought.

"I just saw the chief of surveillance. Bastard repeated back my entire relationship history."

"Relationship?" She raised an eyebrow at Farooq.

"Professional, a colleague."

She shrugged indifferently. "Why can't they find better ways to spend their time than harassing us like this?"

Farooq sat in a faded velvet chair across from the counter.

She set the daily paper on the counter. "Remember when we had five or six papers? Now only this one."

The paper Farooq freelanced for had completely stopped during the siege, when Charagan's semi-autonomous status was dissolved. They literally wrote stories by hand and printed copies on an ancient

"It's so easy to snap our internet. One day to the next, we are used to this now. But it takes much longer to go house to house, burning our books. I'm too old now to write my own book, Farooq. But these are the memories, the fragments of truth. You will find your way. Or maybe it will be your wife."

"What do you mean?"

"If you do her laundry, maybe she will have time to write the book. That would be something new. Something different. Something, how do you say? Not so boring."

His stomach grumbled so loud that it sounded like a response. To what? He was not sure, but he was grateful for the diversion.

press; they could only print three hundred a day. The copies were consumed in minutes. The government tried to regain control of the ground by cutting off the internet and forbidding the papers from printing. Now with the virus, the government used it to limit movement, suspend the internet, cut off communications. As if the virus were transmitted through Wi-Fi. Only one paper was left printing in the region, and they did only five hundred copies, hand printing from an underground press.

Farooq knew he should go to the office, but what would he do there? Make small talk? Discuss the strike planned for tomorrow? There was no real need to go in. He could write stories, but no one had the courage to post them.

"What do you have for me to read, Maasi?"

She shrugged and folded the papers. "You should write our story, Farooq."

"I can't write here, not in the way that I want. I can only capture fragments. I am too close to it all."

She nodded. "It is a good time for you though, before you start your family. When you are old like me, it becomes harder to be so selfish."

He'd not thought of it like that before, but she was right. To write in the way he wanted, he had to deprive himself of so many things. His mother would not be able to rely on his salary, his girlfriend—assuming that he'd have one—would find him unavailable, lost in the trap of art making. She'd have to let their distance grow for his art. He'd marry her after. His wife would understand this side of him. Or maybe he'd never find that and never marry and leave his mother without grandchildren.

"Why didn't you ever marry, Maasi?"

"I figured I'd have to do twice as much cooking and twice as much laundry, unless we had children, and if we did, then think how much more there would be to cook and clean."

Farooq studied her. "Why the bookstore?"

62

ALIM

OVER THE NEXT couple weeks, Alim found that mornings with his father-in-law grew easier. At first Babak had protested Alim staying with them. "It is just improper," Babak had said. "I know that I was absent for years, but you cannot just bring a man into the house like this." It took some convincing for Babak to accept that Alim and Aisha were married.

Babak's rituals each morning were the same. First, Babak read the paper while drinking tea. They could only get a newspaper every couple weeks, so he read and reread the stories as if they were new each day. Babak didn't fast during Ramadan. He'd confessed this quietly to Alim, insisting that he not mention it to Aisha. His first cup of tea, he drank as served. The second, he added a spoonful of sugar to. The third, he added two spoonfuls of sugar to, then complained that it did not dissolve properly. The fourth cup, he ate a biscuit with and added milk, only to complain that it was cold.

"How did you sleep? Were you comfortable?" Babak asked.

"Very comfortable. How did you sleep?" Really, Alim had been up the whole night, having nightmares of missing his train, Kawthar reuniting with her ex, and Fidaa somewhere between life and death.

"Good, the ground is good for me," Babak said, His hair stood in a peppered wave. He'd taken to walking around the house nude at times. They'd often had to remind him to put on clothes. The other day he tried to leave wearing only socks.

"You know what the problem with the new generation is, Alim?"

"No, tell me."

"Pride. There is no longer pride in workmanship. Have you seen the socks they are selling on the street?" He half smiled, revealing his yellowed, crooked teeth. Babak lifted his long legs dressed in loose-fitting pajama bottoms and showed off his foot. "I can barely move my toes in these."

Alim strained the tea of cardamom pods, cloves, cinnamon sticks, and green tea leaves. Then he mixed in some chopped almonds and just a spoonful of sugar. It was their compromise. Aisha preferred no sugar in her tea, and Alim liked a nice, full tablespoon. They settled on a hint. "Would you like to try my socks?"

"No thank you. Everything from the mainland is imported."

"Have you let Aisha help you with your feet?"

"I don't want to bother her. She gets angry when I complain," Babak said. "Tell me about Fidaa."

Alim winced. Hearing his son's name was so painful. "I'm not sure what there is to say."

"Tell me how he was as a child."

"Fidaa clung to Aisha. He always picked her flowers. He was a strong boy." It was hard to even say his name. The memories crowded in. Ones he wished he could forget, like the way Kawthar teased him when they were little. How he would cry and hide behind his mother. Alim never taught him to fight. Never taught him how to stand up for himself. Never defended Fidaa against Haseena.

The last time Alim had seen his son was when Murad was dying. When Alim finally had a moment with Fidaa, he did not tell him how important he was to him. Instead, Alim launched into a lecture about the failure of militant uprisings. Fidaa's last words to him were, "And what did your generation do? You sold us to the colonizer under the veil of democracy." It was true. All his youthful visions of independence for Charagan had dissolved into corruption and then occupation. "What do you remember, Babak? Tell me what Fidaa was like when you met him."

"I recognized Aisha's anger in him. I knew he would hurl it at soldiers, that it would guide him. I should have warned him more. Told him not to follow his anger or he'd end up just like me. But what can you tell a young man waiting to die?" Babak paused, one of his eyes wandered to the left. "Why do you care?"

"I'm his father." Alim poured his tea into the saucer to cool. He had failed his son. "Do you think he was still angry when he died?"

"How can you not be angry if you are born in Charagan? The trick is not to let the anger turn to hatred, to harden your heart." Babak blinked his eyes as if searching for the right words. "But he loved you all very much. He told me his father was a good man. He wanted you to be proud of him. Fidaa loved you."

Alim lifted the saucer to his lips and sipped from the edge. There was the sound of gunfire from outside. His hands quivered, but he continued to drink his tea, as if the sound were a car alarm going off in the distance.

Babak carried on with the conversation as if there were no interruption. "Tell me of my granddaughter." He tilted his chin up toward Alim. "I assume you fathered them both."

Heat rose into Alim's cheeks. "Kawthar is set in her ways like her mother. I have photos to show you."

"I've missed so much," Babak said. "I'm like a beggar, hoping you'll drop a few memories into my hand."

"Kawthar is so strong," Alim said. "She always placed first in her class. She was the child my father wished I was." Alim rubbed his eyes, thinking of other things. The way that Kawthar yelled at her daughter. Her fierce ambition, which left little of her at home. She was just like him, working hard to make herself too busy to deal with her pain. "She's angry too."

"How can she not be angry? What have we given to our children but the boxed memories of torture?" Babak ran his fingers through his hair. The tips refused to be smoothed down. "It's changing, you know. I'm a goddamn relic of the past, and you should at the least be thankful for that."

"What do you mean?" Alim asked. It was worse than ever before. Worse than the masked hope of failed elections. Worse than the brutal reality of militancy. Worse than when the earth opened up and shook at the fault line. Worse than when the river swallowed their land and they floated away on boats.

"Do you remember back in the nineties, when the militants were in charge and all the stores downtown were filled with artillery?"

Alim nodded.

"It is different, now, with the women reclaiming the streets," said Babak. "Men and our wars. What do we know? You know why I put down the gun?"

"Not because we won." Alim felt the tug of guilt that he'd never had the courage to defend his motherland.

"For your children. I've been one messed-up example my whole life. Never knew my way around love. I couldn't even take care of my own daughter. Us men and our guns, what can we achieve?"

Alim was grateful for the brothers, fathers, and sons—his son— who took up arms. For this new wave of militancy that didn't hide behind a mask, that put a face to their movement. Alim needed Fidaa's death to mean something. And it did. "There are many paths to freedom. Really, without the armed resistance, we could never have come so far."

Babak laughed bitterly. "We should've let the women lead us long ago. I need another cup of tea." Babak poured himself one, mixing in two spoonfuls of sugar.

Alim leaned back in his chair. "Are you sure you don't want to try my socks?"

"Keep them, son, I don't want you to end up with feet like mine."

Alim left early in the morning to look for cooking oil and fresh vegetables. His phone vibrated. It was Kawthar. "How are you?" He pulled off into a small alley with hanging potted plants lit by the early morning sun.

"Lubaaba is right here. She misses you so much. I just saw that the virus is spiking in Charagan."

Kawthar always worried. "We are fine, plenty of food. This, too, will pass."

"Grandpa, when are you coming home?" Lubaaba yelled from the background. "Bring Grandma with you."

"I'm sorry, I didn't mean to tell Mom about the visa. I thought you'd told her."

"She didn't mean what she said. She just misses you." He wanted to tell her not to go back to him. That her life would always mean more.

"When are you coming home, Dad?"

Alim had booked a one-way ticket. *For flexibility*, Kawthar kept saying. She hadn't said anything when he packed most of his life into his two suitcases. The hot flat on the mainland, sweating with dust and pollution, wasn't home. "It's in God's hands now."

"Our visas came through, Dad."

"I'm so proud of you." He wished with everything inside him that she would not feel alone amid the biggest accomplishment of her life.

"Your visa was approved, too, Dad."

"Things are just so uncertain right now. The airport isn't even open."

"Would it make a difference if it was? I'm not asking you to go."

"What are you asking?"

Kawthar inhaled sharply. "To say that it's okay for me to go."

"You have my blessing, Kawthar. You can send us Lubaaba if you need. We'll take care of her."

"I just want her to see Mom again. How do they keep us apart like this?"

"I'm so proud of you." Alim's heart cleaved in half. There was nothing they could do. Kawthar had to live her life, even if it meant not seeing them again.

"Love you, Grandpa." Lubaaba sang as Kawthar hung up, and Alim went on his way, searching for cooking oil and vegetables.

Alim returned home with four bunches of cilantro, a small bottle of canola oil, potatoes, and spinach. He set the bounty on the counter for Aisha to appraise.

"Where's Nalja?" he asked.

"She took my dad to the barber before the next lockdown. There's so much sickness in the city right now." Aisha pulled out an herbal tincture. "I'm sorry I didn't give this to you earlier. I ran out. This is fresh." She handed Alim the tincture. "Take two stoppers full, twice a day for two weeks. That should inoculate you."

He put the herbs down on the counter. "Inoculate me?" Was she speaking of the virus? As if billions weren't being poured into finding a cure.

"I've been using it for two years now, with all the women that I work with and their families. I gave it to all the midwives. We haven't had a single case of the virus—even in the villages that were closed." Alim stopped taking her tinctures when he found out about the opium fields, as if the two were related. She'd never taken it up with him though.

"If the villages were closed, then the transmission rates would likely be lower anyway."

Entire villages were cut off by the army as a form of quarantine. Bodies of the dead stacked and buried. The village clinics overflowed, and without any ventilators—they lost so many. "We lost one baby to the virus—but she wasn't breastfeeding."

Alim took the herbs. "How many people are using this?"

"We've given it to nearly 650 families."

He placed the herbs on the counter. "If it were so easy to do. Don't you think the government would be bottling it?" Aisha was so smart, but somehow she went back to her village ways with all this rubbish.

"When has the government ever tried to save us? Stop being so stubborn. Just take them. It'll let me rest easier at night."

"Kawthar got her visa." He took some of the herbs. The bitterness made Alim's face pucker. "The airport is closed again, now that the virus is spiking."

Aisha looked up at him, shaking her head in disbelief. Light flooded her eyes. "I can't believe she did it." She went over to Alim. "Thank you for supporting her so much. I just wish I could help her more with Lubaaba. When will they leave?"

"They want to go as soon as they can. Before the airports on the mainland close again."

"And ours in Charagan are shut still. I just wanted to see her once."

"We will see her when things calm down."

"And then you will go to her? Your visa came through too?"

Alim's stomach tightened. How could he let Kawthar raise Lubaaba all alone. "I'm not leaving you again." Alim swallowed, the bitter taste of the herbs still in his mouth.

63

NALJA

NALJA WAITED FOR Farooq at a small café overlooking the shopping district downtown, sitting at a booth away from the window. The seats were bright orange, and the walls yellow; lacquered pineapples sat on each table. She read the menu, contemplating ordering a cappuccino even though it was afternoon and she should be fasting, and the caffeine would keep her up into the night.

Farooq came in and smiled at her. He wore his same leather jacket with dark blue jeans.

He sat across from her. "Have you been waiting long?"

She shook her head. The waiter came over. He ordered an espresso. "What will you have?"

Her stomach grumbled. "A decaf cappuccino, please."

"You don't fast?" Farooq asked.

"I try not to be too rigid about any one thing."

"How's everyone doing?"

"I haven't seen Aisha Auntie quite like this, but she keeps moving, somehow. She still wants to start a new business."

"That's incredible at her age. And after all they are going through." Farooq stared at a picture hanging on the wall. "I can't imagine how they are living through this loss. I think of my father and those graves, but still I don't know. I just hope he'll come back." His voice cracked. "I hated to be the one to tell them though."

Nalja wanted to reach for him, to soothe him in some sort of way. "It was better coming from you. At least we were together." The waiter dropped their coffees on the table. "Kawthar's visa is approved to go abroad." For years, Nalja had imagined living with Kawthar, but she couldn't imagine leaving Charagan and Aisha, not after what happened to Fidaa. Nalja sipped her cappuccino, even though it was too hot.

"We should go back to Poshkarbal together," Farooq said.

Nalja swallowed, burning the top of her mouth. Would she be able to find her parents' graves? Would that give her closure from two years of their absence, or snuff out hope of them appearing?

"We could film your return, turn it into a documentary. The soldiers are gone now. Not much is left."

Nalja set her coffee down. "It's so hard to imagine being there. We were imprisoned there." Her voice broke off. "How can I face my home without knowing where my parents are?"

"I'm sorry, I didn't mean . . . I wasn't thinking."

"It's okay." She pulled out her notebook. "I've been working on our film."

She'd been up late storyboarding. They hadn't started filming, but she'd been lining up interviews in the village that Aisha worked in.

Farooq took her notebook from her and studied her work. "It's not bad. You have the interviews set?"

Nalja nodded. She was focusing on the women and children, the daily practices that kept their families and communities together. "I'm tired of telling the same story again and again, always in the same way. I want to do something new."

He laughed. "The story will be different when you tell it, my dear. This is new."

"Only for you, because you are listening now."

Farooq clicked his fingers on the table. "What kind of business is Aisha Auntie starting?"

"She wants to move back to a village and start farming those herbs she gave to you and your mom. The village head is willing to set her up with land, labor, space. Everything."

"Do you really think that it works?"

"None of us are sick." Nalja shrugged. "I don't want to live in the village, though.

"Stay in the city with me, then."

Her cheeks burned. "How will you support us?"

"My photography is love, not money. It's nearly impossible to get paid these days."

"Except for my aunt that is. She always seems to find a way."

"You'll have to make a living with Aisha Auntie."

"We're going to the village tomorrow."

"Can I come with you? I haven't been out of the city in a while."

"You can drive us." Nalja flashed him a smile.

He shrugged. "What time can I pick you up?"

"How's ten a.m.?"

"Perfect."

He stood up with her and let her go down the stairs first, holding open the door for her as they entered the busy street.

64

ALIM

ALIM FOUND THAT Aisha, like the mountains, stayed cold at night. The mornings were no longer sweet. He wanted to ask her what happened, why she covered herself. Instead, Alim said, "How can you think these herbs are working when every scientist and corporation is trying to make an antidote or vaccine?"

"You don't want to go with us to the village tomorrow? It's not a problem. Farooq will take us."

He reached for her. "It's not that. How can it be so simple?"

"It is simple. They leave us without vaccines and hope we die."

"I'm sorry." He rubbed her arms. "I just missed you so much. All these years apart, nothing felt right without you beside me."

She rolled toward him; her face filled with grief. "I'm scared."

"What have I done?"

"It's not you."

"What, then?"

"It's what I have become."

"You have only become more beautiful to me." Alim pulled her closer, lifting her face to his. "I love you."

She crawled on top of him, and he held her close. He sucked the thick of her lower lip. She was soft in his arms. Crying. He was her shell and she a mollusk.

He slid his hands under her shirt; she arched toward him as he slid the fabric off, her skin against his. Her pants came off and only the scarf was left between them, a curtain of grief. His fingers traced down her belly to where the new scar began. He reached toward the cloth.

She did not stop him, but helped him, unclasping the safety pin and unwinding the frayed cloth, bringing his fingertips to her lips, kissing them and then releasing them to roam her body.

Every indent of her body could be filled by him. His thumb in her navel. The corner of her hip with his palm, her breast cupped in his hand. Her wetness was his.

The softness, the curl of her hair, all were gone. Damage. Torture. Rape. Words they could not say. The keloids of scar tissue became the language of her suffering.

And for a moment, he wished that he could wind that scarf back on. That he did not have to know this. But his fingers moved to the soft heart of her pleasure. He wished that he could stop his fingers from exploring the topography of her shame.

"You were raped and tortured." A statement, not a question, that unleashed a sonic boom, breaking the sound barrier. He could never go back to unknowing. Revulsion pulsed through him at his own impotence to protect his wife. He wanted to push her away. He could not wipe the soldiers from his mind. He closed his eyes, and all he could hear was the sound of soldiers taking his wife.

Time passed, unbroken by his thoughts. When he opened his eyes, he saw his wife, open to him and anticipating rejection, ready for him to break her, again. Alim forced his hand to keep moving down there as if it were with desire.

He brought his lips to her heart and filled the indent of her breastbone. The tip of his tongue filled in the crevice of her navel, where he'd once felt the kick of his children, the squirm of life. He kissed down her thighs. Her scent like honey.

It awoke something in him. She was still his. And his tongue uncorked her pleasure. She wanted him. She was his, only his, always his, eternally his. The pleasure flowed between them until she demanded that he fill her.

And he did.

He didn't want to hurt her. So he let her slide on top of him. He pulled her in close, pushing into her until a thousand pulses of her muscles tickled him. Alim closed his eyes and came into her. They lay naked in sweat. His fingertips caressing her, letting her orgasm quiver across her skin.

"I love you," he said, kissing her forehead. "I can't be apart from you."

"I'm yours. That is if you'll have me."

He didn't know what would come next for them; he just rolled on top of her and took her lips in his. "You are everything to me."

65

AISHA

THE NEXT MORNING, Aisha woke up with a jolt. Alim still slept by her side. At first it sounded like pebbles being tossed at the window. Every hair on her body stood on end. She went to the bedroom window, peeled off the tape and glue, and opened the shutters. And it came in, the sound of someone crying. Aisha craned her head out the window but could not determine which direction it was coming from. It seemed to be coming from above and below. It was the weeping of a child.

Nalja came out of the bathroom. "Can I help you get things ready for our trip to the village?"

Aisha nodded and followed Nalja into the kitchen. "Could you make lunch? Do you hear that?"

"What?" Nalja asked, digging through the fridge for leftovers.

The crying did not stop. She took a few breaths to steady herself.

"Are you okay?" Nalja packed lentils into tins.

"Just a lot on my mind. Come look at these." Aisha opened her notebook. She knew it was old-fashioned to write by hand, and that spreadsheets were better for numbers, but she wanted Nalja to see the profit and loss for growing, producing, and distribution. The marketing budget had always seemed too high, but Nalja was smart. She'd figure out how to spend that.

"This is incredible. Why didn't you show me this until now? You really think we can produce so much?"

Aisha shrugged. "I thought you'd think I was dreaming too big."

"We've been dreaming too small. This is the problem." Nalja took Aisha's hand in hers. "I'm so proud of you."

"There is something wrong with your sofa," Babak declared as he came into the family room, wearing only pants. "I told you everything I know! Do you hear that sound?"

"You hear the crying too?" Aisha asked.

"I don't hear anything," Nalja said.

"It's not just the crying. She is throwing stones again. I must go pray at the mosque to put all of this to rest." Babak ran out the front door.

"Come back, Dad." He could get shot like this, running around half-naked. There was going to be a protest at the mosque today. "He can't go to the mosque; it's too dangerous."

Aisha grabbed her purse, put on her shoes, and rushed after her father.

Aisha cut through the market toward the old mosque. Fish hung on strings, a mule saddled with burlap, a man with a tin pot boiled water for chai, a woman balanced a basket of plastic blow-up toys. There were mounds of spices, powders of yellow and red, green cardamom pods, black cloves, cinnamon sticks as long as her arm. Aisha was elbow-deep in people. Drums clanged, goats stomped, and once again the distinct sound of a child crying. As if the sky had split open with tears of rain, but there was only the dry, thunderous cry of a child.

The crying became louder until it rang like a siren wailing around her. It seemed to be coming from the chai stand. She walked closer and heard it echo from the bucket used for washing dishes. Walking behind the stand, Aisha crouched over the bucket.

That was when she saw Noorjahan in the water. Noorjahan stayed under the ripples in the water, her serpentine eyes glistening.

"You look beautiful," Noorjahan said.

The cries raked in her head, pulsing like a migraine. "Can you hear that?"

"Yes, of course," Noorjahan said, looking up, the water dappling her face. "The children are crying."

"Can you make them stop?"

"You must heal yourself before you can heal the children. Be patient with your daughter. Even if she is far away, share what I have taught you with her. That's my one regret—leaving you before I became a grandmother, but you are on earth with Lubaaba. Give her your gifts. Alim is a good man. He protected Kawthar."

The cries echoed all around. Aisha wanted to crawl into the bucket and curl up in her mother's arms. She wanted to rest. She wanted the crying to stop.

"I have to go. Your father is calling me."

"But this crying, make it stop, please."

"I can't. The children are crying because their mothers are sick. Heal yourself. Break the cycle." The chorus of cries became a symphony. Aisha blinked. There was only water. Noorjahan disappeared. Aisha removed her mask and washed her face in the water. Washed all the tears away. Four splashes of water, and she prayed to the east in the direction of the rising sun; she prayed for herself—that she would be healed.

Clear water in the bucket. The chaiwallah nodded, appearing undisturbed that she had just bathed in his water.

Her phone vibrated. A text from Alim came through: *We are by the river near the water taxi stand. Don't go to the old mosque. A boy was just run over by an army vehicle.*

Someone shouted, "A man was shot by the army near the river."

Her heart dropped. Alim was by the river. A crowd of shoppers morphed into a march. Everyone turned toward the river, screaming slogans of freedom.

She ran with the crowd toward the river, toward the bullets. And then she saw him, floating in the river, shirtless.

Her father.

Her body resisted movement. Her legs froze, but there was no time for weakness. She pushed through, running toward the banks of the murky water. Time slowed down, allowing her mind to register the details—the lamb kebab roasting, the banana peel blackening under a newspaper, a woman's eyelashes painted with mascara, and then she saw him—his naked chest, shimmering like the belly of a fish, against the water.

His body floated with the ripples. The water around him wine red. A crowd gathered at the banks, shouting and weeping. Her father was dead.

It was Farooq who ran into the crowd, demanding answers. Farooq waded into the water, clicking away with his camera. This was the job of their children—to record death. Can you imagine? He did not pause or retch, just snapped away with his camera—how many bodies had he captured like this? It was as if he knew that one day, he would die like this too. That there was a bullet out there with his name on it, waiting for the day when his body would bleed back into the earth.

And what would he leave behind?

These photos—perfectly composed of death. In another time, such talent would be used to capture the contrast of the mountains, the bloom of a flower against snow, the red of a maple tree against a cobalt sky, the awakening star at dusk, the smoke from a mosque weaving into the sky, the eyes of a woman filled with desire, a puppy suckling on its mother's breast. The world was filled with infinite photographs, but Farooq was born in Charagan; he was destined to capture the suffering, possessing the courage to report on his own conflict. To open the eyes of the world to the pain. Any boy could grab a gun and brandish it at the world. It would only lead to more mothers like her—with children in the ground.

Then Farooq turned to Aisha. She was his next subject. The image of war. The mother who'd lost her child and now her father. You see, in war there is no natural chronology of time. We can die at any time. For this we must love as fast and hard as we can.

Farooq put his camera down. "Maasi, I am sorry."

She let herself go to him as if he were her son. He held her like a baby as she cried for all the pain her father had endured, for everything her mother carried, for everything unsaid between them.

Babak would have wanted to go like this. Naked, floating in the river, weaponless. An old, defenseless man killed by the army. Maybe that was why he didn't wear a shirt, to prove that he had no concealed weapons. Nothing to hide.

The call to prayer rose in the air—sweet, melodic. And Babak's spirit, rising up—free of his body, spoke to her. *Just leave the body. Let it float away. Hold on to the memories, because that is all you have left for your children.*

2030

NALJA

NALJA STARED OUT the windshield at where her home had been. There weren't any remnants of the structure, just ash. "Do you want to come?" Farooq leaned toward her, smelling of soap and mint. Gray hair peppered his temples, even though he was just thirty-four. She shook her head as he went out to take the photos the new government required to issue a deed to the land that their family had owned for generations.

Farooq clicked away, circling the entire lot. How would they rebuild? Rolling down the car window, the damp scent of earth seeped in. The smell of her childhood. She saw her father, serving her a plate of rice sweetened with cardamom and passing it to her as she played with their kitten. Simple moments that pushed against the weight in her chest that constricted her breath when she found out he was dead. He'd made it out of Poshkarbal with her mother. But Nalja hadn't found them in time. Omar died of a heart attack in a southern village among strangers who became friends. She would have held his hand and spoken of his favorite rice pudding. They would have laughed about the time the dog had puppies without them knowing, and how Omar had placed the whole lot on Nalja's bed to wake her up. She would have told him that she had stolen his books, reading the ones that he had forbidden. They would never speak of the other woman, may God wash her memory away. Her mother had done it all by herself. And when Nalja found Mina, Omar was already buried. Mina could barely walk and said she was too old to leave the village. That the southern village was her home, where she could visit with Omar.

Farooq slid into the car. "Do you want to walk around a bit?"

Cold sweat formed along her temples and heat pounded up her spine. Nalja took a swig of water, hoping to stop the nausea. She would vomit if she stood. She leaned back into the seat of the car, closing her eyes, remembering the taste of salt milk tea her mother served in the morning. Pink with saffron like the rising sun. The promise of a new day, the potential for healing, new life beating within. "Let's go to Aisha Auntie's house."

Farooq took her hand and kissed the top of it. His lips warm against her skin. They drove up the road she'd walked so many times before. She rolled her window down, inhaling the scent of her home, remembering the days she spent in the fields with Aisha, eating fresh apples, shelling walnuts, planting the garden. Learning the old ways. The burnt skeleton of Aisha's house stood dotted with clumps of plants reclaiming the wreckage. The orchards still produced apples, heavy on their limbs, and the walnut trees seemed undisturbed by the grasses that overtook the fields.

"Do you want to come out?"

Nalja nodded. "I think the fresh air will help." She got out of the car, and they headed up the path toward the house. Farooq laced his fingers between hers, pressing against her wedding ring.

Only the sink outside the kitchen remained. Nalja walked over and turned on the spicket. Air hissed out, and then brown water flowed. She stood there until the water ran clear. She washed her face in it. Tears slipped over Nalja's cheeks. Everything that her aunt and uncle had created was rubble.

A new administration had been elected last year in Nadistan. All foreign sales of land in Charagan halted. The soldiers were mostly gone from Poshkarbal. They'd left under the old administration. Now, barracks and rubble intertwined with memories. Still, the plants found a way to grow.

Farooq snapped photo after photo, providing some proof that hopefully would result in another deed for Aisha's land. Noorjahan fought so hard for Aisha to have the land, and the soldiers gobbled it up, dissolving her rights. Maybe this administration would be better. Maybe their children wouldn't have to document the pain of war. A special election would be held on September 4. Finally, an election where they could vote for self-rule, independence. New borders would be drawn. Soldiers would wear their national uniform. Hopefully, her children wouldn't be required to serve in the army. Nalja imagined their language being taught in all the schools, books printed in her native tongue, and borders that supported trade instead of militarized checkpoints. Her child would be born with a passport from Charagan.

Farooq came up behind her, rubbing her arms. She pressed back into him, and he placed a hand on her belly. The wings of butterflies fluttered inside her. Nalja pressed Farooq's fingers against her. "I feel the baby." Though it was only ten weeks, Nalja was sure of it. The distinct vibration of new life, independent of her own, grew inside.

Acknowledgments

Thank you to the people of Kashmir who shared their stories with me—those in exile, in prison, and creating home under occupation. Your courage inspires me. This work sits on the foundation of my mentors and ancestors, who taught me so much. Thank you for your wisdom; I promise to pay it forward, as I'm indebted to each of you.

Writing a novel is sort of like parenting—it takes a village and there is no playbook, each path is unique; when you think you know what you are doing, everything changes. So much gratitude to my village, who made this work not just possible, but inevitable. To my early readers along the way—thanks for giving me the gift of your time and feedback. This book would not be in this form without you.

Thank you to the artists, institutions, and communities that supported me over the last decade, and are dedicated to supporting storytellers and truth tellers: Voices of Our Nation Arts Foundation (VONA), the Center for Cultural Power, the San Francisco Arts Commission, Chinese for Affirmative Action, Independent Arts & Media, the Intercultural Leadership Institute (ILI), Youth Speaks, the Brave New Voices network, my mentors at KPFA radio, with special thanks to *La Onda Bajita*, *APEX Express*, *Women's Magazine*, and *Flashpoints*, and finally to Community of Writers, the San Francisco Writers Grotto, and The Ruby—all places that have given me a home with other artists, I'm so grateful. Thank you to my coaches, healers, midwives, and bodyworkers, who guide me on this journey of leading from the heart.

My writing group—how was I lucky enough to be part of this group? Through all the changes, losses, and joys, you are a constant support, grounding, and inspiration. Thank you to the filmmakers, artists, and creatives who worked with me to tell these stories in film, told directly from those living in Indian-occupied Kashmir.

Infinite gratitude to Simon & Schuster for creating the Books Like Us First Novel Contest, believing in *Call Her Freedom*, investing in diverse writers, and building diverse audiences. I am so grateful for your matchmaking, which included finding me the most incredible editor, who challenged me to let the heart of the novel beat on the page. So grateful to be represented by Inkwell Management and my agent, who dreamed of the characters in *Call Her Freedom* before we met.

To my friends, family, neighbors, and community who make my life richer, bring me daily joy, and build a practice of the beauty of human connection. To my friends who gave me refuge and places to write in Esalen, Mendocino, Soda Springs, and Gold Lake. Thank you for these gifts and for nourishing me.

To my family—who trusted and supported me, even when storytelling took me away and brought me to militarized zones. Family is everything. Love you. And to my children—you are beyond my wildest dreams. And to those of you who have taught me to love deeper, thank you. A broken heart heals stronger. For this I am grateful. After all, it's love that guides us to liberation.

About the Author

Tara Dorabji is the daughter of Parsi-Indian and German-Italian migrants. Her debut novel, *Call Her Freedom*, is the Simon & Schuster's Books Like Us grand prize winner. Her documentary film series on human rights defenders in Kashmir won awards at more than a dozen film festivals throughout Asia and the USA. Her work has appeared in publications such as Al Jazeera, *The Chicago Quarterly Review, Huizache*, and acclaimed anthologies *Good Girls Marry Doctors* and *All the Women in My Family Sing*. She lives in Northern California with her family and pet rabbit.